MURDER AT DREEYM GORRYM POINT
A MARGARET AND MONA GHOSTLY COZY
BOOK IV

DIANA XARISSA

Copyright © 2025 by DX Dunn, LLC

Cover Copyright © 2025 Tell-Tale Book Covers

ISBN: 9798305671032

All rights reserved.

No part of this publication may be reproduced, distributed, or transmitted in any form or by any means, including photocopying, recording, or other electronic or mechanical methods, without the prior written permission of the publisher, except as permitted by U.S. copyright law. For permission requests, contact diana@dianaxarissa.com

The story, all names, characters, and incidents portrayed in this production are fictitious. No identification with actual persons (living or deceased), places, buildings, and products is intended or should be inferred.

First edition 2025

❦ Created with Vellum

I

"The views are amazing," Margaret Woods said to her boyfriend.

Ted Hart nodded. "It feels as if I can see forever."

They stopped at the top of the incline and looked out over the surrounding countryside.

"In another ten minutes or so we'll reach the sea," Mark Hammersmith said.

"I hope so," Mark's girlfriend, Ashley Ellison, snapped. "We've been walking for ages already, and all we can see from here is nothing."

Margaret and Ted exchanged glances and then started walking again, following the well-worn path.

"It feels as if we're many miles away from Douglas," Margaret said after another minute.

"Too far away," Ashley said. "Hiking isn't my idea of a good time."

Then why did you come? Margaret wondered.

Ashley sighed. "Did you do a lot of hiking when you lived in the US?" she asked Margaret.

"Not really. I used to like to go to the beach and walk along the sand sometimes, but I didn't do a lot of hiking through the countryside."

"And then you moved to the Isle of Man. I don't understand why anyone would move here if they could live in the US," Ashley said.

"I came to visit my Aunt Fenella and fell in love with the island," Margaret told her. "It feels like home in a way that I'd never experienced before."

Ashley laughed. "Or maybe you just realized that your Aunt Fenella was rich enough that you could move here and live off of her money for the rest of your life."

Ted grabbed Margaret's hand and gave it a squeeze. Margaret counted to ten before she replied. "Aunt Fenella is quite wealthy, but I earn my own money," she said, choosing her words carefully.

"Margaret works hard and far too much," Ted added.

"If I were you, I'd just live off of my aunt's money," Ashley said. "Why work if you don't have to?"

"As I said, Aunt Fenella is wealthy, but I am not. I have to work."

"I wonder if your aunt feels weird about the way her aunt made her fortune," Ashley said. "Fenella inherited Mona Kelly's fortune and everyone on the island knows where Mona Kelly got her money."

Margaret inhaled slowly, counting to twenty this time before she spoke again.

"Mona and Max had a very unique relationship," she said eventually.

Ashley laughed. "That's one way of describing it. Max paid her to look beautiful and sleep with him whenever he wanted her. There are other words for women who sleep with men for money."

"Is that a wallaby?" Mark asked, pointing into the distance.

"I thought the wallabies kept to the Curraghs," Margaret said as they all looked in the direction he was pointing.

"They probably do. It was probably just a bird or something," Mark said. "How are things going at work?"

Margaret grinned at him. She considered Mark a friend and she'd been happy to hear that he'd started dating someone new, but this was the first time she'd met Ashley and so far she wasn't impressed with the woman. At least Mark was doing what he could to diffuse the situation. Mona's relationship with Max was far more complicated than most people realized, but Margaret wasn't about to share what she'd learned about that relationship with anyone, least of all Ashley.

"Things are good, thanks. We're working on some new formulas, which is always interesting," she replied.

"Formulas? What do you do?" Ashley asked.

"I'm a chemical engineer at Park's Cleaning Supplies," Margaret told her.

Ashley raised an eyebrow. "You're a chemical engineer? Wow. Does that pay well?"

"I'm sure it pays better in the US than it does here," Mark said with a laugh.

Margaret nodded. "That's very true, but the island is such a beautiful place to live that I feel that it's worth the lower salary to be here."

"Working for less money is never worth it," Ashley said. "But then, I really can't imagine giving up life in the US for life on a small island, either. I'd give anything to be able to live in the US."

"Why?" Margaret asked.

Ashley stared at her. "Are you serious? So many reasons."

"I think a lot of people have a romantic notion of what it would be like to live in the US," Mark said.

Margaret shrugged. "My life there wasn't that much different from my life here. I got up every morning and went to work. On the weekends, I went grocery shopping and ran other errands. But I didn't have this stunning scenery around me." She waved an arm.

"But you could go to New York City or Los Angeles or Las Vegas whenever you wanted," Ashley said.

Margaret laughed. "I didn't live within easy driving distance of any of those cities. Flying takes time and is expensive. And hotel rooms in any big city are expensive, too."

"Have you ever been to the US?" Ted asked Ashley.

She nodded. "My parents took me to Florida when I was a little girl. We visited all of the theme parks. It was wonderful."

"Vacations are great," Margaret said. "But real life is a lot less exciting."

"And there's the sea," Mark said as the path curved around and the sea became visible in the distance.

"Beautiful," Margaret said.

"Don't you live on the Douglas promenade?" Ashley asked. "Can't you see the water from your flat?"

"I can, yes, but I never get tired of the view," Margaret replied.

"You're living in your aunt's flat, which was Mona's flat, right?" Ashley asked.

Margaret nodded.

"And that building used to be a hotel, didn't it?"

"It was a hotel. Maxwell Martin decided to turn it into flats years ago, though," Mark said.

"Rumor has it that he designed Mona's flat himself," Ashley said. "I was told that it's the most luxurious flat in the entire building."

"I don't know about that," Margaret said. "It's a lovely apartment, er, flat, though. And it's in a great location."

They walked in silence for a few minutes. Margaret could feel herself walking faster as they approached the sea.

"How did you and Ted meet?" Ashley asked, breaking the silence.

"We met when my sister and I came to visit Aunt Fenella," Margaret said. "We'd been planning to visit ever since she'd moved to the island, but it took us a long time to actually make the trip."

"And then you fell in love with Ted? Or you fell in love with the island?"

Margaret shrugged. "I fell in love with the island, definitely. I didn't get to know Ted well enough to fall in love with him that quickly. When I left, I knew I wanted to come back, and I hoped that I'd get a chance to get to know Ted better when I returned."

"Was Ted the main reason you moved to the island?"

"No. I'd just left a job and ended a relationship. I was ready for a change and when I talked to Aunt Fenella, she suggested that I consider moving to the island. The more I thought about it, the better I liked the idea, especially after I'd visited the island."

"What about your sister?"

Margaret frowned. "Megan visited with me, and she plans to visit again soon, but she's busy with other things, too."

Like a man that I don't trust, Margaret added silently.

"What does Megan do?" Ashley asked.

Margaret shook her head. "She's on sabbatical from her job at the moment, but that's enough about me and my life. Tell me more about you. What do you do?"

Ashley shrugged. "I work in human resources for ShopFast."

"That sounds interesting," Margaret replied.

"It isn't, though. Mostly I hire shop assistants to work at the tills. They're all young with few qualifications. But then, I used to be one of them, so I shouldn't say anything."

"You used to work as a shop assistant at ShopFast?" Margaret asked.

"Yeah, years ago. I've been working my way up ever since. They pay for me to go to school, so I've been taking a few classes here and there, too. I'm not taking any at the moment, though, because I want to spend as much time as I can with Mark."

Mark looked surprised. "I appreciate that, but you shouldn't do anything that might negatively affect your career for me. Especially since we've only been seeing each other for a few weeks."

Ashley laughed. "Don't worry, you're just a convenient excuse for me to take a semester off from my classes. I'm tired of working full-time and studying on top of that. I'm still a long way from earning a degree that would be properly useful. Maybe I'll just stay where I am, working in HR, until I get married. Then my husband can take care of me."

Margaret counted to ten again before replying. "That's a rather old-fashioned notion," she said, choosing her words carefully.

"I don't mind if people think I'm old-fashioned," Ashley replied.

Margaret glanced at Mark. His eyes were focused on the sea.

"I know someone who works for ShopFast," Margaret said after a short silence. "Do you know Tim Blake?"

"I know who he is, but we've never met. He's been working for ShopFast a lot longer than I have. And he's a senior manager. He doesn't talk to junior HR employees."

Margaret thought about defending Tim, who was one of the nicest people she knew, but decided not to bother.

"And here we are," Ted said as they reached the beach. "Dreeym Gorrym Point."

"Say that again," Margaret said.

Ted chuckled and then repeated the Manx words. Then he spelled them for Margaret.

"Dreeym gorrym," she repeated slowly.

"The first word sounds like dream, but with a bit of a rolled r," Ted told her. "I can't think of an English equivalent for gorrym. It's sort of gore-uhm, I suppose."

Margaret repeated the words again. "But what does it mean?" she asked.

"Blue ridge," Ted told her.

"Ready for a picnic?" Mark asked.

Margaret nodded. "I'm starving. Breakfast seems to have been a very long time ago."

"It's the sea air," Mark said.

Ashley laughed. "Air is air. I can never understand why people seem to think that sea air has magical properties."

"Maybe because you've always lived near the sea," Margaret said. "As someone who hasn't lived here for long, I believe in the magical properties of sea air."

Before Ashley could reply, Mark set down the bag he'd been carrying and began to unpack their picnic. Ted had another bag that he put down on the blanket that Mark had unfolded and laid out on the sand. A few minutes later, they all sat down for lunch.

"This is lovely," Margaret said as she picked up a sandwich. The waves washed gently against the sand as a light breeze blew past them.

"I'd rather eat in a nice restaurant," Ashley said. "I feel as if there's sand in everything I'm eating here."

"I was very careful not to get sand anywhere on the blanket or in the food," Mark said.

Ashley shrugged. "And I'd rather be sitting in a comfortable chair than on the ground."

"So how did you and Mark meet?" Margaret asked the other woman.

"We met in a pub. I was with some friends. We were celebrating a birthday."

Mark chuckled. "You can't stop there," he said as Ashley took a bite of her sandwich.

"You tell her the rest, then," Ashley replied, reaching for her drink.

"Ashley and her friends were in the corner of the pub, having drinks, when a fight broke out on the other side of the room," Mark said. "I won't go into details about the fight, but there were half a dozen guys, and it got physical very quickly. Ashley was the person who rang 999."

"That sounds scary," Margaret said.

"It wasn't that bad. I've seen much worse, but then I used to hang out with a very different crowd of people," Ashley said. "I only rang the police because one of the guys looked as if he'd been knocked out. I thought he was probably going to need an ambulance."

"I was at the station, typing up reports, when the call came in," Mark said. "I didn't have anything better to do, so I thought I'd go along and see if I could help in any way."

"Mark ended up taking my statement," Ashley said. "And after we'd talked, I gave him my number."

Mark nodded. "That was three weeks ago, more or less."

"And here we are," Ashley said, waving a hand. "Trying to spend as much time together as we can, which isn't easy with Mark's job."

Margaret nodded. "I know what you mean."

"At least the crime rate has been down lately," Mark said. "I've been putting in far fewer hours than normal, really."

"That's very true," Ted said. "And we were both able to get the same day off today. That doesn't happen very often."

"I'm not sure we'll be able to do that again in the near future," Mark said. "So we need to enjoy today."

"It is the weekend," Ashley said. "You both should be off on the weekend."

"And we usually are, but one of us is usually on call," Mark said. "And we both usually have active investigations that we're conducting, which means we're often still taking phone calls and maybe conducting a few interviews, even on our days off."

"At least I always get weekends off," Margaret said.

Ashley made a face. "I usually get weekends off, but a few times each year we have big hiring fairs over a weekend. I have to work those weekends, and I hate them."

"I'm glad things are quiet at the station," Margaret said after a short silence. "I'd be happy if you never got any busier than you are right now."

Mark shrugged. "If the crime rate stays this low for much longer, I think the chief constable might start thinking about reducing staffing levels."

Ted shook his head. "That's not going to happen. Crime rates rise and fall all the time. The chief constable isn't going to cut our workforce just because things are quiet at the moment."

"James left," Mark said.

Ted nodded. "But he was just here on secondment. And he left because there were issues back in Liverpool, not because we no longer needed him here."

Margaret frowned. "James? Are you talking about Inspector Stout?"

"Yeah, he was supposed to be here for longer, but he ended up going back to Liverpool last week," Mark said. "I didn't find out he was going until after he'd gone."

"It was a surprise to everyone," Ted said. "Three of his colleagues in Liverpool suddenly needed time off, so the decision was made to recall James. When the chief constable agreed, they asked James to return as quickly as he could."

"What happened to his three colleagues?" Ashley asked.

"One had a heart attack. He's on the road to recovery, but apparently, it's going to be at least a few months before he can return to work. Another gave his notice. He's going to work for a private security firm. The third also turned in his notice. His wife was offered a job in Manchester, so he's planning to take a job there once they get moved."

"I take a few days off and I miss everything," Mark said.

Ted grinned. "You've had more than a few days off recently. Have you met Michael yet?"

Mark frowned. "I have not."

"James left on Thursday and Michael arrived on Friday," Ted said. "And you were off both days."

"Who is Michael, then?" Mark asked.

"Inspector Michael Madison. He's here on secondment from Derby."

"Is he here to replace James?"

"Not specifically, although it turned out to be good timing that he arrived right when James left. He's part of a new rotational program that's being trialed in the UK. The chief constable signed up to be part of the program, but at the moment there aren't any plans to send anyone from the island's constabulary anywhere else. We're just a host constabulary," Ted explained.

"So we're going to get a bunch of inspectors from all over the UK over here on short visits?" Mark asked.

"Not necessarily short visits. Michael is supposed to be with us for six months."

"So was James. Tell me about Michael, then."

"You'll meet him on Monday. He's in his mid-forties. Married. Two kids who are nearly teenagers. He said he never would have considered anything similar to this secondment when the children were smaller, but he reckons they are now old enough that they shouldn't be too much work for his wife while he's away from home."

"He's going to be here for six months?" Margaret asked. "That's too much work for his wife."

Ted chuckled. "He's going home on weekends, at least twice a month. And his family is going to come and visit him here as well. They've already booked a hotel for when the kids are on Christmas break and for the February half term."

"It's still a lot for his wife to deal with on her own," Margaret said.

"But it's a great experience for Michael," Mark said. "These sorts of programs are often fast tracks to promotions."

"Remember, I spent two years on mine," Ted said. "And while it didn't get me a promotion, it did get me a ton of great experience that I never would have been able to get on the island."

"I keep thinking about doing something similar to what you did," Mark said.

"I'm not sure the chief constable is going to send anyone anywhere while Daniel is away," Ted replied.

Mark made a face. "Leave it to Daniel to marry a millionaire and then take off on a year-long honeymoon. I can't believe the chief constable actually thinks Daniel is going to come back. Now that he and Fenella are married, they'll probably want to keep traveling, not come back to the island."

"Aunt Fenella definitely wants to come back to the island," Margaret said. "And the last time I talked to her, she said that Daniel is already starting to miss his job."

"I wouldn't miss it," Mark said. "Not if I was married to one of the richest women on the planet. I'd thoroughly enjoy traveling all over the world and living a life of leisure."

"Sorry, darling, but I can't give you that," Ashley said with a laugh.

"I don't think Aunt Fenella is one of the richest women on the planet," Margaret said.

"She's a lot richer than anyone here, anyway," Ashley said. "Of course, some of the people here are in line to inherit a fortune one day, at least."

Margaret flushed. "I don't know that I'm going to inherit anything. What Aunt Fenella does with her money is her business."

"She's in her fifties and childless," Ashley said. "Of course she's going to leave her fortune to her favorite niece."

"She and Daniel might decide to adopt a child or two," Margaret said. "Or maybe Aunt Fenella will leave everything to her cat. It's her money. I would never assume that I'm going to get anything from her."

"Ted? Did you know that? And does that information change how you feel about Margaret?" Ashley asked.

Ted laughed loudly. "I am not involved with Margaret because I think she's going to inherit a fortune from her aunt. Even if we both knew that Margaret was going to be one of Fenella's heirs, Fenella isn't that much older than I am, and as far as I know, she's in excellent health. Margaret would probably have to wait for decades to get any inheritance. And by that time, Fenella might blow every penny of the money on trips around the world."

"I hope you're going to be at work a few days this week," Ted said teasingly to Mark after an awkward silence.

"I was only off for two days last week," Mark replied. "And the chief constable approved the time off. You know I was house hunting."

Ted nodded. "How is that going?"

Mark shrugged. "I don't know. I found a few places that were close to what I want, but they were both missing at least one of the things I really wanted. And they were both out of my budget, too."

"I told you we should go house hunting together," Ashley said. "If we buy a house together, we can spend a bit more."

"That's a conversation for the future," Mark said.

"But you know I'm rather desperate to get out of my current living situation," Ashley said. "And I'd love to get a foot on the property ladder."

"Time for dessert?" Margaret asked as she gathered up the empty plates.

"We have dessert?" Mark asked.

Margaret laughed. "We brought cupcakes from the bakery near my building."

"They do wonderful cakes," Ashley said. "I'm not sure what a cupcake is, though."

Margaret opened the box that contained a dozen cupcakes.

"Oh, fairy cakes," Ashley said.

Margaret nodded. "I must remember to call them that. It's such a wonderful name for them."

"Are they all the same?" Mark asked.

"Not at all," Ted said. "That would be boring. There are four varieties. Chocolate sponge with chocolate icing. Vanilla sponge with vanilla icing. Chocolate sponge with a caramel center and vanilla icing. And vanilla sponge with a raspberry cream center and raspberry vanilla icing."

"I'll just have one of each," Mark said.

"We should let Ashley and Margaret take what they want first," Ted said. "And then we can fight over whatever is left."

Margaret took one each of the two chocolate cake options. Ashley stared into the box for several seconds before taking one of the vanilla and raspberry cakes.

"I don't often eat sugary sweets," she said, casting a disapproving look at Margaret's plate.

Mark laughed and then took one each of the different options. Ted selected three cupcakes and then shut the box with the last two cakes inside.

"I really do want to move," Ashley said as everyone started eating.

Mark nodded. "I know. I'm sorry that your living situation is less than ideal."

Ashley's laugh was bitter. "That's not how I'd put it."

"I was hoping things were getting better," Mark said.

Ashley sighed and then shook her head. "If anything, they're getting worse. But you know I don't like to complain. That's why I haven't really said anything to you about it lately." She looked at Margaret and Ted and then shrugged. "Sorry, you have no idea what we're talking about."

"I don't, but I'm sorry," Margaret said.

"You'd be even more sorry if you knew," Ashley replied. "The thing is, I live with the worst flatmate ever."

"That's a shame," Ted said.

"She seemed so nice when I went to look at the flat," Ashley said.

"She's always very nice to me when I'm there," Mark said.

Ashley made a face. "She knows you're a policeman. She's very careful to be nothing but wonderful in front of you. Maybe you should just move in with me. I don't know how long she could continue to pretend to be sweet and kind if you were living there, but it would be fun to watch her try."

"Are you looking for another flat?" Margaret asked.

Ashley shrugged. "I would be, if I hadn't just signed a lease for an entire year. She was smart enough to make me sign the lease with her, even though she'd already rented the flat in her name. She could have just rented out a room to me, but by putting my name on the lease, she knows I can't leave before the year is out."

"There isn't any sort of opt-out clause?" Margaret asked. "Most rental properties in the US allow you to pay a penalty if you want to break the lease early."

"There might be something like that in the lease, but I can't afford any sort of penalty. I can barely afford my rent, really. Living on the island gets more expensive every day."

"The flat is in a good location, at least," Mark said.

"Yeah, it's a great location. I can walk to work and I'm not far from your flat, either, but everything about the place is horrible aside from the location."

"I don't think that's fair," Mark said. "Your bedroom is spacious, and you have your own en suite."

"Yeah, but I still have to share the rest of the flat with her. And most of the furniture is hers. I hate the couch."

Mark looked surprised. "It's very comfortable."

"But it's blue."

"I don't think that's a bad thing," Mark said.

Ashley shook her head. "I do."

"The last two times I was there, she wasn't even home," Mark said after a moment.

"She's been spending a lot more time with her boyfriend lately," Ashley said. "Which is great, of course, because it means she's not home as much, but when she is home, she still nags constantly."

"Nags?" Margaret echoed, flushing when she realized that she'd spoken out loud.

Ashley nodded. "She has ridiculously exacting standards of cleanliness. I should have realized when I went around the flat that everything was spotlessly clean, but at the time I was too busy looking at the space I would be getting. I never imagined that every time I put anything down in the sitting room, I'd get nagged to take it to my room."

"That must be difficult," Margaret said.

"And don't get me started on the kitchen," Ashley said. "I don't dare leave a few dirty pots and pans around the place for more than an hour or two or I get nagged until I've done the washing-up. She always insists that she's worried about attracting bugs or even mice, but I can't believe leaving a pot unwashed for a few days is that much of a problem."

A few days? Margaret thought. *That would be a problem for me.*

"Honestly, how many stray socks are in your sitting room right now?" Ashley asked Margaret.

"Stray socks?" Margaret echoed.

"Yeah, you know, socks you've taken off and just dropped somewhere. Socks you'll get around to picking up sooner or later."

"I have a cat," Margaret said. "I can't leave stray anything anywhere or Katie takes it." *Not that I would leave stray socks lying around anyway.*

Ashley shook her head. "Maybe I should get a cat. Maybe a cat would give Lelia something else to worry about besides the little bit of clutter I sometimes make."

"Maybe you should have stayed in your old flat," Mark said.

"I would have, if I could have," Ashley said. "Or rather, I would have if people had communicated with me more clearly."

Margaret raised an eyebrow. She sort of wanted to hear the story, but she didn't want to appear nosy.

"What happened?" Ted asked.

"It was a big flat with four bedrooms," Ashley said. "One guy had his name on the lease and then he rented out the bedrooms to the rest of us. I'd only been there about six months when he told me that he was not renewing his lease and that we all had to find new places to stay. And we only had six weeks to get moved out, too."

"That isn't very long," Margaret said.

"Exactly," Ashley said. "I had to rush around, looking for another place to live super-fast. I never would have moved in with Lelia if I'd had enough time to look properly. And then, after I'd signed the lease at my new place, the guy at my old place told me that he'd changed his mind and signed another lease. The other two people who were renting rooms from him hadn't found anywhere else to go, so they both stayed where they were. In the end, I was the only one who moved out."

Interesting, Margaret thought.

"The new flat is in a better location," Mark said.

"And it's nearly twice the price that I was paying before," Ashley said. "I really think we should talk about moving in together."

"But you said you can't break your lease," Mark said.

"I said I can't afford to pay the penalty for breaking it, but if we decided to live together, then maybe you could help me out with that little thing," Ashley replied, smiling at Mark.

"That isn't something we need to decide today," Mark said.

"It's something we need to discuss soon, though," Ashley replied. "I don't know how much longer I'm going to be able to live with Lelia Dodson."

Mark nodded. "Let's get everything packed up. It's a long walk back to the cars."

Ashley sighed deeply. "I don't suppose there's any way you can go and get the car and collect me from here?"

Mark looked around. "There aren't any roads out here."

"I'm just tired," Ashley grumbled as Margaret and Ted began packing up the leftovers.

When they all stood up, Mark picked up the blanket and shook as much sand out of it as he could. Then he carefully folded it and put it back into its bag.

"There must be a shortcut back to the car," Ashley said as they began to retrace their steps.

"I don't know that it's a shortcut," Ted said, "but there is another path."

He gestured to the left. Ashley quickly shook her head.

"We can go back the same way we came," she said.

"Let's go the other way," Margaret suggested. "Once we get away from the sand, it looks as if there are a lot more trees in that direction. It might be nice, walking through a small forest."

"I don't think that qualifies as a small forest," Ted said. "But there are a few trees, anyway."

"No, let's just stick to the other path," Ashley said.

Mark shrugged. "It might be nice to walk back a different way."

Ashley shook her head. "I'm going back the way we came," she said loudly. "You can do what you want."

As she strode away, Mark looked at Ted and shrugged.

"I should go after her," he said.

"You should," Margaret agreed.

"She's usually very nice," Mark said before he rushed off after Ashley.

"I'm not sure I believe that," Margaret said quietly as she and Ted watched Mark catch up to his girlfriend.

"I've met her once or twice before," Ted said. "She seemed nice enough on those occasions."

"Do you want to follow them?" Margaret asked as Mark and Ashley turned and started to walk away.

"Not really. Let's take the other path. I don't think it's much longer than the one we took on our way to the beach, and now that we've eaten nearly everything, my bag isn't too heavy."

"I can take a turn carrying the bag."

"I've got it. You can hold my hand, though."

Margaret took his hand, and the pair began to stroll slowly back along the alternate path toward the parking lot. It wasn't long before they reached the wooded area.

"This is lovely," Margaret said as they walked along a row of pine trees.

"Just hang on there a minute," Ted said.

Margaret stopped. "What is it?" she asked.

"Hopefully, nothing," Ted replied.

He gave her hand a squeeze and then released it. Margaret watched as he walked around the last of the trees in the row. As he turned back and started walking along the other side of the trees, she spotted what he'd seen.

"What is it?" she asked again, unable to take her eyes off the large shape on the ground under one of the trees.

"I need to call this in," Ted said. "We need a full crime scene team. I just hope they can get all of the equipment they need out here without too much trouble."

2

Margaret stood in place and listened while Ted made his phone call. After he was finished, he walked back to where she was standing.

"I'm sorry about this," he said, pulling her close.

"It isn't your fault," Margaret said, resting her head on his shoulder. "We should have gone back with Mark and Ashley."

"I think it's better that we found the body," Margaret said.

Ted nodded. "He might have been out here for a while if we hadn't found him."

Margaret shuddered. "I hope it was someone very old who died of natural causes."

Ted slowly shook his head. "We'll be treating it as a murder investigation, at least initially."

"And you'll be very busy for a while, which sounds quite selfish of me, really."

Ted gave her a gentle kiss. "You're allowed to be selfish when it comes to me," he said. "As for being busy, I'm not sure. The chief constable might decide to give this case to Mark or Michael since I found the body."

"Is it anyone you know?"

"I don't think so, but I didn't get close enough to get a good look."

Margaret nodded. "Now I'm cold," she said.

Ted hugged her tightly. "It was a lot warmer on the beach in the sunshine."

"What's that sound?" Margaret asked a minute later.

"It sounds as if someone is coming from the other direction." Ted released Margaret and took a few steps farther along the path. Several rows of trees made it impossible to see much more than a few feet ahead.

"...here somewhere," a voice said.

"I still don't know why that's our problem," another voice replied.

"Ashley," Margaret said quietly.

Ted nodded and then walked a bit farther along the path.

"Mark?" he called. "Stay where you are."

"Stay where I am?" Mark repeated. "Is this some sort of game?"

"I wish," Ted replied.

A moment later, Mark and Ashley walked around a stand of trees. They stopped when they saw Ted.

"We waited back at the cars for a while and then started to get worried about you," Mark said.

"We weren't rushing," Ted said. "And now we're waiting for a crime scene team."

"A crime scene team?" Mark took several steps forward. "What did you find?"

Ted held up a hand. "Just stay there. There's no reason for you to get any closer, not unless the chief constable assigns you to the case."

"Case? Crime scene team? What is going on here?" Ashley demanded. She looked past Ted at the ground under the tree behind him.

"I know that coat," she said.

Mark glanced at her and then turned to see what she was looking at. "I know the coat, too," he said.

Ted frowned. "If you knew the victim, then you really don't want to come any closer."

"There can't possibly be two people on the island with that incredibly ugly coat," Ashley said as she took a few steps forward. "I've always hated it."

"It is quite distinctive," Ted said. "The colors were what caught my eye."

Margaret didn't want to look, but she couldn't help herself. Now that everyone was talking about it, she could only stare at the bright orange accents on the green shape on the ground.

"It can't be Oliver, though," Ashley said. "It simply can't be."

"Let's let the inspector in charge of the investigation worry about identification," Ted said.

Mark nodded. "I'm not going to get any closer. If it is Oliver, I'm already more involved than I want to be."

Ashley shook her head. "It can't be Oliver. For a start, he never, ever goes hiking anywhere. He's an accountant. He sits in an office all week long and then spends his weekends hanging out in my flat with his girlfriend, my horrible flatmate."

Ted's phone buzzed. "A constable is on his way," he said. "Maybe someone should walk back to the car park and meet him there."

Mark nodded. "Ashley and I can do that," he said.

Ashley looked at him and then nodded very slowly. She took a step backward and then suddenly rushed toward the body. Ted very quickly stepped in front of her. As she tried to go around Ted, Mark caught her arm.

"We need to keep our distance from the crime scene," he told her.

"I need to know if it's Oliver or not. If it is, Lelia is going to be devastated," Ashley argued.

"That's a problem for later," Mark said. "For right now, we need to walk back to the car park and wait for everyone to start arriving."

"Okay," Ashley said.

Mark released her arm. As he took a step away, she ran toward the body again. Mark caught her when she was only a few feet away from the scene.

"You're going to make it more difficult for us to find out who did this if you contaminate the crime scene," Mark told her, clearly struggling to contain his anger.

Ashley was staring at the body, her mouth open.

"Come on," Mark said, pulling on her arm.

"It's Oliver," Ashley said.

Mark glanced at the body and then nodded. "You'll need someone closer to the man to make the formal identification, but it is Oliver," he said.

"It can't be," Ashley said. She burst into tears. Mark pulled her backward, away from the body, and then turned her around, into his arms. As he rubbed her back, he slowly backed them both away from the crime scene.

"Do you want me to go to the parking lot and wait for the constable?" Margaret asked Ted.

He shook his head and then sent a text. "There are only two paths from the car park to the beach. I told him to take the one that goes through the trees. He should be able to find us easily enough."

Ashley continued to cry. Margaret dug through her handbag and pulled out a packet of tissues. She handed it to Mark, who gave Ashley a tissue.

"Thanks," Ashley said as she wiped her eyes. "I don't even know why I'm crying. I barely knew the man."

"Finding someone dead is always shocking," Mark said. "Even more so if you knew the victim."

"I can't believe he's dead," Ashley said. "I didn't see any blood. Is it possible that he just had a heart attack or something?"

"At this point, anything is possible," Mark said.

"So maybe he died of natural causes," Ashley said. "Or maybe he had some sort of accident. I know you investigate murders for a living, but surely this wasn't murder."

"Oliver's death will be treated as suspicious and investigated in that way, at least initially," Mark said.

"Maybe he just slipped and fell and hit his head on a tree or something," Ashley said. "I'm going to assume that he decided to go for a walk and met with an unfortunate accident. That's what I'm going to tell Lelia, too."

She pulled her cell phone out of her pocket. Mark quickly put up his hand.

"I'm sorry, but you can't contact anyone right now," he said.

Ashley frowned. "But someone needs to tell Lelia about Oliver. I'm sure she'd rather hear it from me than from the local news."

"Someone will tell her," Mark said. "In person and sympathetically."

"Who?" Ashley demanded.

Mark looked at Ted, who shrugged.

"Someone from the constabulary," Ted said. "Probably the inspector assigned to the investigation."

Ashley made a face. "No police inspector is going to deliver that sort of news as sympathetically as I will."

"It might be possible for you to accompany the inspector when he goes to speak to Lelia," Mark said.

"Oh, that would be good," Ashley said. "She'll need a friend when she hears what happened."

Except you aren't her friend, Margaret thought.

"Please put your phone back in your pocket," Mark told Ashley. "And leave it there until I tell you otherwise."

"I don't like being given orders," Ashley said.

"This is a police investigation," Mark replied. "I need you to understand that and do as I ask. I wouldn't ask if it wasn't important."

Ashley looked over at Margaret. "Does Ted give you orders all the time?" she asked.

"He doesn't normally have to," Margaret replied. "But I would never question his authority at a crime scene."

Ashley inhaled slowly and then sighed deeply before slipping her phone into her jacket pocket.

"At least Lelia and Oliver were only together for a few months," she said. "Maybe she won't be all that upset."

"They seemed quite happy together," Mark said.

"Yeah, because he was just as uptight and difficult as she is. He actually agreed with her when she complained about me leaving dirty plates in the sink. He even spouted some made-up statistics about how quickly germs multiply or something. I wasn't listening."

"I thought he was a nice guy," Mark said, sounding sad.

"Sure, he was nice," Ashley agreed quickly. "He did wear some of the ugliest clothes I've ever seen, though."

Mark grinned. "He did have his own rather unique dress sense."

"I wonder how his ex-wife is going to feel," Ashley said. "According to Lelia, she was still in love with Oliver. He was the one who wanted the divorce."

"Hello," a voice called from the distance.

They all turned and watched as a uniformed constable made his way toward them.

"Inspector, inspector," he said, nodding at Mark and Ted in turn.

"Constable Hooks, good afternoon," Ted said.

"I apologize for taking so long to get here. I missed the turn for the car park and had to go back around. And then I struggled to find the path. I don't do a lot of hiking."

"I hope there's a crime scene team right behind you," Ted said.

The constable nodded. "Officially, I need to see what you've found and then decide whether or not a crime scene team is necessary, but considering you're an inspector, the team has already been requested. An inspector is also on his way."

"Do you need to report what was found anyway?" Ted asked.

"Yeah, I suppose I do," the man replied.

Ted and the constable walked together toward the body. They had a short conversation before the constable pulled out his phone and made a call.

"*He* gets to use *his* phone," Ashley grumbled.

Mark sighed, but didn't respond.

"Inspector Madison will be here shortly," the constable said as he put his phone away. "In the meantime, if you could all just wait here, please. The inspector will have questions for you when he arrives."

"I can't imagine why," Ashley said. "I barely knew the man."

"But you were here when the body was found," the constable said.

"I wasn't. Mark and I were at the car park when the body was found. We should have just driven away and left Ted and Margaret to deal with everything," Ashley said.

"We're here now," Mark said. "We need to wait for Inspector Madison."

"I wish I'd driven myself today," Ashley said. "I would have left you in the car park and gone home an hour ago. I'm tired and hungry and I want to sit down."

"We can walk back to the car park and sit in my car," Mark suggested.

"We can walk back to the car park and get into your car and drive away," Ashley countered. "This inspector guy can take our statements later, from the comfort of your sitting room."

"I'm afraid murder investigations don't work that way," Mark said. "We just need to be patient for a short while."

"Patience isn't one of my virtues," Ashley snapped.

Ted walked back over to Margaret and put his arm around her. She gave him a grateful smile. Time seemed to pass incredibly slowly as they all waited for more people to arrive. Two uniformed constables came down the path a short while later.

"Inspector Madison is on his way," one of them said.

"What is taking him so long?" Ashley demanded.

The constable stared at her for a moment and then shrugged and turned his back to her. The three constables talked quietly together for several minutes before the first members of the crime scene team began to arrive.

"We're just waiting for the inspector," Constable Hooks told them.

"I'll start getting a few pictures," the man with a camera replied.

"Just keep well back from the body," the constable said.

The man nodded.

Margaret rested her head against Ted's shoulder and shut her eyes. She was cold and tired and getting hungry, but she needed to do everything she could to help with the police investigation into whatever had happened to poor Oliver.

"My goodness, this place was hard to find."

Margaret opened her eyes and smiled at the man who'd just joined them. He smiled back at her.

"I'm Michael Madison," he said. "I'll be the inspector overseeing the investigation into whatever happened out here."

To Margaret, Michael appeared younger than his mid-forties. His dark hair was short. His eyes were green, and Margaret got the feeling that he wasn't missing much as he scanned the area. He was wearing a dark grey suit, with black leather shoes that were more than a little muddy from his hike through the woods to reach them.

"Good afternoon, Michael," Ted said. "I didn't expect to see you this weekend."

Michael nodded. "Ted, hello. I have to say that if all murder victims were found by police inspectors, I suspect a lot fewer people would get away with murder. Thank you for securing the scene until I arrived."

Ted nodded. "I don't believe you've met Mark Hammersmith," he said.

"Inspector Hammersmith," Michael said, nodding at Mark. "I was looking forward to meeting you on Monday."

"Likewise," Mark said.

"And this is my girlfriend, Margaret Woods," Ted said.

"Hi," Margaret said.

Michael looked at Ashley.

Mark flushed. "Er, this is Ashley Ellison. We've been seeing each other for a few weeks."

"Nearly a month," Ashley said.

Mark shrugged.

"Let me take a quick look at the scene and then we'll talk," Michael said.

Margaret watched as he walked over to look at the body. He spoke to one of the crime scene team members for several minutes before turning and walking back to rejoin Margaret and the others.

"It's going to take them quite a while to get the equipment they need out here," Michael said. "The best thing we can do for now is get out of their way."

"Yes, let's go," Ashley said loudly.

"Ted, I'd like to chat with you while we walk," Michael said. "Constable Hooks will escort everyone else back to the car park."

Ted gave Margaret a quick hug before he walked over to join the inspector. As they walked away, Constable Hooks took a few steps toward Mark and Ashley.

"If you could all come with me," he said.

"Gladly," Ashley said.

She walked past the constable and started down the path toward the car park.

"You need to wait for the rest of us," Mark called after her.

"Hurry up, then," Ashley called over her shoulder.

"Please wait," Constable Hooks said.

Ashley sighed dramatically as she stopped walking and turned to stare back at them.

The constable gestured for Margaret and Mark to walk with him. Margaret was well aware that he was trying to allow plenty of time for Ted and Inspector Madison to get ahead of them so that they could talk without fear of being overheard. She deliberately walked very slowly along the path toward Ashley. Mark was a step behind her. The constable followed.

"I have never wanted to be out of anywhere as badly as I want to be out of here," Ashley said to Margaret when she reached her.

"Please don't speak to one another," the constable said.

Ashley glared at him. "This is ridiculous," she snapped.

Mark put his hand on her arm. "Hang in there," he said.

She took a deep breath and then blew it out slowly. "It's just so awful," she said.

Mark nodded. He put his arm around her and the pair walked very slowly in front of Margaret along the path. Margaret fell into step with the constable.

"Does it get easier?" he asked Margaret in a whisper.

"I'm sorry?"

"Does it get easier, finding bodies?" he replied in a low voice. "This is the first time I've been called to the scene of a murder. I know you've found dead bodies before, though."

Margaret felt a rush of sympathy for the young man in spite of the awkward question.

"I wouldn't say it gets easier," she said after a moment's thought. "It feels less shocking this time, but I also didn't actually see the body. It's still terribly sad, though."

Constable Hooks nodded. "It is really sad. He must have left behind people who loved him. At least, I hope he left behind people who loved him. It sounds as if he did. It would be even more sad if no one loved him."

"Indeed," Margaret murmured.

A few minutes later, they reached the parking lot. When they'd arrived, Ted's and Mark's cars had been the only cars in the lot. Now the parking lot was almost full of cars. Besides the marked police vehicles, Margaret spotted two crime scene team vans. The rest of the cars were unmarked, but undoubtably belonged to members of the constabulary.

Ted and Inspector Madison were standing together next to Ted's car. When the others reached them, Inspector Madison spoke.

"Margaret, I'm going to start with you. Then you and Ted can get on with your day."

"Thanks," Margaret said.

"That isn't fair," Ashley snapped. "You should start with me. I have better things to do than this. I'll go first. Margaret won't mind waiting."

The inspector shook his head. "We're going to need to talk for a good deal longer than I'm going to need to speak to Margaret," he told Ashley. "You knew the victim."

"So did Margaret," Ashley said.

Margaret looked surprised. "I don't believe that I did," she said.

"He was your accountant," Ashley said. "Or rather, he was your aunt's accountant. I suppose you're going to continue to pretend that you don't have access to her money, but no one believes that."

"I wasn't aware that Aunt Fenella had an accountant," Margaret said. "I've only ever been introduced to her lawyer, er, advocate, Doncan Quayle."

"And Doncan Quayle uses Livergood and Walton as his accountants," Ashley said.

"That may be the case," Margaret said. "But none of that means that I ever met the dead man."

Ashley shrugged. "Oliver was a partner in the accountancy firm that your aunt's advocate uses for all of his clients. There's definitely a connection there."

Inspector Madison smiled. "And I do appreciate you bringing that connection to my attention. It appears that I'm going to need more time with Ms. Woods than I'd anticipated. I'm sorry that you're going to have to wait a bit longer to speak with me," he said to Ashley.

"What? No! You're supposed to talk to me first," Ashley wailed.

"Ms. Woods, I'm afraid the best I can do out here is interview you in my car. I hope you don't mind."

"Not at all," Margaret assured him.

"I mind," Ashley said flatly.

The inspector nodded. "Constable Hooks will take you to the station, then," he said. "I'll interview you there once I'm finished with a few things."

"No, that's okay," Ashley said quickly. "I'll just wait here."

For a moment, Margaret thought that the inspector was going to insist on having Ashley taken to the station. He gave Mark a quizzical look before shrugging and turning back to Margaret.

"Let's talk," he said, gesturing toward a car parked a few spaces away.

He unlocked the car and they both climbed into the backseat.

"I was hoping to meet you under more pleasant circumstances," the inspector said. "Ted has told me a lot about you."

Margaret smiled. "He told me a little bit about you. He said you were from Derby."

"That's right. And I have to say, I wasn't expecting to get assigned to a murder investigation a few days after my arrival. I suspect the chief constable would rather give the case to Mark or Ted, but he can't really do that under the circumstances."

"Well, welcome to the island. I really hope this is the only murder anyone will have to investigate while you're here."

He nodded. "I'm going to take notes and record our conversation. If you'd prefer it, I can ask a constable to sit with us as well. I normally would include one, but it's difficult in the car."

"I don't mind. I can't tell you anything, really, Inspector."

"Oh, please call me Michael. I hope that we're going to be friends, if not immediately, then after the investigation is concluded."

Margaret nodded.

"Tell me about your day, then, please. You can start with when you arrived at Deermly, Dreamly, er, this place."

"According to Ted, it's Dreeym Gorrym Point," Margaret said. "It means blue ridge."

"I don't know that that is at all relevant, but thank you for telling me." He made a note.

"Ted picked me up around eleven," Margaret said. "And then we drove here. It isn't really far from Douglas, but it takes a while to get here because the roads are quite circuitous."

"You can say that again."

Margaret grinned and then told the inspector about waiting for Mark and Ashley to arrive before they set off on their hike to the beach. She told him about their picnic lunch and then the decision to return to the parking lot by different routes.

"You say that Ashley was quite insistent that she wanted to go back to the car the same way that you'd originally walked?" Michael interrupted to ask.

Margaret frowned. "She didn't act as if there was any good reason not to go the other way, but she was quite adamant that she wanted to go back following the same path we'd taken to the beach."

Michael made a note. "Did she try to discourage you from taking the other path?"

"No, not really."

"Okay, what happened next?"

"We walked for a short distance, and then Ted stopped because he'd spotted something out of place."

She continued, telling him about Ted's discovering the body and then calling 999. Then she told him about how Mark and Ashley had come looking for them and everything that had happened from that point until the inspector's own arrival. He didn't interrupt again, as he took several pages of notes.

"Tell me about your aunt, please."

"Aunt Fenella inherited a fortune from her aunt, Mona Kelly," Margaret said. "She's currently traveling all over the world with her husband, Daniel Robinson. It's their honeymoon. When they left the island, their plan was to travel for a year. Daniel is due back at work after that."

"And he's also a police inspector, I believe."

Margaret nodded.

"Is Ashley correct? Was the dead man your aunt's accountant?"

"I have no idea. The money belongs to Aunt Fenella, not me. She made a number of arrangements through her lawyer before she left. His office is making sure that her bills are paid while she's away. I suppose it makes sense that they use an accountancy firm to deal with everything, but if they do, I know nothing about it. I'm not sure that Aunt Fenella knows the finer details of how her accounts are managed, either."

"Tell me again what Ashley said about her flatmate."

Margaret did her best to repeat the conversations that had taken place throughout the day.

"I'm going to let you go now," Michael said when she was finished. "Ted has already given me the short version of his statement. He's going to write up a longer version for me after he takes you home. I'd appreciate it if you'd keep very quiet about everything that happened out here. I'd rather the press not find out about the murder until after we've had a chance to notify the dead man's family and friends."

"I won't say a word to anyone," Margaret promised. *At least not anyone living,* she added silently.

"If you remember anything else or learn anything that might be related to the case, please ring me immediately."

He reached into a pocket and pulled out a business card. Margaret hid a smile when he handed her the card that said "Derby Constabulary" on it.

"Ignore the office number on there," he told her. "My mobile number is the same, though."

Margaret slipped the card into her handbag.

"Thank you for your patience and your cooperation," Michael said. "I'm sure I won't have any trouble finding you if I have more questions."

"Welcome to the island, and good luck with the investigation," Margaret said before they both got out of the car.

"It's about time," Ashley said.

Margaret glanced at her and then looked away. Michael sighed.

"Mark, I need to speak with you before I talk to Ashley," he said.

"This is ridiculous," Ashley said.

"We should go," Ted said, touching Margaret's arm.

"Yes, we should," Margaret said quickly.

As she followed Ted to his car, she could hear Ashley arguing with Michael. Mark tried to interrupt several times, but Ashley ignored him.

"Mark can do a lot better," Margaret said as Ted started his car.

He laughed. "I think you're right about that. I'm finding myself wondering what he sees in her."

"She's very pretty," Margaret said as Ted slowly drove away from the parking lot. "And there were moments when she seemed okay. But there were also a lot of moments when she seemed quite horrible."

"I don't think they're going to be together for much longer," Ted said. "But I also can't see Mark dumping her in the middle of a murder investigation. That would be all sorts of awkward and might make people think that he suspects her of killing Oliver."

Margaret sighed. "I can't believe I'm caught up in another murder investigation."

"Do you know if he really was your aunt's accountant?"

"I have no idea. I'd call Doncan and ask, but I'm not supposed to talk about the case with anyone."

"Michael will ring Doncan and get that information."

"I really hope he and his company weren't stealing money from Aunt Fenella. I know no one has suggested any such thing, but the man got himself murdered."

Ted nodded. "I made the same leap, but I didn't mention it to Michael yet. He'll want to talk to the man's family and friends first, anyway. Having said that, I can't imagine anyone stealing from Doncan Quayle's clients. I'm fairly certain that Doncan keeps a very close eye on his clients' money."

"I'm inclined to agree with you on that."

Ted followed the winding road from the parking lot back to the main road. From there, it was only a short drive back into the center of

Douglas. A short while later, he parked his car on the promenade across from Margaret's apartment building.

"Michael said you needed to go and type up a formal statement," she said.

Ted grinned. "I'm grateful to him for giving you the bad news. We were supposed to spend the entire day together."

"We'll have other days. Oliver won't. Go and get your statement written. If you have time after, call me."

"I hope you won't mind if I grab a sandwich while I'm working. I'm starving."

"I'm hungry too. I'll make myself some dinner while I wait to hear from you."

He pulled her into a kiss. "I don't deserve such a wonderful girlfriend," he said when he lifted his head.

"Good thing she doesn't agree," Margaret told him with a wink.

He laughed. "I'll ring you as soon as I can. And I love you."

"I love you, too," she said before she got out of the car.

As she walked into the building, she spotted Elaine Coleman, her next-door neighbor, walking toward her. Margaret waved. Elaine nodded and then turned and rushed away in the opposite direction.

That was weird, Margaret thought. *But at least she isn't going to ask me any awkward questions about the body.*

Elaine was in her seventies. She'd only fairly recently returned to the island after living in the UK for many years. While Margaret enjoyed the woman's company, Elaine could be a bit pushy, demanding, and nosy, especially when there was a police investigation going on.

Margaret took the elevator to the sixth floor and then walked down the corridor to her aunt's penthouse apartment. She opened the door, went inside, and shut it behind herself. As she walked toward the kitchen, her mind focused on dinner, the room began to fill with a hazy mist.

3

"Mona? Is that you?" Margaret called as she opened the refrigerator and stared at the contents.

"It was only supposed to be a small burst of glittery haze," Mona said as she appeared in the kitchen. She waved a hand to help dissipate the fog.

Margaret shrugged. "Maybe you should stop with the special effects."

"But they're the most fun part of being a ghost," Mona replied.

While Mona had passed away years earlier, Margaret had been surprised to learn that Mona hadn't actually gone anywhere. When Margaret had first visited the island, she'd been unable to see the ghost who shared Aunt Fenella's apartment with her, but now that she'd actually moved to the island, she too could see and communicate with Mona.

"They can be fun, but I'm still not over the clouds that stuck around for ages," Margaret said.

"Katie loved them."

Margaret looked at the tiny kitten, who was curled up in front of one of the floor-to-ceiling windows that showcased the sea below them. "She did love them," she admitted. "And I suppose I would love living with a cloud if I could curl up on it and float around the apartment, too."

"I'm fairly certain I could generate a cloud large enough for you," Mona offered.

"No, that's okay," Margaret said quickly.

"I thought you were spending the entire day with Ted."

"I was, and then we found a body."

Mona stared at her. "You found a body? Why wasn't I notified?"

"Notified? By who? Or should it be by whom? Whatever. Who notifies you when I find a body?"

Mona frowned. "No one – not officially, but I've always been told…" She trailed off and then shrugged. "Tell me everything."

"I can't tell you much. I didn't even see the body. Ted found it and I was more than happy to keep well away from it."

"Does that mean that you don't know who was found?"

"Apparently it was someone named Oliver. I didn't get his last name, but I was told that he was an accountant for Livergood and Walton."

"Interesting."

"Is it?"

"Livergood and Walton is one of the island's premier accountancy firms. Doncan, my advocate, uses them from time to time for certain things."

"Yes, Ashley told the police that Oliver was your accountant."

Mona chuckled. "I don't know who Ashley is, but it is quite a stretch to call anyone my accountant. Doncan has probably used the firm to oversee my accounts, but I'm quite certain I've never met anyone named Oliver who worked for Livergood and Walton."

"I sort of just assumed he was either Livergood or Walton, from what Ashely said."

"How old was he?"

"I don't know. Ashley said that he was dating her flatmate, but she didn't say anything about how old he was. I got the impression that he was in his late twenties or early thirties, maybe."

"I suppose he might be the son of one of the original founders of

Livergood and Walton. And if that's the case, then he must have been Oliver Walton. Donald Livergood's son was Drake, not Oliver."

"Drake Livergood?"

Mona nodded. "Donald died at least five years ago, probably more. I tend to forget that I've been dead for a few years now. I remember meeting his son, Drake, at a number of charitable events over the years. Drake was charming, even as a very young man."

"And you never met Mr. Walton's son?"

"Glen," Mona said.

"Glen?"

"Donald's partner was Glen Walton. He was a few years younger than Donald, and the last I knew he was still alive and well. He and his wife did have a child, but I can't remember anything more than that. Donald was the public face of the company. Glen rarely went to anything. Donald always said that Glen was happiest adding up rows of numbers and making sheets balance."

"Glen might be about to get some very bad news."

Mona frowned. "His wife will be devastated. I met her only a handful of times, but I do remember her talking about almost nothing except her child. I wish I'd paid more attention, really, but at the time I found it quite tedious."

"Do you remember her name?"

"Caroline. Glen called her Caro, but she didn't seem to like it. I remember her frowning at him every time he did so."

"Maybe they're divorced now."

Mona chuckled. "I doubt that very much. Glen and Caroline always seemed the sort to stay married forever, no matter how happy or unhappy either of them became."

"What else can you tell me about them?"

"Nothing, I'm afraid. As I said, I barely knew them. I could tell you that Donald Livergood was a terrible flirt who probably cheated on his wife, but I can't see that it matters. She died more than a decade ago, and as I said earlier, Donald is also no longer with us."

Margaret stared at her. "With us?" she echoed.

Mona sighed. "Yes, of course, he's actually no longer with you, which I suppose means he's with me, on this side of the line between life and death. Whatever. You know what I meant."

"I don't suppose you can suggest any reason why someone would want to murder Oliver Walton."

"I haven't the foggiest idea. I barely even knew the man existed. I can't believe his death has anything to do with the accountancy firm, not unless Drake is running the business in a very different way to how his father ran it."

"What do you mean?"

"I mean, Donald did everything in his power to make the business almost invisible to anyone and everyone. The right sort of people who needed his services knew where to find him, but he didn't advertise, and he and Glen worked very quietly and efficiently without any fanfare. Donald went to charity events because that sort of thing is expected of business owners on our little island, but while he did flirt a great deal, I can't be certain if he cheated on his wife or not. If he did, he was incredibly discreet. It's very difficult to keep secrets on a small island. If he was cheating his clients or on his wife, I never heard about it."

"Interesting."

"I would imagine Glen is still working for the company," Mona added.

"So the murder was probably personal," Margaret guessed.

"Most murders are."

"I suppose so."

"Even if the motive was primarily financial, killing someone is a very personal act."

Margaret shivered. "I'd rather not think about that."

"Did you learn anything about the man's personal life?"

"He was involved with Ashley's flatmate."

"You said that earlier. Who is Ashley?"

Margaret sighed and then told her aunt all about Mark's new girlfriend. Mona bristled when Margaret repeated what Ashley had said about Mona's relationship with Max.

"I don't know why I'm surprised," Mona said when Margaret was finished. "Everyone assumed the very worst about me when I was alive.

I shouldn't be surprised that they continue to do so now that I'm gone."

"I don't think Mark is going to be seeing Ashley for much longer."

"I should hope not. I really must make an effort to find a nice woman for him. Perhaps Ashley's flatmate would be a better choice."

Margaret laughed. "I don't think he'd date Ashley's flatmate, not after dating Ashley. It would be awkward."

"What do you know about the woman?"

"Her name is Lelia Dodson. About the only thing I know about her is that she won't let Ashley leave dirty dishes in the sink or socks all over the floor."

Mona frowned. "I was already feeling sympathetic towards Ms. Dodson after hearing what you had to say about Ashley. Now I'm tempted to go and haunt her flat until Ashley can be persuaded to move out."

"Can you do that?"

"Maybe."

Margaret thought about asking more questions, but she knew that Mona could be evasive and even untruthful when it came to talking about the afterlife.

"And how long had Lelia and Oliver been together?"

Margaret thought for a minute. "I think Ashley said they been seeing each other for just a few months."

"That probably isn't long enough to make someone murderously angry."

"I don't know about that, but Ashley did say that Oliver had an ex-wife."

"Excellent," Mona said. She snapped her fingers. A small notebook and pen appeared, floating in the air next to her. She grabbed the notebook and flipped it open. "What is the ex-wife's name?"

"I don't think Ashley said."

"I'll just put Mrs. Walton for now," Mona said. "And Lelia Dodson. And Ashley, of course. What is her surname?"

"Ellison."

Mona made a note. "I suppose I need to put Glen and Caroline Walton on the list."

"They were his parents."

"And they're suspects. But I'll put them at the bottom of the list. I haven't spoken to either of them in a long time, but I can't actually imagine either of them killing anyone."

"It isn't a very long list."

"I'm going to add Drake Livergood," Mona said. "If they were business partners, maybe there were problems there."

"I'm sure the local paper will have a full list of suspects on their website as soon as the news breaks," Margaret said.

"I'm surprised that Heather Bryant didn't follow you home," Mona said.

Margaret made a face. "I'm sure she would have, given the opportunity. Maybe no one knows about the body yet."

"Why don't you pull up the newspaper's website and see."

"After I start dinner. I'm starving."

Margaret searched through the refrigerator again and then gave up. She always did her grocery shopping for the week on the weekends, but she hadn't had time to do any shopping today. She'd been expecting to have dinner with Ted, of course, so not shopping until Sunday hadn't seemed as if it was going to be a problem. Sighing, she opened the freezer and pulled out a small frozen pizza.

"Pizza isn't that bad for me," she said. "I'll put some veggies on it to make it better."

While the oven was preheating, Margaret washed and chopped up some slightly limp broccoli and a few florets of cauliflower that were in better condition. Then she added them to the top of the frozen pizza before popping it into the hot oven.

"And now to see what the local news has to say about the body," she muttered as she set the oven timer for twenty minutes.

Her laptop was on the desk on the other side of the room. She opened it and then opened her web browser.

"'Body Found in Remote Beauty Spot,'" she read the headline.

"Heather probably couldn't spell Dreeym Gorrym," Mona said.

Margaret laughed. "You might be right about that. It isn't mentioned in the article at all."

"What does the article say?"

"Nothing really, beyond the headline. I don't know how she managed to write six paragraphs of text, all basically repeating the same thing. A body was found. That's all she knows."

"Are there any pictures?"

"There's a picture of the parking lot full of police cars and crime scene team vans. That's it, aside from a paragraph full of speculation."

"What does that paragraph say?"

"That she suspects the person found must have been murdered. And then she speculates that maybe what was found was an older skeleton or maybe only partial remains from a murder that took place a long time ago. She concludes by stating that she really hopes that no one was actually murdered on the island recently."

"She's going to be disappointed when she finds out that the body you found had only been there for a short while. I don't suppose you've any idea when Oliver died?"

Margaret shook her head. "As I said, I never looked at the body. And I don't know enough about decomposition to guess, even if I had looked at the body."

"Ashley didn't say something about having just seen him that morning or anything?"

"No, she did not, and that's enough about the poor dead man. I'm going to eat my pizza and read a book and try to forget everything that happened after we started walking back toward the car this afternoon."

"You do that," Mona said. "I'm going to do a bit of poking around. Let's see if I can find out anything interesting before you do."

"Don't interfere in a police investigation."

"Yes, of course," Mona said. She waved a hand and then slowly faded away. When she was nearly gone, she seemed to shimmer into dust that gently drifted to the floor.

"That had better disappear on its own," Margaret muttered as she shut her laptop. "I have enough vacuuming to do to pick up cat hair."

"Merooww," Katie said.

Margaret laughed. "I don't mind. You're worth a little extra work."

The timer in the kitchen startled her.

"I forgot I was cooking," she told Katie. "As hungry as I am, I can't believe I forgot about my pizza."

She took the pizza out of the oven and sliced it into eight pieces. Then she got herself a drink and sat down to eat.

"I can't stop thinking about Oliver. I need to think about something more pleasant."

After several seconds of staring at the sea while mindlessly chewing, Margaret got up and found a book. It was one of her aunt's books, a cozy mystery set in Florida. The story moved quickly, and the characters were almost unbelievably quirky, but Margaret found it difficult to get lost in the plot.

"And that's my fault, not the book's," she admitted as she put the book down and finished her dinner. After cleaning up the kitchen, she paced back and forth through the living room for a few minutes before sitting back down at the desk and opening the laptop again.

"Let's see what I can learn," she muttered as she searched for "Livergood and Walton." A moment later, she clicked on the link to the company's website.

"Simple and discreet," she said as she studied the homepage. There was very little information on the page, aside from the company's address and telephone number. It didn't even identify them as accountants.

There were a handful of links on the site. The first was "Contact Us," and it simply opened a contact form. After closing that, she clicked the second link, one labeled "Our Story."

"This is more like it," she said as she began to read about the history of the company.

"Well, that was boring," Margaret said a few minutes later as she sat back and turned her attention to the stunning view outside her windows.

"Merrowww," Katie said.

"It just basically says that the company was founded by Donald Livergood and Glen Walton many years ago. Then it goes on and on about what a great privilege it is to serve the men, women, and businesses on the Isle of Man to the best of their talents and abilities. I'm paraphrasing. They used much fancier language."

"Mewww," Katie said.

"Exactly. It also says that the company has been fortunate enough to welcome a second generation of skilled and highly trained accountants to the firm. They don't mention their sons by name, though."

Katie made another noise.

Margaret laughed. "I feel the same way."

After watching the people strolling along the promenade for a minute, Margaret looked back at the computer. "There's another link. It says 'Our People.' I should probably see what's there."

"Meeeeew," Katie said, walking over to sit at Margaret's feet.

"I can't believe you're interested in this."

Katie seemed to frown at her.

Margaret laughed and then clicked the link.

"Donald Livergood is at the top of the list," she told the cat. "There's a picture, too. He looks like an accountant."

Katie jumped up on the desk and looked at the computer screen. Then she jumped down and began to groom herself.

"If you ever need to know where Donald went to college, it's all here," Margaret continued. "And there's a list of some of his former clients, too. It's only at the very end that they actually say the man is dead, which is weird."

Katie's "mew" sounded not at all interested.

"Glen Walton is next. He's listed as a founding director. Again, it gives all the details of where he studied and lists some of his clients. Doncan Quayle is on the list."

"Merrroooww," Katie said.

"Have you met Doncan?" Margaret asked her.

Katie looked up at her and then switched to licking her other front paw.

"Right, so Drake Livergood is next on the list. His biography has the dates that he attended college. From those, I'd guess he's around thirty-five. His client list is shorter and less impressive than Glen's, but I suppose that's to be expected."

Margaret scrolled down the page. The next entry was for Oliver Walton. She stared at his photograph.

"He was very young," Margaret said. "At least he was when the picture was taken." She read through his biography, paying attention to the dates given for his education.

"Assuming he started college at eighteen, he must have been around twenty-six or twenty-seven," she said after some quick math. "They all look like accountants, but in this picture, Oliver looks like he had a bit of a mischievous streak."

She sighed. "I'm probably seeing things that aren't there. I'm just really sad that the man is dead."

Katie made a noise and then jumped into Margaret's lap. She curled up into a tight ball and began to purr loudly. Margaret ran her hand along Katie's back and let herself shed a few tears for Oliver Walton.

She and Katie both jumped when Margaret's phone rang a short while later.

"Hey, gorgeous. How are you?" Ted asked when Margaret answered.

"I'm okay."

"You don't sound okay. You sound upset."

Margaret sighed. "I'm just sad. I looked at the website for Livergood and Walton and they have a picture of Oliver there. Seeing that made me sad."

"I just finished my statement. Why don't I come over and we can spend some time together talking about everything other than Oliver?"

"I'd like that."

"I'll be there in five minutes."

Margaret made sure that Katie had plenty of water and then dropped a few treats into her food bowl.

"You've earned them, listening to me babble all evening," she told Katie.

Katie didn't bother to reply. She was too busy eating her treats.

Margaret touched up her makeup and combed her hair. She was just walking out of her bedroom when she heard the knock on the door.

"Hello," she greeted Ted.

"Hi."

He pulled her into an embrace. "Are you okay?" he asked when he released her.

"I'm going to be fine, but I'm also going to be sad for a short while."

He nodded. "It is very sad. I had a short conversation with Michael before I left the station. He'd just returned from notifying Oliver's parents. That is far and away the worst part of the job."

"They must have been devastated."

"He'd also spoken to Lelia and to Oliver's ex-wife."

"Poor Michael. That's a lot of sharing of bad news."

"And, of course, it's always possible that one of those people murdered the man."

"So he had to be watching them all closely, looking for hints that what he was telling them wasn't actually news to them."

"Exactly."

Margaret sighed. "I don't understand why anyone wants to be a police officer."

"There are days when I wonder that myself."

"You have talked about maybe moving into security work."

"And on days like today, I give that idea a lot more thought. It would be less interesting in a lot of ways, but the idea of never having to knock on a door and tell someone that his or her loved one has died is quite tempting."

"And on that note, let's go for a walk or something. Some fresh air might clear our heads."

Ted nodded. "And if that doesn't work, we can always go to the pub."

Margaret laughed. "Even if it does work, we can always go to the pub."

While there were a number of pubs on the island, and quite a few within walking distance of Margaret's apartment, they both knew exactly which pub they would visit should they decide to get a drink.

The Tale and Tail had once been the grand mansion Douglas home of one of the island's wealthiest families. Some years earlier, the family had decided to sell the mansion. The developers who'd purchased the property on the promenade turned the building into a luxury hotel. The enormous library on the ground floor, however, they'd left mostly untouched. Shelves of books still lined the walls. A spiral staircase wound its way up to a second level where even more books covered the walls.

The new owners put in an elevator to allow visitors to bypass the staircase after a drink or two. They also installed a bar in the center of the ground floor room. On the upper level, couches, chairs, and low tables were scattered around the space. And then they'd added a dozen or more cat beds and opened their doors to a number of rescued cats and kittens. Most of the animals didn't stay at the pub for very long. Customers often found themselves falling in love with the various residents, all of whom were available for adoption.

To Margaret, the Tale and Tail was just about the most perfect place in the world. She could grab a book off the shelves and then curl up on a couch with a glass of wine and the book. Usually, it didn't take long for a cat to find her and snuggle up with her, making the entire experience complete. While she wasn't the type to frequent pubs on her own, she was willing to make an exception for the Tale and Tail, just occasionally stopping in for a drink on nights when Ted was otherwise occupied.

"Where should we go?" Ted asked as they walked out of Margaret's building together.

"Let's walk on the promenade until we get tired. That probably won't take long, considering we went hiking this morning."

Ted nodded. "I had a sandwich at the station, but I'm still hungry. Maybe we could get ice cream or something."

"We could. Or we could go somewhere, and you could get something more substantial."

Ted shrugged. "I think I'd rather have ice cream."

Margaret laughed. "Now that you've mentioned it, ice cream does sound good. I used to eat so very healthily, but since I've been on the island, I've been having desserts and treats a lot more."

"I think we both eat healthily most of the time. A scoop of ice cream now and then isn't going to hurt us."

"We did go hiking this morning."

"We did."

They both laughed and then crossed the street so that they could walk along the promenade. Ted took Margaret's hand and squeezed it tightly.

"I needed this," he said after a few paces.

"I think we both did."

Ted sighed. "I feel sorry for Michael. He's only been on the island for a few days, and now he's caught up in a murder investigation."

"You said something about him going home for weekends. He won't be able to do that for a while, will he?"

"Obviously, he wasn't planning on going home this weekend. He only just arrived. He wasn't planning on going home next weekend, either. His wife and the kids are supposed to be coming here on Friday to spend the weekend with him."

"That will be nice for him, although he might not get to spend much time with them if the case isn't solved."

"Yeah, that's what he was saying. He wants to solve the case before Friday so he can spend the weekend touring the island with his family."

"Obviously, I think everyone on the island would like to see him find the killer as quickly as possible."

"Aside from the killer, of course."

"If he was murdered. Maybe he had a heart attack or tripped and fell and hit his head or something."

"Anything is possible."

Margaret frowned at the doubt she heard in Ted's voice. "You're pretty sure he was murdered, aren't you?"

"Yeah, I am."

She sighed. "Maybe Ashley did it."

"She's on my short list of suspects, although I must admit she isn't at the top of the list."

"Who is at the top of the list?"

"That's a hard question. I don't really have a list. If I did have a list, though, Ashley would be on it, but not at the top."

Margaret laughed. "I think you need some ice cream."

"I know I need some ice cream."

They walked back across the street to a row of little shops. One of the shops sold ice cream that was made right on the island.

"Two scoops of Chocolate Explosion in a cone," Ted requested.

Margaret read the description. "'Chocolate ice cream with chocolate cake pieces, chocolate chunks, and a chocolate fudge swirl.' That's a lot of chocolate."

"Is that a problem?" Ted asked as he was handed his cone.

Margaret laughed. "Not at all. I'll have one scoop of Chocolate Explosion and one scoop of Caramel Madness in a cup, please."

"I don't suppose you'd be willing to share a bite of your Caramel Madness with me," Ted said after Margaret had her ice cream and he'd paid for the treats.

"I can let you have one bite, but only of the caramel ice cream and the caramel swirl. I'm not giving you one of my chocolate-covered caramel chunks. There aren't very many of those, and I'm saving them until the end."

Ted laughed. "I'm happy with just the ice cream. I just want to try it."

She gave him a spoonful of the cold treat.

"That's really good. Maybe I should have ordered two different scoops instead of getting two of the same."

"You'll know better for next time."

"Maybe. Or maybe I'll just keep getting two scoops of my favorite chocolate ice cream anyway."

They crossed back over to the promenade and continued walking for a short while. Ted finished his ice cream and then convinced Margaret to share another bite of hers with him. She left half a dozen chocolate-covered caramel cups in the bottom of her cup as she ate.

"Okay, because I love you, you can have one caramel cup," she told him after she'd eaten the last of the ice cream.

"Wow, that's true love," Ted said before opening his mouth. "Delicious," he added after he'd swallowed.

"Next time, get your own," Margaret suggested.

"Maybe. Probably, even."

Margaret threw away her empty cup and wiped her mouth before dropping the napkin in the garbage as well. Then she walked to the railing and looked out at the sea.

"It's always different, isn't it?" Ted asked.

Margaret nodded. "And it's always beautiful." She took a deep breath. "I can't believe how much my life has changed in the past year. I still feel like pinching myself sometimes. Maybe this is all a dream."

"If it were a dream, surely there would be fewer dead bodies," Ted said.

Margaret gave him a rueful smile. "You're right about that."

He put his arms around her, and they stood together, watching the water for several minutes.

"I love you," Ted whispered in Margaret's ear.

"I love you, too," she replied.

"And I love standing here watching the water, but I'm also getting tired. Maybe now would be a good time to head to the pub," he said after several additional minutes had passed.

"Now would be a great time to head to the pub."

They walked hand-in-hand back along the promenade before crossing the road at the zebra crossing not far from the pub's entrance. As they walked inside the building, Margaret stopped to take a moment to appreciate the wonderful space.

"We have a few new cats," the bartender told them as he poured them their usual drinks. "Asparagus is having some trouble settling in. He's smaller than most of the others even though he's fully grown. He's wearing a green collar. If you see him, please give him some extra love."

"We'll do that," Margaret promised.

She and Ted carried their drinks up the stairs. The upper level was nearly empty. They settled together on a couch in a corner as far away from the other three people who were there as they could be.

"Cheers," Ted said, tapping his glass against Margaret's.

"Cheers," she replied.

A moment later, a small cat walked past them. He gave Margaret a curious look as he strolled by.

"Are you Asparagus?" she asked.

He stopped and then turned around and studied her.

"You can have a snuggle if you want," she told him.

The cat looked at Ted and then back at Margaret. She patted her lap. "Even if you aren't Asparagus, you're welcome," she said.

After another quick glance at Ted, the cat slowly and carefully began to climb up the couch and onto Margaret's lap. As he settled in, she checked the tag on his green collar.

"Asparagus?" Ted asked.

Margaret nodded as she began to pet the small animal. His purr was very quiet, but she could hear it.

Ted reached over and picked up her drink. "I assume you don't want to disturb your new friend to take a sip now and then," he said as he handed her the glass.

"You'll just have to keep handing it to me at regular intervals," she told him.

He laughed. "I'm happy to be of service."

They were talking about vegetables when they heard the sound of people coming up the stairs. Asparagus lifted his head and stared at the new arrivals. Ted and Margaret both waved.

"I thought we might find you here," Mark said as he walked toward them. "I hope you don't mind if we join you."

Margaret looked past him and forced herself to smile at Ashley and the other woman with her.

4

"Of course not," Ted said. "Pull up some chairs."

Mark dragged three chairs over, arranging them in a rough semicircle in front of the couch where Ted and Margaret were sitting. Then the trio sat down.

"Margaret Woods, Ted Hart, this is my flatmate, Lelia Dodson," Ashley said.

Margaret studied the young woman, who looked as if she'd been crying. She looked no more than twenty with long blonde hair pulled back in to a ponytail. She was wearing stylish glasses with blue frames that exactly matched her dress, shoes, and handbag.

"It's nice to meet you," Margaret said. "I'm sorry for your loss."

Lelia nodded. "I don't quite know how to feel," she said in a low voice. "We'd only been together for a few months, but we'd been planning a future together."

"When you meet the right person, you just know," Ashley said, grabbing Mark's hand and squeezing it tightly.

Margaret and Ted exchanged glances.

"Lelia doesn't normally spend much time in pubs," Ashley said. "But I told her the Tale and Tail isn't a typical pub."

"It's lovely, isn't it?" Lelia asked, looking around. "Ashley told me that there were books, but I wasn't expecting this many."

"The books are one of my favorite parts of coming here," Margaret said. "And the cats are another." She nodded toward Asparagus.

Lelia frowned. "I'm not really an animal person. My mother didn't allow me to have any pets when I was a child. I'm actually quite timid around cats and even more so around dogs."

"I keep telling her that we should get a kitten," Ashley said. "I even offered to do all of the work. She could just cuddle with it at the end of a long day."

"Our lease doesn't allow for animals," Lelia said.

Ashley shrugged. "No one has to know."

Another cat walked past. He looked at the group and then walked over and stood at Lelia's feet, meowing softly.

"Oh goodness, what does he want?" she asked, looking terrified.

"He just wants some love," Ted said. He bent down and picked up the cat. "You just want some attention, don't you?" he asked, putting the cat on his lap and rubbing its back.

"Thank you," Lelia said. "I didn't know what to do."

"You could have just ignored him," Margaret said. "He would have wandered off eventually."

"Or you could have picked him up and cuddled him," Ashley said.

Lelia shook her head. "I'm not ready for that."

"Do you want to give him a pat?" Ted asked. "I'll hold on to him, but you can pat his back."

Lelia hesitated and then shook her head. "No, but thank you. Maybe I'll feel braver after I finish my drink."

Ashley laughed. "You're drinking seltzer water."

Lelia shrugged. "But I'm sitting right next to a cat. That's a new experience for me."

"Some people live very sheltered lives," Ashley said.

Lelia flushed. "My mother did her best."

"I'm sure she did," Margaret said. "Were you an only child?"

"Oh, yes. And it was just me and my mother. She never talked about my father."

"Never?" Ashley asked. "Does that mean you don't even know his name?"

"I don't. My mother refused to tell me anything about him. Whatever happened between them, he hurt my mother very badly."

"But if you don't know anything about him, he could have been anyone," Ashley said. "And it's a small island. You might be related to half the people on the island. Maybe Oliver was your half-brother. Maybe that's what got him killed. Maybe his father realized that he was in a relationship with his own sister."

Lelia stared at her. "Oliver was not my half-brother," she said eventually.

"I'm sure Ashley said your apartment is in Douglas," Margaret said, eager to change the subject. "Were you able to walk to the pub tonight?"

Lelia shifted her gaze to Margaret. "We walked," she said.

"Did you grow up in Douglas?" Ted asked.

"I grew up in Onchan, which is really much the same thing," Lelia replied.

Onchan was the neighboring village, and as far as Margaret could determine, there was no clear dividing line between Douglas and its neighbor.

"You should do one of those DNA tests that tell you all about your ancestors," Ashley said. "I'm sure you'd find out all sorts of interesting things."

"I'm not interested in finding out anything about my father. I promised my mother that I'd never go looking for him. She told me that finding him would cause nothing but trouble."

"Well, I really hope you aren't related to half the island," Ashley said. "If I were you, I'd want to make sure of that before I got married and had children."

"My mother moved to the island just a few months before I was born," Lelia said flatly. "Before she moved here, she'd been living in London. She didn't know a soul on the island when she arrived."

"So she met your father in London," Ashley said. "In that case, you'll probably never find him, even if you go looking."

"As I said, I'm not interested in finding him."

Margaret looked at the cat on Ted's lap. He seemed to be slowly inching his way toward Lelia. She frowned at him. Ted noticed her expression and looked down at his lap.

"I think this guy really wants to meet you," he said to Lelia.

She frowned. "I don't know."

"It's entirely up to you," Ted assured her.

"I'm thinking about it."

Ashley shook her head. "I'll take the cat," she said.

"I think he's happy here," Ted countered.

"I can't believe you and Oliver never came here," Ashley said to Lelia.

"We didn't spend much time in pubs," Lelia replied. "We did occasionally get a meal in a pub, but they don't do food here, do they?"

"Not usually," Margaret said. "Although you can order food from the hotel's restaurant from the bartender. He calls the order into the kitchen, and someone brings it over."

"I didn't know that," Mark said. "And I've been drinking here for years."

Ted nodded. "The food is good, too, but it's hard to eat sitting on a couch. We've been known to order snacks at the bar, though."

"Right now, I feel as if I'll never want to eat anything again," Lelia said.

Ashley sighed. "That's a bit dramatic," she said.

Mark frowned at her. "Are you ready for another drink?" he asked.

"Yes, please," Ashley said, quickly draining her glass.

"Come with me and help carry everything," Mark said to her as he got to his feet.

Ashley frowned. "But I'm comfortable here."

Mark laughed. "Then I'll only bring back as many drinks as I can carry. That's one for me and one for Ted."

Ted grinned. "I will have another, thanks."

"I'm good," Margaret said.

"Lelia, would you like another drink?" Mark asked.

She looked at her half-empty glass and then shook her head. "No, thanks."

Ashley sighed deeply before slowly standing up. "You should get me a drink, not Ted. I'm more important to you than Ted is."

Mark opened his mouth to reply and then snapped it shut again. He winked at Ted and Margaret before heading toward the elevator. Ashley stomped after him, clearly not happy.

"I am very sorry for your loss," Margaret said to Lelia.

"Thank you. I'm devastated. Part of me wants to talk about Oliver and part of me doesn't even want to think about him."

"We can talk about whatever you like," Margaret told her.

She glanced toward the elevators. "Ashley told me that I shouldn't talk about Oliver anymore. She said that nothing I say will bring him back, so I should stop talking about him."

Margaret took a deep breath. "You should do whatever feels right to you. Every person in the world mourns differently and every person in the world mourns in the way that is right for him or her. Don't let anyone tell you how you should mourn."

Lelia gave her a small smile. "Thank you. I want to talk about Oliver, just for a minute or two. But I know talking about him will make me cry."

Margaret pulled a packet of tissues out of her handbag and handed it to Lelia. "That should help," she said.

Lelia nodded. She took out a tissue and carefully unfolded it before slowly refolding it into a neat square. "We met at the grocery store," she said. "I usually shop on Sundays and get everything I need for the entire week, but that week Ashley ate up all of the turkey that I'd bought for my lunches. I don't think I'd ever been in ShopFast on a Wednesday evening before, but being there that night turned out to be a good thing."

"I hope Ashley has stopped eating your food," Margaret said.

Lelia shrugged. "She's not as organized as I am, so she often runs out of food midweek. I don't mind sharing some of my things with her, but it is inconvenient when I go to put my lunch together for work and find that I don't have anything to make into a sandwich."

"Where do you work?" Ted asked.

"I work for the *Isle of Man Times* in the subscription office. I'm the person you talk to if you want to subscribe or cancel your subscription or if your newspaper isn't delivered when it should have been."

"That sounds as if you'd have to work odd hours," Margaret said.

"I used to work odd hours, when I first started, but I've been there since I left school at sixteen. There are three of us in the office and I've been there the longest, so I work regular eight-to-five hours now. One of the other girls works from three until midnight. The other works from six in the morning until three in the afternoon. Anyone who rings between midnight and six has to leave a message with our answering service."

"Do you enjoy your job?" Margaret asked.

She shrugged. "I don't hate it, at least most of the time I don't hate it. I hate getting shouted at by angry customers, but that doesn't happen every day. Some days it's very quiet in our department. When it's really quiet, we sometimes get asked to type things for the reporters. I enjoy that a lot more than answering the phones, even though most of the reporters have terrible handwriting."

"Maybe you should become a reporter," Margaret suggested.

"Oh, no. I have no desire to actually be a reporter. It's just fun to type up their reports. I love trying to work out what their scribbles say. I usually get it right, too. There are a few reporters who always ask me to help them, rather than either of the other two girls."

"You must be good at your work," Margaret said.

"I work hard. I know I'm not the smartest woman in the world, but I'm a hard worker. My mother always told me that I was going to have to work hard because I wasn't pretty, and I wasn't smart."

Margaret frowned. "Your mother told you that?"

Lelia flushed. "She wasn't wrong. She was just trying to prepare me for the future."

"I think you're very pretty," Margaret said. "And I think you're probably a lot smarter than you give yourself credit for."

"Oliver always told me that I was pretty," Lelia said softly. "The last guy I was involved with used to tell me that I was lucky to be with him because I wasn't pretty enough to attract anyone else."

"I hope you ended things with him the first time he said that," Margaret said.

"We were together for six years," Lelia said. "And then my mother died. I thought he'd be there for me, but he'd been planning a holiday in America with his brother. They left the day after my mother died. While he was gone, I realized that I was happier without him, even while I was mourning my mother's death."

"I'm sorry. That must have been a very difficult time for you."

She nodded. "I'd been living with him, but while he was gone, I moved myself out. I moved back into the house that my mother had purchased when she'd first moved to the island. He was gone for a month. When he came back, he called me and wanted to know why I'd moved out. While I was trying to work out how to explain myself, he interrupted and told me that it didn't really matter because he'd come back planning to ask me to move out anyway. He had a new American girlfriend who was moving in soon."

"I'm so glad you got away from him," Margaret said.

"I am, too, now," Lelia said. "I was sad at the time, but I knew I'd be happier alone than with him. He rang me a few months later and suggested that we try again. I'd heard through the grapevine that his American girlfriend only stayed on the island for a few weeks before she flew home again. Apparently, she hated just about everything about the place."

"I can't imagine that," Margaret said.

"Can I just touch him?" Lelia asked Ted.

The cat on Ted's lap had inched his way until he was right on the edge of Ted's lap and nearly touching Lelia, whose knees were only inches away from Ted's.

"Of course you can," Ted said.

She reached over and gave the cat a very tentative pat. "His fur is so soft," she said as she patted him again.

"He's very friendly, too," Ted said. "I'm sure he'd sit quietly on your lap if you wanted him to."

"Oh, no. I'm not ready for that," Lelia said. She gave the cat a few more pats and then sat back in her chair. "I was wandering through the frozen food department. I try not to eat too much prepackaged food, but I do keep a few frozen things for last-minute meals. Ashley had eaten everything I had in the freezer, though, so I was looking for things to replace my supplies. I was so busy looking at the options that I ran my trolley right into Oliver's."

"Some women do that sort of thing on purpose," Ted said.

Lelia blushed bright red. "I would never have done it on purpose. After my last relationship ended, I decided that I didn't want to risk getting my heart broken again. Even if I had been looking for a new boyfriend, I never would have approached Oliver. He was so incredibly handsome. He was way out of my league."

"He clearly didn't think so," Margaret said.

"Yeah, but he was wrong," Lelia said with a small laugh.

"What happened after you ran into his trolley?" Margaret asked after a short silence.

"I apologized, of course. Oliver just laughed and said something about how we'd both been too busy looking at the food to pay attention to our surroundings. Then he suggested that we abandon our trolleys and go and get dinner together. I refused, of course. I had frozen things in my trolley. They would have spoiled if I'd just left the trolley in the aisle and left the store."

Margaret nodded. "Did he then suggest dinner another time?"

"Yes, he did, which surprised me. He suggested that we have dinner together on Friday night. I was going to say no, but I found myself almost mesmerized by his eyes. They were kind with a hint of mischief. I couldn't resist agreeing to have dinner with him."

"He sounds quite wonderful," Margaret said.

"He was incredibly wonderful. Being with him made me so very happy. We went out for dinner a few times, but then we fell into a fairly simple routine. Neither of us wanted to spend our time in pubs or clubs. Instead, we took turns cooking for one another, and then we used to watch telly or play cards in the evenings."

"That sounds nice," Margaret said.

Lelia shrugged. "Ashley used to make fun of us for being boring. And I'm sure she wasn't happy to find Oliver at our flat nearly every night. But we were both happy just being there together. Having dinner at home and then playing cards isn't her idea of fun, though."

"Then she didn't have to do either," Margaret said.

"Oh, she doesn't do either. She's always out with one man or another, having dinner in fancy restaurants and going out to the clubs." Lelia's cheeks turned bright red. "Oh, but, I mean, she seems quite devoted to Mark. She hasn't been doing any of that since she started seeing him."

"It sounds as if you and Oliver had a great relationship," Margaret said.

Lelia shrugged. "He'd started talking about getting married. He wanted a wife and children. I wanted to marry him, but I'm not certain I want children. I know that they are a lot of work and expense. My mother used to tell me how different her life would have been if she hadn't had me. I know she had to give up a lot for me."

"But that was her choice," Margaret said. "And whether or not you have children is your choice."

"Now that Oliver is gone, I don't think I'll ever get involved with anyone again. Losing someone you love is too painful."

"You need time to mourn before you make any decisions about the future," Margaret said. "It sounds as if being with Oliver made you happy, so it might be nice to one day find someone else who can do the same for you."

"It might be easier to accept what happened if Oliver hadn't been murdered," Lelia said. She reached forward and gently stroked the cat on Ted's lap again. "Murders only happen in books or on telly or in movies. People don't get murdered in real life. Not in my real life, anyway."

"Sadly, people do get murdered every day," Ted said. "But we're doing everything we can to find Oliver's killer."

Lelia sat back again. "It doesn't make sense. Oliver was just an ordinary person living an ordinary life. No one had any reason to want to hurt him."

"It's possible that he was just in the wrong place at the wrong time," Ted said.

"But I can't even imagine why he was at Dreeym Gorrym Point," Lelia said. "He didn't enjoy hiking. He wasn't all that fond of being outdoors, really. He didn't have any reason to be there."

"Inspector Madison is doing everything he can to find out why Oliver was there and who was there with him," Ted said.

"I didn't even see him last night," Lelia said, pressing the tissue to one eye and then the other. "We were supposed to have dinner together, but he rang me and cancelled at the last minute. He told me that something had come up at work and that he was probably going to be tied up all night."

"Did that happen very often?" Margaret asked.

Lelia slowly shook her head. "Not very often. It wasn't the first time, though. The first time it happened, I thought maybe he was just making excuses because he didn't want to see me. I think it only happened maybe four or five times over the time we were together, but it happened often enough that I didn't give it any thought. I just assumed that we'd see each other tonight."

She sighed and then slowly looked around the room. "This is not where I thought I'd be tonight."

"I'm glad you're here," Margaret said. "I'm not sure you should be at home alone."

"That's what Ashley said. And she also said that she wasn't about to sit around our flat and listen to me cry about Oliver all night, either. That's why I'm here."

"I think she was right not to leave you home alone."

"I suppose so. I'm tired, though. I think I want to go home soon. Maybe after a few more minutes."

"So Oliver worked late last night?" Margaret asked after a short silence.

Lelia shrugged. "He told me that he was working late, anyway. I didn't have any reason to doubt him."

"His office wasn't far from here," Ted said.

"Yeah, but he didn't always work in his office. He had a laptop, so he sometimes would work from home or even from my flat. As long as the work got done, it didn't really matter where he was when he did it."

"So he might have been working from his place last night?" Margaret asked.

"Yeah. He bought a little semi-detached house in Onchan a few years ago. He'd been living with his parents until then, but the house was a smart investment. He bought it while house prices were shooting up, but they kept going up even after his purchase."

"I keep thinking that I'd like to buy something, but I don't know that I can afford anything," Margaret said.

Lelia nodded. "I still own the house that I inherited from my mother, but I don't want to live there. It has a lot of bad memories for me. I rent it out, and I put every penny I get from that into a savings account. I'm hoping to buy a little house somewhere else on the island one day."

"Did you like spending time at Oliver's house?" Margaret asked.

Lelia made a face. "Let's just say that I have higher standards of cleanliness than Oliver did. He was very careful to respect my standards in my flat, but he wasn't always as meticulous when he was at home. His house wasn't dirty or unsanitary, but he did have a bad habit of leaving things lying around the place. I found it difficult to relax there. I always wanted to tidy before I sat down."

Margaret nodded. "I know the feeling."

"Hey," Ted said.

Margaret laughed. "Your flat isn't too bad, really."

"I tidy every time I know you are coming over," Ted admitted.

"If I'd known – if I'd even had a hint of what was coming, I never would have complained about the mess in his house," Lelia said. She wiped her eyes again. "I thought we had forever together."

"Do you think something was wrong at work?" Margaret asked.

Lelia slowly shook her head. "Oliver didn't really talk about his job. He worked with very important clients. He couldn't talk about anything, really. He was very careful not to even share his clients' names with me, even though some of that information is on the company's website. He did talk about work, though, just in very vague terms."

"How vague?" Ted asked.

She shrugged. "He'd tell me that he'd spent the entire day trying to balance one single sheet for a small client and that he couldn't make it work until he'd rung the client and questioned something. Or he'd tell me that he was going to be busy for a fortnight auditing some big company that kept records that were almost too perfect. He never shared anything more than that."

"What sort of emergency would mean he had to work late last night?" Margaret asked.

"It wasn't an emergency so much as a project that needed more time than he'd realized," Lelia replied. "He told me when he rang me last night that he'd gone through the same set of numbers over a dozen times and that he was still two pounds off. This was a summary worksheet, so he knew that he needed to go back to the original sheets to find where he'd made his mistake. And he didn't want to leave it until Monday because he'd promised the client that he'd have everything finished by Monday."

"I wonder if he finished the job," Margaret said thoughtfully.

"He must have. He never would have gone out if he hadn't finished his work," Lelia said.

"He had all weekend," Ted said.

"He tried hard not to work on weekends. He used to, before we started seeing each other, but once we became involved, he used to try to keep his weekends free for me."

"Were you supposed to do something special today?" Margaret asked.

Lelia shook her head. "We didn't have any specific plans. I wish we'd made plans. If we had, I would have realized that he was missing long before I started to worry about him. But when we talked last night, he said that he wasn't certain about his plans for today. He was really apologetic, but he said he thought he might have more work to do. He promised that he'd be free in time for dinner, if not before. I, well, I got a bit angry with him. I deeply regret that now."

"You were disappointed. You'd been expecting to spend the day with him," Margaret said.

"Yeah, and now I'll never get to spend another day with him." She wiped her eyes again and then leaned forward to pat the cat.

"Do you know any of the people he works with?" Margaret asked.

"I've met Drake a few times. I didn't care for him, really."

"Oh? Why not?"

She shrugged. "He just made me uncomfortable. He always tells jokes that are slightly risqué, but not so bad that I felt as if I could say anything. And he was with a different woman every time I saw him, too. One of them told me that she'd been seeing him for six months. I had to bite my tongue because I almost told her that I'd seen him at a party with a different woman just a few weeks earlier."

"Did he get along well with Oliver?" Margaret asked.

"Yes and no. Oliver didn't care for his jokes, either, but he didn't feel as if he could say anything. They worked together, and Drake has been there for almost a decade longer. Besides that, Drake is one of the partners in the firm. He inherited a partnership when his father died. Glen, Oliver's father, is the other partner."

"I assume you've met him," Margaret said.

"Yes, a few times. Glen was always very polite to me, but I still felt as if he was puzzled as to why his son was interested in me. His mother, Caroline, was also polite, but she didn't seem to think that our relationship was anything serious."

"Oliver had been married before, hadn't he?"

Lelia made a face. "He and Karina were married for about five minutes. And Oliver was unhappy for four of them."

Margaret grinned. "That's a very short marriage."

"They grew up together. Karina's father's company was one of Liverpool and Walton's biggest clients. Oliver's parents told him that he was going to marry Karina one day from the time he was a baby."

"How dreadful," Margaret said.

"Yeah, it was dreadful. It was dreadful for Oliver, but it was also dreadful for Karina. Neither one of them ever felt as if they had a choice in the matter. Both sets of parents wanted them to get engaged before Oliver went away to university, but Oliver insisted on waiting. After he finished school, though, when he got home, he found out that his mother and Karina's had been planning a wedding."

"Seriously?" Margaret was aghast.

"Oliver sat down with Karina, and they had a long talk. In the end, they both decided that they might as well make everyone happy and get married."

"I can't imagine deciding that," Margaret said.

"Oliver told me that he didn't really feel as if he had much choice, but also that he felt silly arguing. Karina is smart and funny and beautiful. They'd been close friends for their entire lives. He felt as if he should have wanted to marry her, even though he didn't."

"How did Karina feel?" Margaret asked.

"That was the worst part for Oliver. She was excited about marrying him. She told him that she'd been in love with him since she'd been old enough to understand what love was and that she couldn't wait to be his bride."

"Oh, dear," Margaret murmured.

"They were actually married for just over a year," Lelia told her. "Oliver told me that he did everything he could to fall in love with her, but he simply couldn't make himself feel something he didn't feel. He finally ended things with Karina when she started talking about having a baby. He realized that he didn't want to have a child with her, so he ended things as gently as he could."

"Karina must have been devastated," Margaret said.

Lelia nodded. "The divorce was final over two years ago, but as I understand it, Karina still hasn't forgiven Oliver for breaking her heart. Her father took his business elsewhere, which was a big blow to Livergood and Walton. Glen was furious with Oliver for a long time."

"How dreadful. It must have been awful for everyone involved," Margaret said.

"Oliver threw himself into his work. He spent ages doing everything he could to bring in new business to try to make up for the damage he'd done. He didn't get involved with anyone else, either. I was the first woman in his life since the divorce. I believe Glen and Caroline were both hoping that he might go back to Karina eventually."

Margaret sighed. "That must have been difficult for you."

"It made our interactions uncomfortable," Lelia admitted. "I know they both thought that Oliver would be better off with Karina. Oliver just used to laugh and tell me that his parents would accept me by the time we celebrated our tenth wedding anniversary. I don't know that he was right, though."

Margaret frowned. Everything that she'd learned was interesting, but was there a motive for murder anywhere in what she'd heard?

"Sorry we were gone for so long," Ashley said loudly as she and Mark walked back across the room toward them. "Did we miss anything interesting?"

5

"What took so long?" Ted asked as Mark handed him his drink.

Mark shrugged. "We may or may not have gone out for a snack before getting another round of drinks."

"I was hungry," Ashley said. "And I wanted fish and chips."

"I'm sorry, but I'm getting tired," Lelia said. "I think I'm going to go back to the flat."

"You can't walk home alone," Ashley said. "It's dark out there. Just wait. We'll finish our drinks quickly."

Lelia shook her head. "You stay and enjoy your drinks and time with your friends. I'll be fine on my own."

"Margaret and I are ready to leave, anyway," Ted said. "If we can get these cats to wake up, we can walk you back to your flat."

"I really don't want to be a bother," Lelia said. "The island is a very safe place. I'll be fine on my own."

"Your boyfriend was just murdered," Ashley said. "Now isn't the time to try to tell us that the island is a safe place."

Lelia blinked several times before using the tissue again. "I'll be fine," she said, getting to her feet.

Asparagus opened one eye. Then he opened the other, stood up and jumped out of Margaret's lap. As he ran off, the cat that Ted was petting got to his feet. He looked at Ted and then seemed to shrug before climbing off Ted's lap and onto the floor.

"I'm ready to go home and get some sleep," Margaret said, standing up. She paused to brush off some of the cat hair that was clinging to her trouser legs.

"We'll walk you back to your building," Ted told Lelia. "Mark and Ashley can enjoy their drinks together."

"What about your drink?" Lelia asked.

Ted grinned. "It's just a soda and Mark paid for it. I don't mind leaving it behind."

"Hey," Mark said, laughing.

"We should move over to the couch," Ashley said. "That would be much cozier."

Mark shrugged. "I'm fine here," he said.

Ashley frowned. "Maybe I don't want to stay and have a drink with you."

"Shall we?" Ted asked, looking from Margaret to Lelia and back again.

"Good night," Margaret said to Mark and Ashley.

Mark winked at her. "Good night," he said.

Ashley just sighed and then took a sip of her drink.

Margaret, Ted, and Lelia walked to the elevator together.

"I might have to come here again," Lelia said as they walked through the ground floor together. "Mostly, I want to look at the books."

"If you find something you want to read, you can borrow it," Margaret told her. "I've been reading my way through an entire series by an author I'd never heard of before I found the first book in the series on a shelf at the Tale and Tail."

"Is there any order to how the books are arranged?" Lelia asked as they walked outside.

"The fiction is all arranged by the author's last name," Margaret told her. "It starts on the ground floor near the door and carries on around the room to the stairwell and then up to the upper level. There is a large section of non-fiction on the opposite wall on the ground floor."

"So I could go and look for books by my favorite authors?"

"You can, but in my experience, you might not find anything if those authors are well-known. I don't know if the library used to have more popular authors and those books have all been borrowed and never returned, or if the original owners of the house preferred to buy books by less noted authors, but I've never heard of most of the authors of the books on the shelves at the pub."

"That's a shame," Lelia said.

"It is and it isn't," Margaret replied. "I can get more popular books from the Douglas library. The Tale and Tail has introduced me to several new authors, though, and I've thoroughly enjoyed every book I've borrowed from there."

"I'm sorry to interrupt, but which way are we going?" Ted asked.

Both women laughed. They'd stopped right outside the door to the pub for their conversation and hadn't moved.

"My flat is to the left, but I truly can get home on my own," Lelia said.

"But you'll let us walk you home because you know that we'll worry otherwise," Margaret said.

The trio turned and began to walk along the wide sidewalk.

"Do you want to cross over and walk on the promenade?" Ted asked after a minute.

Lelia shrugged. "It's getting dark. We can't really enjoy the water in the dark."

"What was it like, growing up on the island?" Margaret asked.

"That's a rather hard question to answer," Lelia said after a minute. "I've never lived anywhere else, so I never really thought about what it was like growing up here. I was simply busy growing up."

Margaret laughed. "It was a dumb question," she said.

"Not at all. I know what you meant. You grew up in the US. I'm sure your childhood was very different to mine," Lelia said. "I just don't know what was different."

"Our childhoods probably weren't that different," Margaret said. "I think all children spend most of their days in school, don't they?"

"Probably, but I missed quite a bit of school, too," Lelia replied. "I had some health issues when I was younger and as I got older, my mother fell ill. I spent a lot of time taking care of her when I should have been in school."

"That's unfortunate," Margaret said, unable to come up with a better word.

"She didn't have anyone else. Her parents disowned her when she fell pregnant. She didn't even tell them where she was moving. She just left London and never went back."

"Your poor mother," Margaret said.

Lelia shrugged. "I struggle to feel sorry for her, really. She could have made other choices. She told me that her mother did try to get in touch at one point before she left London, but my mother refused to reply to her. I've always wondered how different things might have been if she'd answered that letter."

"Perhaps you should try to find your grandparents," Margaret suggested.

"I've thought about it, but that was another thing my mother made me promise her before she died. I wasn't to try to find my father, and I wasn't to try to find her family, either. She told me that we'd done just fine on our own and that I was better off without them in my life."

"If I were you, I'd give some thought to trying to find them, even if you don't want to find your father."

Lelia sighed. "Oliver and I were talking about it. He wanted to go to London and start looking for my grandparents. I laughed when he suggested it, though. We can't just walk around London looking for them. I told him that we'd have to do a lot of research before we went anywhere."

"Do you have any idea where to start?" Margaret asked.

"Not really. I have some of my mother's papers. I should probably go through them. I think she might have changed her name when she moved to the island. I keep coming back to my promise, though."

"You shouldn't feel bound to a promise that was made under duress," Ted said.

"That's exactly what Oliver said. He also said that I'd made the promise, but he hadn't promised anyone anything, so there was no reason why he couldn't go looking for my grandparents."

"Maybe he did," Margaret said.

"He shouldn't have. We were still talking about it. I was supposed to make a decision soon, but I hadn't decided yet. He wanted to start looking through my mother's things, but I wasn't ready to let him – not yet, anyway. And now it's too late."

"If you ever decide you want to try to find them and you need some help, please call me," Margaret said. "I'm not an expert at finding missing people or anything, but I'll do what I can."

"And she can consult me if she needs to," Ted said. "I'm not an expert at finding missing people either, but I do know a few people who are."

Lelia shrugged. "I'll think about it."

They'd reached the end of the promenade. Lelia gestured toward the hill in front of them.

"I live near the top. You don't have to walk all the way up there with me."

"But we will," Ted said as they crossed the road to the sidewalk on the other side. "We spend far too much time walking on the promenade, which is flat, easy walking. Walking uphill will be good for us."

"Just don't expect me to talk," Margaret said as they began to climb.

Ted laughed. "It isn't that steep," he said.

Margaret wasn't sure she agreed as they followed the sidewalk away from the sea. Eventually, just before they reached the top of the hill, Lelia stopped.

"My building is right down there," she said, pointing down a short side street.

"I didn't even know these apartments were here," Margaret said as they began to walk down the side road. There were three identical apartment buildings in a row. They were nondescript blocks with small windows and only a single door in the center of each frontage.

"The buildings are older and badly designed, but I do have a view of the sea from both the sitting room and my bedroom," Lelia said.

"And the rent is affordable, especially since I share my flat with Ashley."

"I think I'm too told to share a flat with anyone now," Margaret said. "I managed with Aunt Fenella, and I think I could live with my sister for a short while, but I can't imagine sharing with a stranger or even a friend."

"It isn't always easy, but I've never lived alone. I've always had flatmates everywhere I've lived since my mother died. Maybe one day I'll have enough money saved that I'll be able to buy myself a little house and live all alone."

"It was nice meeting you," Margaret said as Lelia stopped at the door to the third building in the row.

"It was nice," Lelia said. "Thank you both so much for walking me home."

"I'm going to wait here," Ted said. "But I think Margaret should walk you to your door."

Lelia shrugged. "You've come this far, you both might as well come in."

She used a key to open the door and then led them into the building. The carpet in the entryway was old and worn in places, but it looked clean. Lelia led them to a small elevator.

"I'm on the top floor. Oliver and I used to laugh about me living in a penthouse flat."

There was barely enough room for all three of them in the elevator car. Margaret worried briefly that they might be more than the mechanism could manage, but it actually lifted them to the fourth floor quietly and efficiently.

"They replaced the lift last year," Lelia said as they walked out of the car. "The old one was scary, but this one works nearly all the time."

She led them to the end of the short corridor and then unlocked the door to her apartment. As she pushed the door open, she switched on a light.

"It isn't much, but it's home," she said as she led Margaret and Ted into the apartment.

"This is charming," Margaret said as she looked around the cozy space. "And the views are wonderful."

They'd entered into a room that was part living room, part dining room, and part kitchen. Lelia had divided the spaces with a few low screens and had put down a large area rug in the living room area. Margaret walked to the window and looked past a few buildings and roads toward the sea.

"I love the view," Lelia said. "And while I do want to buy a house one day, I know I'll never get a sea view when I do. Houses with sea views are always going to be above my budget."

Margaret dug around in her handbag until she found a pen. Then she took one of her business cards out of one of the bag's pockets. It took her only a few seconds to scribble down her cell number on the back of the card.

"If you need a friend, please call me," she said as she handed the card to Lelia. "You can call my office, but it's probably best if you call my cell."

Lelia took the card and looked at it for a moment before slipping it into her pocket. "Thank you. I really appreciate that. I might reach out as I try to work out how to live without Oliver."

"You're going to be fine, eventually," Margaret told her. "But you need to give yourself time to grieve."

Lelia nodded. "I'm not an impulsive person, but right now I want to pack up my things and move somewhere else. Everything in here reminds me of Oliver."

"It's best not to make too many changes too quickly," Margaret said. "You've had a shock. You need to recover from that before you make any life-changing decisions."

"Can you wait here for a minute?" Lelia asked.

Margaret nodded. As Lelia walked out of the room, Margaret looked at Ted. He shrugged and then walked over and joined her at the window.

"It is a nice view," he said. "They should have made the windows at least twice this size, though."

"Bigger windows would be nice," Margaret agreed.

Lelia was carrying a small box when she walked back into the room a moment later. She put it down on the small dining table and then sighed. "I shouldn't do anything impulsive," she said.

"You must know that you aren't at your best," Margaret said, walking over to stand next to Lelia.

"Would it be too weird to ask you for a hug?" Lelia asked, her voice breaking on the last word.

"Not at all," Margaret said, pulling her close.

Lelia started to cry quietly. Margaret rubbed her back and whispered meaningless things until the tears stopped.

"I am so sorry," Lelia said as she pulled away from Margaret.

"You've no need to be sorry."

Lelia took a deep breath. "When my mother died, I was told not to do anything impulsive, too," she said. "And I didn't." She nodded toward the box on the table. "I was supposed to burn that box."

"Burn it?" Margaret echoed.

"My mother gave it to me. She told me that she'd been planning to burn it. She said it was just full of old papers that were meaningless to anyone but her. And she made me promise that I'd burn it."

"She demanded a lot of promises from you," Margaret said.

Lelia nodded. "And when I made the promise, I really intended to burn the box. She also made me promise not to look inside."

"Which means the papers aren't meaningless," Margaret said.

"Yeah, I did question her when she said I couldn't look at them. She just shook her head and then insisted that I make the promise."

"And you promised because you didn't have a choice," Margaret said.

"I promised because I'd been promising her things my entire life. Our entire relationship was based on her making demands and me promising to live up to them. And I really was going to burn the box, but it isn't that easy to burn something safely. Her house had a gas fire, not a proper fireplace. That's probably why she never managed to burn the contents of the box, now that I think about it."

"And now you want to go through the box," Margaret said.

"Oliver and I were talking about going through the box. I was thinking about letting him go through it or maybe going through it together. It feels like a horrible betrayal of my mother, but it also feels like something I should do. Or rather it did, and now that Oliver is gone, I'm just confused and sad and I don't know what to do."

"You need to give yourself time to think."

"I know. But I'm also afraid that I'm going to make an impulsive decision and set fire to the box. I'm angry that Oliver is gone. I'm angry that my mother kept so many secrets. Right now, I feel as if I could happily set fire to the box that I promised I would burn, especially since I can't open it with the man I loved."

"Do you want me to take the box and put it somewhere safe until you can make a decision about what to do with it?" Margaret asked.

"That's why I went and got it. I was going to ask you to take it home with you and put it somewhere until my head is clearer. But I don't want to impose on you."

"It's not an imposition," Margaret said. "There is a safe in Aunt Fenella's apartment. Mona used it for jewelry, but Aunt Fenella keeps most of Mona's jewelry in safe deposit boxes at various banks around the island. That means the safe is nearly empty. I'd be more than happy to store your box in the safe for you until you're ready to open it or destroy it."

Lelia took a deep breath. "I think that might be for the best, if you truly don't mind. Part of me wants to just open it and start reading, but I know I'm not ready for what I might find."

"I'm happy to take it. Just call me when you want it back."

"I will, but please don't give it to me right away. Make me wait a few hours at least, just in case I change my mind again."

"I can do that."

Lelia sighed. "I'm sorry. I'm asking far too much from you. We just met. You don't even know me."

"But that's okay," Margaret said. "You can trust me to keep your box for now and to return it when you want it back. I'm happy to do something to help you."

"Are you sure?"

Margaret chuckled. "We could go back and forth all night with this or I could just take the box and leave. I think it would be better for both of us if I just took the box and left."

Lelia nodded. "I'm making too big a thing out of this. There's probably nothing in the box except for old utility bills and grocery lists."

"Call me anytime," Margaret said. She picked up the box that was about the size of a shoebox and took a few steps toward the door. Ted followed.

"Thank you so much," Lelia said.

"You're very welcome."

Ted opened the door for Margaret. She turned and smiled at Lelia.

"I meant what I said. Call me if you need a friend," she said.

"Thank you." Lelia grabbed a tissue and wiped her eyes. "Thank you so much."

Ted walked out of the apartment and then shut the door behind them. They were silent as they walked to the elevator together.

"Are you going to peek inside the box?" Ted asked as they walked out of the building a minute later.

"No," Margaret said. "Even though I really, really want to."

"I think you missed at least one really."

Margaret laughed. "Yeah, at least one. I'm dying to see what's in this box, but I'm not going to look."

"Maybe you should. If it is just old utility bills and grocery lists, you could tell Lelia. That would make her decision about what to do with the box a lot easier."

"Except I'd have to tell her that I opened the box, which means that I broke her trust."

"She didn't ask you not to open the box."

"It was implied. I'm not opening the box."

Ted chuckled. "I didn't think you would, but I had to ask. I really want to know what's in that box."

"With half a dozen more reallys."

"Exactly."

The pair walked back down the hill and then crossed the road to walk along the promenade. Margaret kept the box tucked under her arm as they went.

"I think Lelia should look at the contents. And I think she should try to find her grandparents and her father," Ted said.

"I agree with all of that, but it has to be Lelia's decision. Or decisions. She can do some of those things and not others."

"At least now I have something else to think about besides Oliver's murder," Ted said.

"I don't suppose it's possible that the two are connected."

"What do you mean?"

"I don't know what I mean. I'm just thinking out loud, really. Is it possible that Oliver took a look inside this box? Or maybe he decided to do some of his own research. The amount of information available online these days is shocking. What if he found Lelia's father and Lelia's father didn't want to be found?"

Ted sighed. "Then the case is a good deal more complicated than I think anyone was expecting. I'm going to have to talk to Michael about this."

"And after you have that conversation, maybe you could say something to Mark."

"Something to Mark?"

"I'm just being horrible, but I really don't like Ashley."

Ted chuckled. "Oh, that. Yeah, I don't like her either, but ending things now, during a murder investigation, might be awkward for Mark."

"Staying with her during the investigation might be awkward, too."

"I'll talk to Mark. At least he was smart enough to take her away tonight so that we could talk to Lelia."

"Do you think he did that on purpose?"

"Oh, absolutely. Otherwise, he would have invited all of us to go and get something to eat with them."

Margaret thought for a minute. "I suppose you're right. And I'm glad we got to talk to Lelia. I feel really sorry for her. I hope we can help her."

"You're already helping her by taking that box away, at least for a short while. She's upset. She needs to spend some time mourning for Oliver before she decides what to do with the box."

Ted took her hand and squeezed it tightly. "You were wonderful to Lelia tonight."

"I was just trying to help. I can't imagine how she must be feeling. I also can't imagine how awful her childhood was. Everything she said about it sounded just dreadful."

"It did sound as if she had a difficult childhood."

"And now she's stuck living with Ashley."

Ted laughed. "I think she's happier with Ashley than she was with her mother."

"And that's incredibly sad."

When they reached Promenade View Apartments, they crossed the road together. Ted kept his hold on her hand as they took the elevator to the top floor.

"Do you want to come in for a few minutes?" Margaret asked in the doorway to her apartment.

Ted hesitated and then slowly shook his head. "It's late. I'm tired. And if I come in, I might try to talk you into opening that box. You go and lock it away in the safe. I'm going to go home and try to forget that the box exists."

Margaret laughed and then leaned in to to give him a kiss. "I'm going to forget about the box, too," she told him. "Otherwise, it will keep me awake all night."

"Let's go and get brunch somewhere tomorrow."

"I'd like that."

"I'll collect you around ten. We can drive down to that hotel in Port Erin that does the brunch buffet."

"Perfect. I'll be ready."

He kissed her again. "I love you."

"I love you, too."

"I also love that you are a good enough person not to open the box, even though I really want you to open the box."

"What box?" Margaret asked.

Ted laughed. "I'll see you in the morning."

She watched him walk back to the elevators before pushing the door shut. After checking that it was locked, she headed straight for her aunt's bedroom.

"What box?" a voice demanded.

Margaret jumped and almost dropped the box. She spun around and frowned at Mona, who was standing near the kitchen.

"I'll explain later," she said. "I need to put it in the safe first."

Margaret had to move a few things around inside the large safe in order to fit the box inside it. Then she shut the door and twisted the knob. "And now I'm going to forget all about you," she muttered as she walked back out of the room.

"Not before you explain why you put an old shoebox in my safe," Mona said.

Margaret sighed. "It's a long story."

"Does it have anything to do with Oliver's murder?"

"No. At least I don't think so. Not directly, anyway."

"Tell me everything."

Margaret switched off the lights and then sat on the couch facing the windows. She watched the water while she told Mona about her evening.

"You have to see what's in the box," Mona said when she was finished. "Lelia gave it to you because she wants you to open it and see what's inside."

"She just asked me to keep it safe for her. That's what I'm going to do."

Mona frowned. "But I want to know what's in there."

"You stay away from it."

"I can't get into the safe," Mona said. "At least I don't think I can get into the safe. I haven't actually tried. Maybe I can get into the safe."

"Please, Mona, just leave the box alone."

Mona sighed. "I'll leave it for tonight, anyway. But you need to invite Lelia here when she decides to open it. I want to know what's inside."

"We'll see. For now, she needs to deal with the death of the man she loved."

"She'll get over her loss faster once the police find the killer."

"Maybe Lelia killed him. Maybe he looked inside the box, and she found out."

Mona frowned. "I don't think so. Everything you've said about her suggests that if he'd done that, she would have actually been pleased. She wants to know what's in there, and she wants to find her family. She's just a tiny bit more frightened of what she might find than eager to find it. But that's a problem for another day. For now, we need to work out who killed Oliver."

"Ted and I were speculating that maybe Oliver did some research and found Lelia's father. Maybe he didn't want to be found."

"If Lelia's mother told her the truth about moving here from London while pregnant, then it seems unlikely that her father is on the island."

"But we don't know if Lelia's mother told her the truth. And even if she did, London is only a short flight away. Maybe Oliver found him and invited him to come and meet his daughter."

"The police are going to struggle to find him if that's what happened. After the murder, he probably got back on the next flight to London."

"Ted is going to talk to Michael. I hope the murder had nothing to do with Lelia's past. She has enough to worry about right now. She'd be devastated if she found out that her father was a murderer."

"Michael might want to try to find the man," Mona speculated. "Maybe you should warn Lelia about that."

Margaret shook her head. "This is all getting too complicated for me. I'm going to bed."

"I wonder if Lelia's mother's spirit is still around anywhere. I don't suppose you know where her house is?"

"I have no idea. Lelia said she grew up in Onchan, but that's all I know."

"Perhaps I'll take a tour of the island while you're sleeping. I won't have time to go everywhere, but I can visit a few friends and see if any of them are familiar with Lelia's mother. If she's still around, someone will know where I can find her."

"Good luck."

"Ah, thank you. I'm going to need it."

Mona shimmered for a moment before seeming to explode into millions of bright points of light. Margaret blinked several times as the tiny lights faded away.

"I want to come back as a ghost," Margaret told Katie, who'd jumped into her lap as Mona had disappeared. "Not because I want to haunt anyone. I just want to be able to blow myself up into glitter and still be absolutely fine."

She gave Katie a quick snuggle and then started to get ready for bed.

"Of course, Great-Aunt Mona isn't fine. She's dead, but you know what I mean," she added as she washed her face.

Katie stared at her from the bathroom doorway and then slowly turned and walked away. When Margaret walked back into the bedroom, Katie was asleep on the spare pillow on Margaret's bed. Margaret crawled under the covers and quickly fell asleep herself.

6

"Good morning," Margaret said to Katie when the tiny cat began tapping on her nose at seven o'clock the next morning. "You're hungry, aren't you?"

"Mmeewwwww," Katie said, jumping off the bed and running out of the room.

As Margaret slid her feet into her slippers, she could hear Katie shouting at her empty food bowl in the kitchen.

"I'm coming," Margaret called as she pulled on her bathrobe.

In the kitchen, she filled Katie's food and water bowls before switching on the coffee maker. Then she stood and watched the handful of people walking on the promenade while the coffee brewed.

"That's so much better," she said after her first sip of the hot liquid.

After her first cup, she showered and got dressed and ready for the day.

"I'm starving, but we're going for brunch," she told Katie when she returned to the kitchen. "And it's an all-you-can-eat buffet with excellent food. So I should be starving when I get there. The problem is, I'm not going to get there for several hours yet."

She made herself a single piece of toast and ate that with a small tub of yogurt. Then she sat down and opened her laptop.

"I'm just keeping myself busy," she told Katie as she typed in the address for the local newspaper's website.

"Local Accountant Brutally Murdered," the headline screamed.

She sighed. "The victim's identity has been released," she said.

As she turned her attention back to the screen, she heard something buzzing. Frowning, she picked up her phone. The screen was blank. The buzzing noise seemed to be getting louder. Margaret looked at Katie. The tiny cat was curled up in front of the windows with her eyes shut.

"Mona? Is that you?" Margaret asked.

Something flew past Margaret's head. She blinked several times. "That really looked like a bee with Mona's face on it," she told Katie. "But that would be weird, even for Mona."

The creature flew past Margaret again. Whatever it was, it seemed to be growing at an alarming rate. Margaret sat back and watched as it circled the room and then landed on the couch. A moment later, it disappeared, and Mona appeared in its place. Her hair was a mess, and she looked dizzy and confused.

"Are you okay?" Margaret asked.

"No, I am not," Mona snapped. "Never, ever, trust an imp."

"An imp?"

Mona waved a hand. "She was a baby angel, really, or something similar. She offered to teach me how to fly. I shouldn't have trusted her."

"She turned you into a bee?"

Mona shuddered. "I don't ever want to speak of that experience again. I'd appreciate it if you'd simply forget it ever happened."

Margaret nodded slowly. "You might want to fix your hair."

Mona sighed and then snapped her fingers. Now looking like herself again, she turned to Margaret. "You said the victim's identity has been released. I assume Heather gives a list of possible suspects."

"I don't know. I was going to read the article, but then I was dive-bombed by a large bee," Margaret said.

Mona narrowed her eyes. "I don't have to stay."

"Sorry," Margaret said. She turned her attention back to the laptop.

"Yes, there's a list of possible suspects. According to Heather, they are in no particular order."

"Ha. If that were the case, she should have alphabetized them."

"She should have. That would have been safer for her. As it is, the first name on the list is Karina Walton."

"The ex-wife," Mona said. "And from what Lelia told you last night, she'd be at the top of my list, too."

"But according to Lelia, Karina probably wanted Oliver back."

"Exactly, and while he was still single, she thought she had a chance. But then he started seeing Lelia. When she found out, she killed him."

"Surely she should have killed Lelia."

"Maybe she wanted Lelia to suffer as much as she has."

"Maybe."

"Who else is on the list, though? There must be quite a few more names there."

"Glen and Caroline Walton are next. Heather notes that Glen's business lost a lot of money when Oliver divorced Karina. Apparently, Glen had been getting ready to retire early when Karina's father took his business elsewhere. That meant that Glen had to continue working. Heather reckons that both Glen and Caroline were still upset about that."

"I can't see why murdering Oliver solved that problem, though."

"According to Heather, the company has huge life insurance policies on its most important employees. Heather suggests that when the policy pays out on Oliver's death, Glen will finally be able to retire."

"I can't imagine parents killing their child over money."

"It happens."

"Drake Livergood is also on the list," Margaret said.

"He'll benefit financially from Oliver's death."

"Yeah, and Heather offers lots of speculation as to other possible motives for the man. Everything from professional jealousy to personal issues. She even suggests that Drake might have fallen in love with Lelia and wanted to get rid of his competition."

"What did Lelia say about Drake?"

"She didn't care for him. He tells risqué jokes and always has a different woman on his arm."

"Maybe he's in love with Karina."

"Surely, he could have just asked her out, then. She and Oliver got divorced a few years ago."

"Maybe he tried, but she refused because she was still in love with Oliver."

"Maybe. Heather also suggests that Ashley might have had a motive."

"What sort of motive does she give for Ashley?"

"Actually, Heather gives several possible motives. She suggests that Ashley might have fallen in love with Oliver and been upset when he turned down her advances. Heather also speculates that Ashley might have fallen in love with Lelia and wanted to get rid of her competition. Or maybe Ashley just didn't like that Oliver spent so much time at the apartment, so she decided to get rid of him."

"Those are all terrible motives."

"I agree, but I don't mind seeing Ashley's name on the list."

Mona laughed. "You really don't care for the woman, do you?"

"Not at all. And maybe, if she's a suspect, Mark will have to stop seeing her, which would be a good thing, in my opinion."

"Is that the whole list?"

"No, Heather also suggests that Karina's parents, Howard and Doris Stone, might have done it. Obviously, they're still upset that Oliver broke their daughter's heart."

"If that were the case, why wait so long?" Mona asked.

"Maybe because they'd just found out that Oliver was seeing someone else."

Mona nodded. "That's a good point. Was Oliver's relationship with Lelia some part of the motive for the murder?"

"I don't know. I also don't know anything about Howard and Doris Stone."

"I know them," Mona said. "Or rather, I knew them. They have lots of money, and they love to flaunt it and do everything they can to make other people feel small. Max just used to laugh when they acted snobbish around him, but I know they upset a lot of people. Doris used to volunteer with various charities, but over time no one wanted to work with her. In the end, she started her own charity."

"That's mentioned here, actually. The charity, not that no one wanted to work with her anywhere else. Apparently, it raises a lot of money for beautifying the island, whatever that means."

Mona laughed. "Doris had a great deal of difficulty finding a cause to support. When she was volunteering, she'd help whatever charity her husband told her to help, but when it came to establishing a charity of her own, she struggled. It's difficult to find something to support when you disapprove of nearly everyone."

"Oh?"

"Single mothers, the homeless, people with addiction issues, orphaned children, even stray dogs and cats. She seems to think that all of them are where they are in life due to making poor choices."

"Stray dogs and cats made poor choices?"

"Maybe not, but they once had owners who made poor choices, leading them to be strays. In the end, her charity is all about keeping the island beautiful. As I understand it, it pays to have a professional gardener go around certain parts of the island and plant flowers and trees to make those areas more attractive for everyone."

Margaret raised an eyebrow. "And are those parts of the island particularly near Doris's house?"

Mona laughed. "I don't know for certain, but I suspect they are. I know one area that her gardener maintains is the large roundabout on the way into Douglas from the airport. Howard and Doris don't live very far from there."

"It sounds as if they could have paid someone to get rid of Oliver if they'd decided that they wanted him dead."

"Indeed. But that sort of thing comes with its own dangers. And I can see Howard taking matters into his own hands if he felt it was worth doing. It would be helpful to know how Oliver died. If he was poisoned, I'd suspect Doris. If he was strangled or stabbed, I'd suspect Howard."

"Heather also adds that it could have been someone unknown to her and perhaps even unknown to Oliver."

"Yes, of course, but that seems unlikely. Very few people are killed by total strangers. It does happen, of course, but I truly hope it hasn't happened this time. I hate the idea of an unsolved murder on the island."

"Don't we all?"

"All except for the killer," Mona said. "It doesn't sound as if Heather knows anything about Lelia's past."

"She does mention Lelia as a suspect. I skipped over her, because I don't believe she had anything to do with Oliver's murder. Heather suggests that Oliver had ended things with her as a possible motive."

"I've never met Lelia, but everything you've told me about her makes that seem unlikely. I hadn't given much thought to Howard and Doris, but now that Heather has mentioned them, I'm wondering about them. I suspect that's mostly because I didn't like either of them. I'd be quite happy to see one or both of them behind bars. They are terrible snobs who were incredibly rude to me over the years."

"I've never met most of the suspects," Margaret began. Then she stopped and frowned at Mona. "And I'd rather not meet any of them, so please stay out of it."

Mona shrugged. "What could I possibly do to interfere?"

"I don't know, but you do interfere."

"Ah, Ted will be here soon. Must dash." Mona clapped her hands together. Nothing happened.

"Are you okay?" Margaret asked.

"I'm fine," Mona replied.

She clapped her hands together a second time. As Margaret watched, she began to flicker in and out like a bad television signal. When Mona clapped again, she suddenly disappeared.

Margaret spent a few more minutes reading the local news before shutting down the laptop and putting on the television. She watched a cooking show until it was time to get ready to leave for brunch. Just before ten, Margaret got Katie her lunch.

"Now, I'm putting this out early, but you shouldn't eat it until noon," she told Katie, who was still stretched out in the sun. "I'll be back to give you your dinner at your regular time. If you eat lunch too early, you'll be hungry before it's time for dinner."

Katie didn't even open her eyes. Margaret sighed and then put on her shoes and checked that she had everything she needed in her handbag. As she dropped her cell phone into her pocket, she heard a knock on her door.

"Good morning," Ted said, pulling her close.

His hair was still damp from his shower, and he smelled of a delicious mix of some woodsy aftershave and soap as Margaret kissed him.

"Brunch," he said. "I'm starving."

"Me too. I've been up since seven, when Katie woke me. I did have a slice of toast, but that was hours ago."

"Whereas I got up at half nine and haven't eaten a thing."

As Margaret locked her door, the door next to hers opened. She smiled at Elaine as she walked out of the other apartment.

"Oh," Elaine said. "Hello. I forgot..." She trailed off as she quickly walked back into her apartment and shut the door.

"That was weird," Margaret said. "I get the feeling that Elaine is avoiding me."

"She probably just forgot something," Ted said. "I wouldn't worry about it."

"I won't worry much," Margaret promised as they walked to the elevators.

They chatted about nothing much as Ted drove them south from Douglas toward Port Erin. He parked his car in the parking lot in front of the small hotel.

"I don't know why it isn't crowded in here every Sunday," Margaret said as they walked into the building. "The food is excellent."

"I'd come more often if it wasn't such a long drive from Douglas."

Margaret laughed. "In the US, we drive farther to shop. Island residents are just spoiled."

"That's very true."

They walked through the hotel's lobby to the restaurant's entrance. There were only a handful of occupied tables in the dining room.

"For two?" the hostess asked.

Margaret nodded.

"On Sunday mornings we offer a Sunday brunch," she told them. "Our Sunday roast dinner doesn't start until midday."

"We're here for brunch," Ted assured her.

"Very good. Right this way, then."

She led them to a table for two in a quiet corner. The next closest table, for four, was empty.

"I can get you something to drink while you help yourselves to the buffet," she said.

"Coffee," Ted said.

"I'll have orange juice," Margaret said.

"They'll be waiting for you at the table when you get back from the buffet," the hostess promised.

Margaret led Ted to the buffet line. It offered a generous selection of both breakfast and lunch options. Margaret helped herself to a waffle, some bacon, some salad, and a bowl of fresh fruit. After drizzling syrup on her waffle, she walked back to the table. She sat down and then switched the orange juice and coffee cups around. Ted joined her a moment later.

"I'm going to have to go back for more," he said as he sat down. "I want another dozen things."

Margaret looked at his heaping plate. "Are you sure you'll have room for a second helping?"

He grinned. "I'll find room."

They ate in a companionable silence for several minutes. Ted's plate was nearly empty when the hostess showed a party of three to the table next to them. Ted nodded and smiled at the new arrivals. Margaret didn't recognize them, but she gave them a polite smile before returning her attention to her fruit bowl.

"Ah, Inspector Hart, I'm surprised to see you here," the man at the next table said.

Margaret looked up and studied the man, who'd taken a few steps closer to her and Ted. He looked to be somewhere in his sixties. His grey hair was long and had been combed into an oddly-shaped swirl on the top of his head, no doubt a sorry attempt to hide his baldness. He was wearing a dark suit and a gold watch that looked both heavy and expensive.

Ted nodded. "I don't get down to Port Erin very often," he said.

"But you should be working." The older woman who came and stood next to the balding man glared at Ted.

That has to be his wife, Margaret thought. She was wearing a dark blue dress with matching heels and a great deal of diamond and sapphire jewelry. If the stones were genuine, the set had probably cost more than some houses.

"I have the day off," Ted said with a small shrug.

"But Oliver was murdered!" The younger woman who joined the couple looked very much like the older woman.

Margaret immediately assumed that she was their daughter. Unlike her mother, she was simply dressed in a black dress. The only jewelry she was wearing was a thin gold wedding band on her left hand.

"And the investigation into his death is ongoing," Ted said. "Inspector Michael Madison is heading the team."

"I don't know him," the man said. "And I do know you. The chief constable speaks very highly of you. He has dinner with us regularly, you understand."

"That's good to hear, but the case has been assigned to Inspector Madison," Ted replied.

"I'll just have to ring a few people, then, shall I?" the man asked. "I would apologize for breaking up your brunch plans, but I'm not the least bit sorry. A man was murdered. You should be investigating. Everyone in the constabulary should be investigating until the killer is behind bars."

"I'm afraid that isn't how it works," Ted said.

"It should be," the older woman said. "Karina is devastated once again. She won't rest until the killer is behind bars."

"I don't believe the cause of death has been determined," Ted said.

"We're interrupting," the younger woman said, giving Margaret an apologetic look.

"Some things are more important than brunch," the man barked.

The woman glanced at him and then looked back at Margaret. "I'm Karina Walton. The man trying to ruin your morning is my father, Howard Stone. And this is my mother, Doris."

"It's nice to meet you all. And I'm sorry for your loss," Margaret said. "I'm Margaret Woods," she added.

"Yes, of course," Howard said. "Mona Kelly's great-niece or something. Heiress presumptive to Mona's fortune. Everyone on the island knows why Ted is courting you."

"Father!" Karina exclaimed.

Howard shrugged. "It's true."

"As we were saying," Doris said icily, "you should be working." She glared at Ted.

"Even if I were assigned to the case, I am allowed to have some time off," Ted replied. "There is a team of crime scene experts hard at work analyzing everything that was taken from the site where the body was found. The crime lab operates twenty-four hours a day, seven days a week. If they find anything critical, they'll reach out to Inspector Madison, and he'll investigate further."

"They should be talking to the woman he was seeing behind my daughter's back," Doris said.

"He wasn't seeing her behind my back," Karina said. "We were divorced. He was allowed to see other people. I'm allowed to see other people, too."

Doris shook her head. "It was just a matter of time before you found your way back to one another. You still loved him. He would have realized that he still loved you, eventually."

Karina shrugged. "We'll never know now."

"Your drinks," the hostess said loudly, putting coffee cups on the table behind the Stones.

"Thank you," Karina replied.

"Tell your Inspector Madison that he needs to take a close look at where that girlfriend of his was yesterday," Howard said.

"He'd probably dumped her," Doris said. "He was probably getting ready to come back to Karina. He probably dumped her and that's why she killed him."

"Inspector Madison will be looking at everyone who knew Oliver," Ted said.

"I can't imagine his parents had anything to do with it," Howard said. "Although they were still angry with him because of the way he treated Karina. That was the one thing we could still agree on. He behaved very badly towards my daughter."

"Let's get brunch," Karina said.

"Glen was still angry with Oliver," Doris said. "Not only did Oliver break Karina's heart, he cost the company a lot of money."

"Murdering Oliver wasn't going to fix either of those things, though," Karina said.

"I don't know about that," Howard said. "I'm not terribly happy with the accounting firm I'm using now. With Oliver gone, I might be persuaded to move my business back to Livergood and Walton."

Karina sighed. "I'm going to get something to eat," she said. "It was nice meeting you," she told Margaret.

"Likewise," was all Margaret had time to say before Karina walked away.

"She's devastated," Doris said. "Absolutely devastated. She and Oliver were raised with the understanding that they were destined to spend their lives together. She never questioned that. She fell in love with him when she was a child and she was just as much in love with him when he died as she'd ever been, even after the horrible way he treated her."

"And now she won't rest until the killer is behind bars," Howard said. "You have to find the killer."

Ted nodded. "We'll be doing everything we can to find the killer, but as I said, it isn't actually my case."

"I'm going to ring the chief constable," Howard said. "It will be your case before the end of the day."

"Honey, you need to eat more than that," Doris said as Karina returned to their table. Her plate held a few chunks of fruit and a pot of yogurt.

"I'm not very hungry," Karina replied.

"But you need to keep your strength up," Doris said. "It's going to be a long and difficult day."

Howard nodded. "Inspector Madison is coming to speak to us," he said. "Of course, I'll have my advocate sit with you while you speak to him, but it will still be an ordeal."

"I don't need an advocate. I have nothing to hide," Karina said flatly.

"And then that nice young woman from the newspaper is coming to speak to us," Doris said. "She wants to talk about my charity work. She said she really hopes that the murder doesn't interfere with the wonderful work that I'm doing."

"What young woman is that?" Margaret asked.

Doris shrugged. "I've forgotten her name. Helen or something similar."

"Her name is Heather Bryant and she's an investigative journalist," Karina said. "She's not coming to talk about your charity work. She's coming to ask questions about the murder."

"If that's the case, then I'll have her shown out," Doris said. "I have no intention of discussing the murder with anyone."

"I'm going to get some more to eat," Ted said, getting to his feet.

"That's a good idea," Margaret said. She stood up quickly.

"Expect the chief constable to reassign you soon," Howard said. "And once that happens, I expect you to get to work immediately."

Ted just nodded at the man as he walked past him. Margaret took another serving of fruit and then a second waffle as well. She poured syrup over the fluffy treat before walking back to the table. Karina gave her an apologetic smile as Margaret walked past her.

"Maybe we should eat fast and get out of here," Margaret said to Ted in a low voice when he joined her.

"I'm not letting Howard Stone make me cut short my brunch," Ted replied. "I probably should have just told him that the reason I can't be assigned to the case is because we found the body. No doubt the chief constable will share that information with him when Howard rings him."

Margaret took a bite of her waffle. "This is delicious."

"What should we do after brunch?"

"Why don't we take a walk on the beach down here?"

"That's a great idea. And since it's summer, the ice cream stands on the beach will probably be open. We can get some ice cream as we walk."

"Perfect," Margaret replied, deliberately ignoring the voice in her head that reminded her that she'd just had ice cream the previous day.

"I thought there would be more of a selection," Howard said loudly as he sat down with his plate of food.

89

Margaret looked over at the very full plate. *It's probably good that there wasn't. You'd have needed a second plate,* she thought.

"It isn't nearly as nice as it used to be," Doris said as she put her plate on the table. "I remember coming here years ago. They used to have a carvery station and many other options."

"We used to come for Sunday lunch, not brunch," Karina said. "They still do Sunday lunch with the carvery and everything else you remember."

Doris shrugged. "Well, this is disappointing," she said.

"You've filled your plate," Karina said. "You must have found something you liked."

"Of course I filled my plate. The price is the same however much I eat. I'm going to do everything I can to get my money's worth, especially since you aren't eating very much."

Karina sighed. "I'll go and get another plate of food in a minute. First, I need to spend a penny."

Doris nodded. "Do you want me to come with you?"

Karina shook her head. "I'll be fine."

Margaret glanced over as Karina stood up. Karina looked at her and then slowly inclined her head toward the back of the restaurant. Margaret glanced over and saw the sign for the restrooms.

"I'm going to the loo," she whispered to Ted.

He looked surprised, but just nodded and then took another bite of bacon. Margaret waited until Karina had walked past the table before slowly getting to her feet. She picked up her handbag and then turned and walked to the restrooms. There were two stalls. One of them was occupied. Since she was there, Margaret decided to take advantage of the opportunity to use the facilities before she and Ted headed to the beach. When she came out of the stall, Karina was washing her hands.

"Hi," Karina said.

"Hi," Margaret replied.

Karina stepped away from the sink and started looking through her handbag. Margaret started to wash her hands.

"I need to talk to someone," Karina said.

"Someone like the police or someone like a friend?"

Karina laughed. "I'm going to talk to the police later. Inspector

Madison is coming to interview me at my parents' house. My father made all of the arrangements. His advocate will be with me the entire time to make certain that the inspector doesn't ask me any difficult questions."

"Your father is trying to protect you."

"My father is trying to control me. But that isn't anything new. And it isn't as if I'm going to lie or try to hide anything from the police. It's just that when I'm questioned, I know the inspector is going to ask very specific questions. I suppose what I really want is to sit and talk about Oliver. My parents are tired of listening to me talk about him. The police are only interested in hearing about him in the context of his murder. And I know you're a total stranger, but maybe that's the appeal. You'll be hearing everything I say about Oliver for the first time. If you'll agree to sit and let me babble at you for half an hour, that is."

Margaret smiled at her. "I'd be more than happy to sit and listen to you talk about Oliver for half an hour or more. I can't imagine what you're going through right now."

Karina took a deep breath. "I'm not even sure how I feel, which is the worst part." She shook her head. "But that's a conversation for later. Except now I feel stupid for having said anything."

"Please don't feel stupid. I truly do understand why you want to talk to someone. There are professionals…"

She trailed off when Karina held up a hand.

"I've been in therapy since I turned eighteen. It helps, but my therapist knows everything there is to know about Oliver already. I really want to talk to someone who hasn't heard the story before. And I want to do it today, after I talk to the police and after I throw Heather Bryant out of my parents' house."

Margaret grinned. "Have fun with that."

"Oh, I intend to," Karina said with a small smile.

"Where do you want to meet and when?" Margaret asked.

"I think it would be best for me if it looked as if we bumped into each other by chance. I can be strolling on the Douglas promenade around seven, if that works for you."

"I can do that."

"Great. I'll see you in Douglas around seven."

Margaret pulled a business card out of her bag and quickly wrote her cell number on the back of it. "Ring me if you can't make it," she said.

Karina nodded and then handed Margaret a card. "My number if you need it," she said. "And now I need to get back before my mother comes looking for me."

As she walked out of the room, Margaret looked at the card. It was pink and had Karina's name centered on it. Under her name was a cell phone number. There was nothing else on the card.

Margaret combed her hair and touched up her lipstick before she rejoined Ted. He gave her a curious look as she sat down next to him.

"Have you had enough to eat?" she asked as she picked up her fork and stabbed a piece of cantaloupe.

He shrugged. "I could probably manage another mini croissant or maybe a few more pieces of bacon, but we're going to be getting ice cream soon, aren't we?"

"I thought that was the plan."

"It *was* the plan," he said, his tone suggesting that he thought their plans might have changed.

"It's still the plan," Margaret said.

"In that case, I won't have any more bacon," Ted said. "I think one of the ice cream places on Port Erin beach has bacon ice cream."

"Bacon ice cream?"

"I've never tried it, but Mark said it's really good."

Margaret shook her head. "I'll stick to vanilla. Or maybe chocolate. Or caramel. Or mint. There are so many wonderful choices and none of them include bacon."

Ted laughed. "There are a lot of great choices, but now that I'm thinking about it, I really want to try bacon-flavored ice cream."

"Just don't think you're going to eat all of mine if you don't like it."

"I'll get two different scoops, just in case I don't like the bacon one."

"What sort of ice cream goes well with bacon ice cream?"

"Pancake ice cream?"

They both laughed. Ted paid the bill and then the pair walked back to his car.

"Do you want to tell me about your conversation with Karina?" he asked as they climbed inside.

"Yes, I think I do."

Margaret repeated what she could remember of the conversation while Ted drove them to the nearby beach.

7

"Everyone seems to want to confide in you," Ted commented as the pair started walking hand in hand along the water's edge.

Margaret nodded. *And how much of that is due to Mona's interference, I wish I knew,* she thought.

"If Karina gives you a box full of secrets, please don't even tell me," Ted said. "I was awake half the night wondering what is in the box that Lelia gave you."

"I've put it completely out of my head. I'll worry about it after Oliver's killer is found."

"I'm curious what Karina wants."

"So am I. Although I do understand just wanting to talk to someone who will be hearing her story for the first time."

"Except you've already heard a lot of it."

"But not from her perspective. I did wonder if she thinks one of her parents might have had something to do with Oliver's death."

Ted frowned. "If that's the case, she should be talking to the police."

"She is talking to the police later today, but I can't see her accusing her parents of anything, not while she's in her father's house sitting next to her father's advocate."

They walked in silence for several minutes. Margaret jumped when Ted's phone suddenly began to buzz loudly. He glanced at the screen and then sighed.

"It's the chief constable," he said. "I have to answer."

Margaret nodded. She sat down on a nearby bench while Ted walked away, phone in hand. When he walked back to join her a few minutes later, he was smiling.

"Is everything okay?" Margaret asked.

He nodded. "Howard rang him when they finished brunch to demand that I get assigned the case. Apparently, Howard said that he wanted me to conduct the interviews at his house this afternoon. The chief constable had to explain to Howard that there were several reasons why he couldn't assign me to this case. Apparently, when Howard tried to argue, the chief constable rang off. When Howard rang him back, he had his assistant speak to the man."

"'Rang off,'" Margaret echoed. "That's very British."

"Is it?" Ted asked. "What would you say?"

Margaret grinned. "Well, now I'm going to say rang off, because I like it, but in the US we typically say, 'hung up.'"

"Well, however you want to say it, Howard did not get his way with the chief constable. Michael is still in charge of the investigation. And Howard is probably going to be quite horrible to him when he visits them this afternoon."

"Poor Michael."

Ted shrugged. "It comes with the job. Taking statements is never easy and for the kinds of people who seem to think that they are above the law, it's even more difficult."

"Maybe Michael will head back to Derby sooner than expected."

"I doubt it. This secondment is a great opportunity for him. And from a few things he's said, he isn't going to miss his wife all that much."

Margaret frowned. "Are they not happy together?"

"I shouldn't have said anything. I don't know if they are happy or not. Over the past few days Michael has just made a few remarks that suggested that he's not unhappy to be away from home, that's all."

"What a shame. I hope he'll miss his kids, at least."

"Oh, he definitely misses them, but he told me that he's been talking to both of them every night. He said he's talked to them more since he arrived on the island than he did in a typical year at home."

"That's good."

"His wife and the kids are supposed to be coming to visit next weekend. He told me he's really excited to show the kids around the island."

Margaret opened her mouth to reply but shut it when Ted jumped to his feet.

"Ice cream," he said.

"I suppose we can get ice cream now," Margaret said as she got up from the bench. "It's starting to feel quite warm in the sun. Ice cream sounds good."

"There are three different stands, and we have to walk past all of them to get back to the car," Ted said.

"I'm not getting ice cream three times."

Ted laughed. "I wasn't suggesting that we should, although now that you've said that I'm quite tempted. But what I did mean was that we can check each stand as we go past until we find the one that sells the bacon ice cream."

"Are you really going to try bacon ice cream?"

"If I can find it, yes."

The first stand had a fairly limited selection of scoopable ice cream. They mostly carried prepackaged frozen treats.

"Almost everything they had can be bought at the grocery shop for less," Ted muttered as they walked away from the stand empty-handed.

"Maybe we'll have better luck at the next stand," Margaret replied.

When they got there, they found a much wider selection of flavors. Margaret opted for scoops of chocolate cake and mint chip ice creams. As she dug into her bowl of icy goodness, Ted sighed.

"We might have to walk back here if the last stand doesn't have bacon ice cream," he said. "That chocolate cake flavor looks wonderful."

"It is wonderful. It's chocolate ice cream with a swirl of vanilla icing and quite a lot of chunks of chocolate cake. It's better than I thought it would be."

"I don't suppose you want to let me try a bite?"

Margaret laughed. "Didn't we just have this conversation last night? I will let you try a bite, but then I want to try a bite of the bacon ice cream. At least I think I do. I'll decide when I see it."

"Delicious," Ted said after trying Margaret's ice cream. "I hope you won't mind walking back there if I can't get what I want at the last stand."

"It's a beautiful day, and I'm eating ice cream again. I need the exercise."

The third stand had a reasonable selection of flavors, but no bacon-flavored ice cream. Ted asked the man behind the counter about the flavor.

"Oh, that isn't something we've tried. I think the stand at the center of the beach tried it a few weeks back. From what I heard, it sold well initially, but very few people tried it once and then went back to get it again. It was just a novelty sort of thing. I don't know that they'll make it again."

Ted sighed. "In that case, I'll have two scoops, one chocolate and one raspberry ripple in a cone, please."

The man scooped up generous balls of ice cream, carefully stacking them on top of the cone. Then he handed the confection to Ted.

"Thank you," Ted said. He paid for the ice cream and then took a big bite. "Delicious," he added.

The man smiled. "We try."

"Do you want to try either of my flavors?" Ted asked Margaret as they walked away from the stand.

"Since you had a bite of mine, it's only fair that I get a bite of yours. I'll try the raspberry ripple and pretend that I'm having more fruit."

She used her spoon to secure herself a small bite of the fruity flavor.

"It's very good and very refreshing," she said.

"You can have a second bite if you let me try your mint chip," Ted offered.

"I could do that."

The pair walked the rest of the way to the car exchanging bites of ice cream and chatting easily.

"Now what?" Ted asked as they finished their treats leaning against his car.

"What time is it?"

"Nearly two o'clock."

"So we have hours to fill before I'm meeting Karina on the promenade."

"We need to have dinner in there somewhere. I'll probably want to eat early since we had brunch but not lunch."

"But we just had ice cream."

"Ice cream doesn't count."

Margaret laughed. "Okay, so an early dinner. That still gives us a few hours to fill."

"Shopping? Sightseeing? Or we could just sit on the beach and soak up the sun."

"We're in Port Erin. What if we drove the rest of the way down to Cregneash and had a wander around there?"

"We could do that. We're only a mile or so away."

A short time later, Ted pulled his car into the parking lot for the small village in the far south of the island. A living history museum, the village provided visitors with an opportunity to experience what life on the island had been like in the nineteenth century. Margaret and Ted walked around the village, sticking their heads into a handful of thatched cottages and the church. They visited the loaghtan sheep on the small farm where the fields were still plowed by horses.

Ted paused as they walked back toward the car.

"They have ice cream in the café," he said.

Margaret laughed. "We just had ice cream."

"But they make their own ice cream here. I've never had ice cream from Cregneash Village."

"It's nearly five. We should get dinner as soon as we get back to Douglas."

"You say that as if a single scoop of ice cream will spoil my dinner."

"Go and get some ice cream, then," Margaret said with another laugh.

Ted grinned. "Don't you want anything?"

She shook her head. "I've had enough ice cream for today."

"No amount of ice cream is ever enough," Ted said before he disappeared into the small café.

Margaret strolled slowly along the lane, admiring the tiny cottages. It was almost impossible to imagine entire families living in such small spaces together. As she turned back around, Ted walked out of the shop carrying a small bowl of ice cream.

"That's a single scoop?" she asked when she reached him.

"I couldn't choose between the caramel swirl and the apple crumble, so I had to get two scoops. But that means I can share them both with you if want."

Margaret tried a bite of each flavor.

"They're both really good. I think I like the apple crumble better, though," she said as they walked back toward Ted's car.

"Okay, maybe I have spoiled my dinner a little bit," Ted admitted as he drove them back toward Douglas. "I was planning to take you somewhere nice tonight because we rarely have time for that during the week, but now I'm not certain I'm hungry enough to appreciate somewhere nice."

"We can just go to a café or something," Margaret said. "I'm not all that hungry myself. Mostly, I'm getting nervous, wondering what Karina wants to discuss with me."

"I'll be nearby if you need me."

"You can't be too nearby. You might put her off talking at all."

"I'll wear a disguise."

Margaret laughed. "Do you have a disguise?"

Ted nodded. "I have several, actually, and some of them aren't bad. I did undercover work for a few years earlier in my career. And when you do undercover work on a very small island, you either learn how to create quite good disguises or you get spotted everywhere you go."

"What was it like, working undercover?"

"There were things I enjoyed about it, but it's also incredibly difficult to have to think twice before you say anything to anyone. We were taught how to walk differently, how to talk differently, even how to sit differently. All of those things help you remember that you aren't yourself, but they also take a lot of extra effort."

"That does seem like a lot to remember."

"I used to wear a fake moustache a lot. It itched and I was constantly worried that it was going to fall off in the middle of a conversation."

Margaret laughed. "I can't even imagine."

"You'd be surprised by how different I look with a moustache, though."

She studied his profile as he drove. "I can't picture it."

"Maybe I will put on a disguise and then wander up and down the promenade while you're talking to Karina."

"I would like you to be somewhere sort of nearby, but I don't know about the disguise."

"We can talk about it over dinner. Now that we're getting close to Douglas, I'm getting hungry."

"Let's go to the café in Onchan," Margaret suggested. "The little one on the corner that has such good soups and stews."

"That sounds great. Even though it's hot outside, soup still sounds good."

"That's because you've had so much ice cream that your insides are frozen and craving heat."

Ted parked in the small parking lot for the café. There were only a handful of people inside. They sat at a table for two near the window.

"I'm going to give you these, but you should have the beef stew," the waitress said as she handed them menus.

"Oh?" Margaret replied.

The woman shrugged. "The cook tried a new recipe for the stew tonight. It's usually one of our most popular dishes and I've always loved it, but the new recipe is better. I've already had two bowls of it, and I'm taking home a bowl for my husband. Unless I eat it in the car on the way home. It's that good."

"I'm not going to argue," Margaret said, handing back her menu. "I'll have the beef stew."

"So will I," Ted said.

The waitress nodded. "It's served with freshly baked bread. We have sourdough, whole wheat, or we can serve it with our sourdough garlic bread."

"Garlic bread," Ted and Margaret said together.

The woman laughed. "That's the best of the three, but after bullying you into ordering the stew, I didn't want to say anything about the bread. What about drinks?"

They requested soft drinks. The waitress brought those almost immediately. She was back with their stew and garlic bread before much longer.

"Please don't hate it," she said as she put a large bowl of stew in front of Margaret.

"It smells amazing," Margaret said.

"Do you need anything else right now?"

Margaret shook her head. Ted did the same as he picked up his spoon. Margaret reached for a slice of garlic bread.

"The bread is good," she said after a bite.

"The stew is amazing," Ted said. He put down his spoon and picked up a piece of bread. "The beef is tender and flavorful. There are baby onions. There are carrots and potatoes, and goodness knows what else. I think it's the best stew I've ever eaten."

Margaret tried a bite. "It is really good," she said before taking a second bite.

When the waitress walked past a minute later, they assured her that they loved their meals.

"I'm too full," Margaret said after she'd eaten every bite of stew and a piece of garlic bread. "That was really delicious."

"It's a good thing I have room for the last piece of garlic bread, then," Ted said as he grabbed it. "It would be a shame to waste it."

"What about pudding?" the waitress asked as she cleared away their bowls.

"I wish I could, but I'm too full to even think about it," Margaret said.

"I bake the pies," the woman told them. "And I've been working on my apple pie recipe for months now. I think I've got it just about perfect. You can always take a couple of pieces home with you for later."

Ted laughed. "We'll have two slices to take away," he said. "If you don't want yours later, I'll eat them both," he told Margaret.

She laughed. "I'm going to want to try a bite or two, but I don't think I'll be able to eat an entire piece of pie later today. Right now, I feel as if I'm going to be full forever."

The waitress returned with a large box and their check. Ted paid for dinner and then they walked back outside. At the car, Ted peeked into the box.

"There's almost half a pie in here," he said.

Margaret took a look. "It smells of cinnamon and happiness. I want a very thin slice after I talk to Karina."

"Let's get you back to the promenade, then. You don't want to be late for your meeting."

"I'm not convinced she's going to turn up," Margaret said as Ted drove them back toward Margaret's building.

"I suppose that depends on how badly she wants to speak to you."

"I have a feeling she might struggle to get away from her parents, too."

Ted parked on the promenade across from Margaret's building.

"You'd better take the pie inside," he said. "Otherwise, I might just sit in the car eating pie while you talk to Karina."

Margaret laughed. "I have to feed Katie, too. She's probably starving. I gave her an early lunch, and now she's going to have a late dinner."

"I'm going to move my car and then change my clothes," Ted said. "I might not put on a disguise, but I am going to do a few things to make myself less recognizable from this morning. I'm also going to keep my distance from you and Karina, wherever you end up. If you need me, just wave."

"Wave?"

"Yeah, stick your hand up and wave it back and forth. I'll come running."

Margaret nodded. "I wish I could think of a better signal, but I suppose that will work."

"I'll see you later," Ted said.

Margaret got out of the car and then carefully crossed the road and walked into her building. The smell of cinnamon seemed to surround her as she took the elevator to the sixth floor. Katie was asleep in front of the windows when Margaret walked into her apartment.

"I guess you aren't too hungry," Margaret said to the sleeping animal before she went into the kitchen. She put the pie in its box in the cold oven to keep it safe from the mischievous cat and then quickly filled Katie's food bowl. She added a few treats to the top of the bowl before topping up her water. With that job out of the way, she freshened up before heading back down to the promenade. It was just a few minutes before seven as she began to stroll toward the Sea Terminal.

It was a perfect night for a walk on the promenade. While it wasn't exactly crowded, there were quite a few other people enjoying the warm, dry weather and the amazing scenery. Margaret found herself looking twice at every man she saw, often taking a third look at those who had moustaches. None of them looked like Ted, but because that was the point, she couldn't stop herself from staring. When she reached the Sea Terminal, she turned around. She'd walked only a short distance before she spotted Karina walking toward her.

"I should have picked a specific spot, shouldn't I?" Karina asked when she reached Margaret. "We could have been walking up and down all night looking for one another."

"I was going to text you if I didn't spot you in the next few minutes."

Karina laughed. "I should have thought of that."

She turned around and fell into step with Margaret.

"How was your afternoon?" Margaret asked.

"It was, hmm, interesting might be the best word for it. Inspector Madison was very polite and seemed competent enough. I'm certain he had a long list of questions for me that he didn't ask because of my father's advocate, but he asked some difficult questions anyway."

"And did the advocate tell you not to answer?"

Karina laughed again. "Oh, yes. He probably advised me not to answer at least half of the questions. I answered them all anyway. I don't have anything to hide."

"That's good."

"I just wish I could have told him something that would have helped with the investigation. I simply don't have any idea who killed Oliver."

"Everything you told him will help. He's working on a giant jigsaw puzzle and I'm sure you gave him some extra pieces to work with."

"And then I had the pleasure of chasing Heather Bryant out of the house."

"Oh, goodness, that must have been awkward."

"I'll give the woman credit for being persistent. When she rang, she told my mother's secretary that she wanted to talk to my mother about her charity. My mother loves talking about her charity, even though it does very little that is at all useful. Mother's secretary was happy to give Heather an appointment, based solely on what Heather said over the phone. When I found out about it, I did some research."

"That was smart of you."

She shrugged. "My mother's secretary is fairly new to working with Mother and to the island. It never occurred to her that it was odd that a newspaper reporter suddenly wanted to talk to my mother about her charity work just after my mother's former son-in-law was murdered. I had a long conversation with her after I got rid of Heather."

"She must have been very upset."

"Actually, she just shrugged and reminded me that she was new to the island. That's her excuse for everything, of course. She can never seem to find anything my mother asks her to get, even when my mother tells her exactly which store carries whatever it is she wants. She's messed up several lunch reservations for my mother and her social circle because she doesn't know the names or locations of any of the island's restaurants. It seems as if when my mother asks her to book somewhere, her secretary just rings some random restaurant and makes a booking instead of booking the place my mother requested. I could go on and on, but just talking about it is making me tired."

"I'm surprised your mother hasn't fired her."

"I think she wants to, but my father is quite fond of her. And not in a creepy way. She was just smart enough to be incredibly kind and sweet to him when she first started, so now my mother's complaints fall on deaf ears as far as my father is concerned."

"If she's your mother's secretary, then your mother should be able to fire her, regardless."

"Except my father pays her salary, so the decision is ultimately his."

"So your mother's secretary made an appointment for Heather to come and interview your mother."

"Yes, and I was there when the woman arrived."

"Smart."

"While I walked with her to the drawing room, I made it very clear to her that my mother would talk about nothing other than her charity. Heather agreed, of course. What else could she do?"

"And how long was she there before she started asking questions about the murder?"

"Not long," Karina said with a chuckle. "In fairness to Heather, she did ask a few questions about Mother's charity. She even took a few notes, although I suspect she probably threw them away as soon as she left the house. Then Heather asked my mother how much she thought the charity would be affected by the recent murder."

"Ouch."

"Yeah. My mother just stared at her and then said that she didn't believe that the murder had anything to do with the charity."

"And then Heather said something horrible," Margaret guessed.

Karina grinned at her. "You know Heather, then."

"I wouldn't say I know her, but I've been questioned by her a few times."

Karina flushed. "Of course, because you've found a few dead bodies, haven't you? And your aunt used to find them everywhere she went. I didn't really make the connection earlier today."

"What did Heather ask next?" Margaret asked, eager to change the subject before Karina started to wonder who'd found Oliver's body. That information hadn't yet been released to the public, as far as Margaret knew.

"She said something along the lines of, 'I thought people might be less willing to donate to a charity whose founder is a suspect in a murder investigation. Your husband and your daughter are suspects, too, of course, which could be a concern for your husband's business, couldn't it?'"

Margaret frowned. "That sounds like Heather."

"I immediately stood up and told Heather that the interview was over. My mother started stammering out a reply, but I wouldn't let her speak. I rang for the butler and had him escort Heather out of the house and off the property."

They have a butler, Margaret thought.

"I was worried that Heather might hang around the house and then follow me down here, but I didn't see any sign of her when I drove onto the main road."

Margaret looked around. "I suppose we should be paying attention to the people around us, especially if you want to speak confidentially."

"I don't know what I want."

"We can just walk, then."

They were both silent until they'd walked past Margaret's building.

"Are the flats nice?" Karina asked, nodding toward Promenade View.

"I think they're very nice, but I haven't seen a lot of other, um, flats on the island."

Karina nodded. "I've been thinking of moving. I've been thinking about it since the divorce, but now I'm really thinking about it. My house is just full of memories that I don't really want to remember any longer."

"You might feel differently in a year or two."

"I might. But if I do, I can always move back into the house. It will still be there."

"You won't sell it?"

"I can't sell it. It isn't mine to sell." She shook her head. "I don't know why I always assume that everyone on the island knows everything about me and my life. It's a ridiculous assumption, even though I often find that people know more about me than I think they should."

"I'm going to guess that your parents own your house," Margaret said.

"Yeah. It's a small house on the grounds of their estate." She sighed. "Except it isn't really a small house. It has six bedrooms, three reception rooms, and seven bathrooms. It's a mansion by any standards other than my parents'. It was a wedding gift to me and Oliver, except they didn't actually give us the house, just the right to live there."

"And now you want to move."

"Last year my mother's father died. He left me some money. It's the first money I've ever actually had, really. My father very quickly offered to help me manage it, but I refused. I don't usually stand up to him, but that money represents possibilities to me. I've spent the last six months trying to work out what I want to do next, but I'm not very good at making my own decisions. My parents have always made my decisions for me."

"I can't imagine."

"They have my best interests at heart. No one loves you as much as your parents love you. And honestly, I've never been unhappy with any of their decisions. They've given me a wonderful life."

"But they haven't equipped you to live on your own."

"I don't live on my own. I have a housekeeper, a cook, a driver, and a gardener who look after me. My parents pay for all of them. On paper, I'm a director at my father's company, but I never go to the office. I don't even know if I have an office. I have an assistant there who rings me once a week to let me know what is happening, but I rarely have any idea what he's talking about. He never asks me to make any decisions or come into the office or anything of that sort. And for all of my hard work, I get paid a generous salary and drive a company car."

"I don't think your parents are actually helping you."

"You're probably right. No, you are right. It's just taken me a long time to recognize that. And now that I have, I'm frozen with indecision. Part of me wants to quit my job and move out of my house, but I have no idea if I can afford to do either thing. It's far easier to just keep living my comfortable, stress-free, financially secure life."

"I can understand that. Change is hard. And it's scary, especially if you've never had to deal with any sort of upheaval in the past."

"I am divorced," Karina said. "That was a major upheaval. My parents did what they could to help me through it, but it was devastating."

"I'm sorry."

She shrugged. "And now we reach the topic I've been wanting to avoid at least as much as I want to talk about."

She stopped and then looked up and down the promenade.

"There's an empty bench over there. Let's sit down and talk," she suggested.

Margaret nodded. "I'm ready to sit down for a bit."

"I run on a treadmill every day for an hour," Karina said as they walked toward the bench. "I always think that it's a perfect metaphor for my life. I'm running in total safety, in a completely controlled environment. And I'm going exactly nowhere."

They sat down together. For a short while, no one spoke.

"I don't even know where to start," Karina said eventually.

"Why don't you start at the beginning?" Margaret suggested.

8

"I don't want to bore you or keep you here all night," Karina said.

"We can always take a break and resume another time if it gets too late," Margaret replied. "And after everything you've already told me, I'm curious to hear more."

"My parents didn't really want children."

Margaret held up a hand. "I should warn you that I am going to share everything you tell me with Ted. Everything that might be relevant to the murder investigation, anyway."

"I want you to do that. I want you to do everything you can to help the police find out what happened to Oliver. I loved him. I loved him a lot."

Margaret nodded. "But you were saying that your parents didn't want children."

She shrugged. "My father didn't really care either way. It wasn't as if he had any intention of being involved in the upbringing of any children they might have. And actually, I think he did want children; or rather, he wanted a son. He wanted an heir. I'm fairly certain he was disappointed when he got a daughter instead."

"I hope that attitude is mostly dying out now."

"I suspect there will always be a certain group of men who want sons to carry on the family name. I don't think my mother wanted children. She'd been raised in a similar way to the way that I was raised by parents who'd indulged her every whim. She was spoiled and selfish, and the idea of having to sacrifice anything for someone else appalled her."

"Even if that someone was her own child?"

"When she and my father got married, they agreed that my mother's money was her money and that my father's money was their money. It was quite unlike my father, but I'm told that he was crazy in love with my mother at the time."

"Whose money paid for the things you needed, then?"

"My father's. Oh, my mother used to buy me presents out of her accounts once in a while, but my father paid for everything else. They made that arrangement when my mother found out that she was pregnant. I believe she would have terminated the pregnancy if my father hadn't agreed."

Margaret frowned. "I'm sorry."

Karina shrugged. "My mother has slowly grown more generous towards me over the years. She'd inherited a great deal from various grandparents and other relatives even before she married my father, but after her own parents died, she inherited quite a lot more, including several houses in England and two yachts."

"Two yachts," Margaret echoed.

Karina laughed. "We went sailing on one of them the summer I turned sixteen. I was seasick for weeks, but once I started feeling better, I enjoyed myself. My mother sold both of the yachts as soon as her parents died, though."

"So now your mother is more generous?"

"She can be. Sometimes. But it really doesn't matter because my father spoils me terribly. I think at least some of that is because he feels guilty about wanting a son."

"Did they spend much time with you when you were a child?"

"Not at all. My mother likes to travel, with or without my father. He has a company to run, of course, so he can't always drop everything to fly to the Caribbean for a month in the sun with my mother. I had to stay at home with my nanny and my tutors, of course. My father wasn't about to pay to fly all of them to the Caribbean, not even if my mother had been interested in taking me along, which she was not."

"I'm sorry."

Karina shrugged. "I'm not. I didn't know any better, of course. And I had a wonderful nanny who was like a mother to me. I loved her dearly. She lived with me until her untimely and unexpected death just after my eighteenth birthday. I was also close to a few of my tutors. I'm still in contact with two of them, actually. They did their best to teach me things, but I wasn't all that interested in learning."

"Someone told me that you met Oliver when you were quite young."

"I've known Oliver for my entire life. I suppose I should say that I *knew* Oliver for all of my life. Or maybe for all of his life. He was six months older than I am. I never knew life without Oliver."

She stopped and took a shaky breath. "He was one of the few constants in my life, actually. Even after the divorce, I knew I could ring him if I needed anything. He was always my friend, even after the divorce."

Margaret found a pack of tissues in her bag. She handed Karina a tissue. Karina dried her eyes.

"I'm never going to be able to talk about him without crying. After everything that happened, I should hate him. I do question everything I thought I knew about him. But I loved him. He was my first love. And he might be the only man I ever love. Even two years after the divorce, I can't imagine falling in love again."

"Give yourself time to grieve before you worry about that," Margaret said.

"I've had two years. Part of the problem is that I don't know anything about how to have a relationship. Oliver and I were a couple before either of us knew what that meant. Our mothers decided that we should be together, and we were both raised believing that that was true."

"That must have been difficult."

"It was all that I knew. I'm sure it was harder for Oliver. We used to talk about how hard it was for him, because he went to school and then university where he met lots of other women. I had tutors until I turned eighteen, and then I did nothing much for the years after that until the wedding. I've never really spent time alone with any men aside from my father and Oliver. Maybe, one day, if I decide to try meeting someone, I'll ring you for advice."

"I'd be more than happy to help you."

"They did it for my protection."

"I'm sorry. You lost me."

Karina laughed. "My brain is jumping all over the place. What I meant was that my parents wanted me to marry Oliver at least in part to protect me. I'm the sole heir to a considerable fortune. There are a lot of men out there who would love to take advantage of me."

Margaret nodded. "Is Oliver's family equally wealthy?"

"Oh, goodness, no," Karina said with a small laugh. "But my father liked and trusted Glen. He trusted Glen with his business, which is far more important to him than I am. My mother and Caroline were close friends, too. Glen was just successful enough to allow them to exist on the very fringes of my parents' rather elite social circle. But my parents both liked the idea of me marrying an accountant. They thought that Oliver would look after my money for me. He was going to have to, of course, because they'd never taught me anything about looking after it myself."

"So your mother and Oliver's mother decided that you two should get married?"

"Yes, when we were both very small. I don't remember a time when Oliver wasn't in my life, and from the very beginning he was always referred to as my future husband."

Margaret frowned. "I can't imagine how that must have felt."

"It felt perfectly normal. I didn't know anything else. I've already told you how sheltered my life was. I simply assumed that everyone married the person their parents chose. It was Oliver who told me otherwise. We were in our early teens, and he'd met someone else."

"Oh dear."

She laughed. "It's funny now, but at the time I was upset and confused. I didn't understand how he could be attracted to anyone else. We were meant to be together. He told me that he hadn't meant to fall for her, but that she was cute and smart and fun to be around.

And then he told me that most people were allowed to find their own partners, that arranged marriages like ours were an old-fashioned idea from the colonial era that only truly mattered to the nobility. I cried in my nanny's arms for hours that night."

"He'd shattered your view of the world."

"Yeah, he had. My nanny was very careful with her replies. She told me that some families did things differently to other families. When I asked her, she admitted that if she had ever wanted to get married, that she would have expected to find her own husband without her parents getting involved. I had to wait three weeks for my mother to get home from the South of France to talk to her about it."

"And what did your mother say?"

"She said that I was lucky that she and my father had chosen a husband for me. When she'd turned eighteen, she'd been given three names on a piece of paper and been told to choose one. She also said that she'd spent her entire life questioning her choice."

Margaret winced. "What a horrible thing to tell you."

"She also said that I was lucky because I'd had a chance to get to know Oliver. She'd met the three men on the list, but only very briefly. She had to make her choice based on having done little more than nod and smile at each of the men."

"Do you know why she chose your father?"

"He had the most money," Karina said flatly.

"I should have been expecting that."

Karina nodded. "She also promised me that either Oliver or I could change our minds at any time. We didn't have to get married. She and Caroline were just hoping that we'd want to get married when we were older. And she told me that it was perfectly normal for men to want to get involved with other women before they married the woman they wanted to spend their lives with. I didn't know anything about sex at that point, but she muttered something about men needing to have a certain amount of experience before they settled down. I wanted to believe that Oliver and I were still going to be together, so I didn't question anything she said."

"And you and Oliver were still friends?"

"Oh yes. We were always friends. In retrospect, we should have simply stayed friends. And a lot of the reason why we got married is my fault. But I was still blindly listening to my mother at that point."

"Because you didn't know any better."

"I should have known better, but I still wanted to make my parents happy. My mother and Caroline wanted Oliver to propose before he went away to uni, but he wanted to enjoy his three years across. I was hurt, but I also understood. I even told him that I might try going out with a few other men while he was gone. He told me that he thought I should."

"But you didn't?"

"I might have, if I'd met anyone, but I was still living in my parents' house, doing not much of anything, really. My mother started taking me with her when she traveled, now that I was old enough to traipse around museums and historical sites with her. She always made certain that we were back on the island whenever Oliver was on breaks, but otherwise we did a lot of traveling in those years."

"I hope you had fun."

"It was fun, but my mother made sure that I was very closely supervised at all times. I think she was afraid that some handsome Frenchman was going to try to sweep me off my feet. If one had been able to get close to me, he might have succeeded, actually. Oliver had never courted me in any way. Being chased by a man would probably have been exciting."

"And then Oliver graduated?"

"And by the time he moved back to the island, my mother and Caroline had the entire wedding planned."

Margaret sighed. "I can't help but feel a bit sorry for Oliver."

"I feel sorry for him, too, now. At the time I was just really excited that we were going to be getting married. I wrongly assumed that he'd been consulted, you see. I didn't know that he was going to get blindsided when he came home."

"I'm surprised he didn't just immediately return to the UK."

Karina nodded. "He thought about it, but his life was here. His father had a job and an office waiting for him. And I was here. If nothing else, we were friends. He hadn't made many friends while he'd been at uni. He was actually quite shy."

"So you got married."

"Not without a lot of back-and-forth first." Karina smiled, a dreamy look in her eyes as she stared out at the sea. "We sat down together, just the two of us, and had a serious talk. It was the first time we'd ever done that, really. We used to talk all the time, of course, but we'd never really talked about our future. I didn't think we needed to talk about it, because I'd assumed it was all decided. He didn't want to talk about it because he didn't want to let anyone down."

"Does that mean he didn't want to get married?"

"He definitely didn't want to get married, not when we first started talking. He thought we were too young. Looking back, I think he was right, but at the time I didn't see it that way. As far as I was concerned, we were going to get married one day, so why not get married now?"

"Especially since the wedding was all planned."

"Exactly. And I can admit now that some of my arguments in favor of getting married were purely selfish. Our mothers had planned an almost perfect wedding for us. My mother even used her own money to buy me the most amazing wedding gown. We flew over to London for a long weekend so that I could find my dress. Caroline came with us. She and my mother both loved the dress I selected."

"And that was before Oliver found out about the wedding?"

Karina sighed. "I thought he knew. We hadn't spoken for a few weeks. He was busy with exams, and I was busy with wedding plans. We texted once in a while, but not as much as we normally did. I didn't mention the plans because I thought his mother was keeping him informed. I'd do things differently if I could do them over again."

She sighed. "Or maybe I wouldn't. The year that Oliver and I were married was the happiest year of my life. If he'd known what our mothers were up to before he came home, he probably would have decided to spend a year traveling or take a job in London or something. As sad as I am about how everything turned out, I'd hate to have missed out on that year we had together."

"What convinced him to go through with the wedding?"

"I suppose I did, although as much as it pains me to say it, Oliver made what he considered the most logical decision."

"Logical?"

She made a face. "He was an accountant. He made a spreadsheet with all of the pros and cons of marrying me. Money was the biggest pro. My parents offered him a large lump sum as a wedding present. It was a present for him, not us, and he got to keep it if we were still together on our first wedding anniversary."

"That sounds like a bribe."

"Yeah, it was a bribe, but I didn't want to see it that way. I told myself that my parents were just being generous. They wanted to give Oliver more equal footing with me. I'd already inherited some money, and we both knew that I was going to inherit a lot more eventually."

"What else went on the spreadsheet?" Margaret asked.

"Oh, lots of things. On the plus side, he put that he did care about me, even if he wasn't certain that he loved me enough to want to spend the rest of his life with me. And he knew that marrying me would make both of our families happy. And he knew that marrying me would be good for his career. The biggest con was simply uncertainty. He didn't know if he wanted to be married at all. He wasn't ready for children. And he worried that he might one day meet someone else and fall properly in love."

"You should have ended things."

"I should have, but I didn't. And I'm glad I didn't, because I got to be his wife for a year, at least."

"I hope the wedding went well."

"It was a magical day. Once Oliver made the decision to go ahead and marry me, he threw himself into the process. We had three engagement parties in the weeks before the wedding. And then we had our wedding weekend, starting with a bridal brunch and carrying on through two days of celebrations. Then we went on a lengthy honeymoon."

"That all sounds wonderful."

"It was wonderful. I was deliriously happy. And I want to believe that Oliver was happy, too. He told me every day that he loved me and that he had no regrets about marrying me. We traveled around Europe from one five-star hotel to the next, eating amazing food and drinking champagne. I'd never traveled anywhere without my parents or my nanny before. Just that was intoxicating to me, before I even took a sip of champagne."

"How long were you gone?"

"Four months. They were far and away the happiest four months of my life. Oliver told me that they were the happiest days of his life, too. I wanted to believe him. And even now, after the divorce and after his untimely death, when I think back to those months, I truly believe that we were both incredibly happy. Maybe he wasn't as madly in love with me as I was with him, but we loved each other, and we had fun together. And then we came back to the island."

"And everything went wrong?"

"It was gradual, but it started almost immediately. Oliver went to work for his father's company. Glen wanted Oliver to prove himself, so Oliver had to work long hours, which meant I spent most of my time alone. My parents had given us the house as a wedding present, so I kept myself busy decorating and then redecorating every room, but I missed Oliver. After a month or two, though, I started to realize that he didn't miss me, at least not in the same way."

"I'm sorry."

"Thanks. Really, thank you. I feel like you're truly hearing my story. Everyone on the island watched it unfold in real time, and I doubt very much that anyone felt sorry for me as it was happening. I was the spoiled rich girl whose parents had bought her a husband. Everyone seemed to think that I should have been expecting it all to go wrong."

"I'm sorry about that, too."

Karina shrugged. "I sometimes think I should have tried harder. I did ask Oliver to go to marriage counseling with me towards the end, but by that time he'd already given up on the marriage. We were both just going through the motions. Mentally, he'd already moved on."

"And that was after a year?"

"Oh, no, that was after about six months, maybe seven. For the first few months after we got back from our honeymoon, Oliver kept insisting that everything was fine, that he was just busy. He moved into one of the spare bedrooms and spent most weekends at the office but kept telling me that he was still happy with me. After a few months of that, we finally sat down together and had a long talk. He told me that he still loved me, but that he hadn't been able to fall in love with me in the way he'd hoped he would when we'd decided to get married. Then he told me that he thought it would be best if we got divorced."

"That must have been a shock."

"It was a horrible shock. I begged him to try counseling. I insisted that he hadn't given it enough time. I did everything I could to change his mind, but nothing I said mattered. As I said before, he'd already moved on."

"With another woman?"

"No – at least I don't think so. No. I'm certain there wasn't anyone else. He told me that he wanted to be single again. That he wanted to stop having to worry about someone else. That he'd never really had a chance to live on his own and make all of his own decisions. That was what he really wanted. He insisted that it wasn't me. It was just being married that he wasn't enjoying."

"I can kind of understand that. You were both very young."

"I kind of understood, too, but I still hated it. I still wanted to make our marriage work. After going back and forth for ages, I reminded him that if we separated before our first anniversary, he wouldn't get the money from my parents. And I suggested that he give our marriage another six months. I promised him that I'd do everything I could to make him happy for those six months and that if after that he still wanted a divorce, I'd sign the papers the day after he got the money from my father."

"Wow."

Karina sighed. "Yeah, wow. It was a desperate attempt by a desperate woman to keep a man who didn't want her. Of course, Oliver agreed. It was only six months and there was a lot of money at stake. To be fair to him, I truly do think that he tried to give our relationship a chance during those six months. He wouldn't agree to counseling, but he did start coming home earlier in the evenings and we started doing things together on weekends, too. I'd like to believe that we had some happy moments during those months, even though I spent them feeling as if I had the sword of Damocles hanging over my head."

"How awful for you."

"Oliver waited until a few days after my father gave him the check before he filed for divorce. I was devastated, but I signed the papers. He bought himself a little house and moved out the next day."

Margaret wordlessly handed her a tissue. Karina wiped her eyes.

"The worst part of his sudden death is that I'll never know if we would have reunited or not," Karina said.

Maragaret stared at her.

Karina chuckled. "Yes, okay, I know. After everything I've told you, that seems unlikely, but we were still friends. We still texted each other every day and talked at least once a week. Just last year, Oliver told me that he missed me and that he sometimes thought he'd been too hasty in filing for divorce."

"He was involved with someone else."

"He was. He told me all about Lelia. They met at ShopFast. Oliver rarely did anything impulsively, but he asked her out almost without thinking about it. He felt quite sorry for her, really."

"Sorry for her?"

"I've never met her, but Oliver told me about her. Apparently, she had a rather horrible childhood. She doesn't have a lot of money, either. Oliver actually told me that he was thinking of marrying her just so that he could divorce her and give her a small settlement. He wanted to give her enough money so that she wouldn't have to keep working at whatever badly paying job she has."

"Marrying her just to divorce her seems a bit extreme."

"Yeah, that's what I said. I suggested that he just give her a lump sum, but he didn't think she'd take it. Obviously, I didn't care for the idea of Oliver getting married again."

"Do you think he was serious?"

"I don't know. When he said it, I got the feeling that he was sort of testing the waters, wanting to see what I'd say. I wondered if he was hoping that I'd offer to befriend Lelia and give her some money. It was a strange conversation, really."

"When was that conversation?"

"Just a few days ago. We only talked one time after that and for only a few minutes. I rang him, just to say hello. He was on his way out. I asked if he was taking Lelia somewhere, but he just laughed and said that he had plans with Drake. That was about it. The conversation ended after we'd both said 'I love you,' to the other."

"Drake?"

"Drake Livergood. He's another director or partner or something at Livergood and Walton. His father, Donald, was one of the original founders, but he died some years ago now."

"And he and Oliver were friends?"

"They were work colleagues. I don't know that they were friends. I suppose they were. I've never really thought about it. I don't know Drake well. He's about ten years older than Oliver. He'd already been with the company for a decade when Oliver started there. I would say that they were friendly, but maybe not friends."

"What do you think of Drake?"

Karina frowned. "I don't know how to answer that. He's tall, dark, and handsome, but he's also a player. Oliver told me that years ago, before I even knew what the word meant. Actually, Oliver warned me about Drake. He said that Drake was jealous that Oliver and I were supposed to get married one day. According to Oliver, Drake didn't understand why he couldn't marry me. Oliver reckoned that Drake was just after my money."

"He is ten years older than you."

"Yeah, which was a huge difference at the time, but wouldn't be as big a problem now. In another few years, it won't matter in the slightest."

"Did Drake ever ask you out?"

"Oh, goodness, no. That would have caused no end of problems between him and Oliver. And that would have caused problems for the company." She frowned. "I've only seen him once since the divorce. My father was quick to move his business elsewhere after Oliver left me, which meant no one from Livergood and Walton was welcome in our house or at our parties any longer. But I bumped into Drake at a charity event about six months after the divorce. He stopped me to ask me how I was doing. I told him that I was fine and kept walking. As I walked away, he called after me. He said that I should ring him sometime, that he'd like to buy me dinner to apologize for his friend being dumb enough to let me get away. I just kept walking."

"Interesting," Margaret said as Karina turned her gaze back to the water.

"I think that's everything," Karina said after several minutes had ticked past. "And I feel a good deal better for having shared all of that with you."

"I'm glad I could help."

"Maybe I'll sleep better tonight." Karina sighed. "Except I don't think I'll ever sleep properly until the person who killed Oliver is behind bars."

"Do you have any idea who might have killed him?"

"I wish I did. No one had any reason to want to hurt him. Okay, maybe I did. He did break my heart, but I still loved him. The last thing I wanted to do was kill him. I was still hoping we might get back together one day."

"He did have another woman in his life."

"Lelia was just a passing fancy. He felt sorry for her. He might even have married her, but they were never going to be together forever."

Karina held up a hand. "Okay, I know that sounds delusional, but Oliver and I talked a lot. He still loved me. And he told me all about Lelia. He wouldn't have done that if he was truly in love with her."

"Does that give her a motive for his murder?"

Karina frowned. "I don't know. Maybe he told her that he didn't want to see her any longer and she killed him. That happens, doesn't it? People get so upset that they kill the person they love when they get rejected."

"It does happen."

"I've never met Lelia, so I rather like that solution."

"I have met her. I don't think she did it."

"My parents would never have done anything to hurt Oliver."

I didn't say they might, Margaret thought. "Were they still angry about how he'd treated you?"

"Yes, of course. My father was particularly upset that Oliver waited until after our first anniversary to file for divorce. I've never told anyone that staying together until Oliver got my father's check was my idea. Please don't tell my parents."

"I doubt I'll ever speak to them again, but if I do, I won't tell them anything."

"Thanks. I know my mother and Caroline were both upset that Oliver was involved with someone they both considered unacceptable."

"Unacceptable?"

"Anyone outside of our very small social circle is considered unacceptable. They both would have been furious if they'd heard that Oliver was considering marrying Lelia. Glen would have been angry, too. Both sets of our parents really wanted Oliver and me to get back together."

"Can you think of anyone else who might have had a motive for the murder?"

"Drake, maybe. I'm only saying that because they worked together. As far as I know, they got along just fine, but maybe Oliver stole a client from him or something. And now I'm just speculating wildly, because I have no idea if that's something that's even possible at Livergood and Walton."

"Lelia has a flatmate."

Karina laughed. "Oh, yes, the lovely Ashley. I've completely forgotten her surname. Oliver talked about her almost as much as he talked about Lelia. From what Oliver said, she's rude and messy and lazy."

"I wonder if there's a motive for murder anywhere there."

"Maybe. Maybe she wanted Oliver for herself. That was never going to happen, but maybe she didn't know that. Maybe she threw herself at the poor man and he rejected her. From everything Oliver told me about her, I can imagine her being upset enough to stab him. Or hit him over the head. Or whatever happened to him."

"It's still possible that his death was simply an accident."

"My parents are convinced that it was murder, and they're friends with the chief constable. I don't think it was an accident."

Before Margaret could reply, a song started to play somewhere. Karina frowned and then pulled her phone out of her pocket.

"It's my mother," she said. She tapped on the screen to answer the call.

"I'm walking on the Douglas promenade," she said after hello.

Margaret got up and took a few steps away to allow Karina some privacy. The woman's voice carried across the short distance.

"I'll be home when I get there. I'm an adult. I don't have a curfew any longer."

A moment later, Karina stood up and slipped her phone back into her pocket.

"I need to go," she told Margaret. "My mother is having fits because I'm not home and there is a murderer running around loose on the island."

"You have my number. Call me if you need to talk again."

"Thank you. I really appreciate you giving up so much of your time tonight."

Margaret watched as the woman walked away. After a minute, she began to slowly follow.

"Hey, can you spare a few pounds for a hungry Manxman?" a voice asked.

Margaret looked over at the grey-haired man who'd walked up behind her. His clothes were shabby, and he was wearing thick glasses that had smudges on both lenses. She shook her head and then took a few steps forward.

"Ah, come on," the man said. "I need some ice cream."

9

Margaret did a double take. "Ted?" she said tentatively.

He laughed. "I told you I had some good disguises," he said, winking at Margaret.

"It is a good disguise. You don't need any more ice cream today, though."

"Ah, I should have gone for ice cream before I tried to talk to you."

Margaret laughed. "Were you close enough to hear any of the conversation?"

"I walked past a few times, but I never heard much. You're going to have to repeat everything for me."

Margaret looked up and down the promenade. There weren't many people near them. "Do you want to talk here or back in my apartment?"

"My apartment is closer. We could go there."

Yes, but then I'd have to repeat everything a second time for Mona, Margaret thought.

"Unless you have ice cream," Ted added. "I know I've already had lots of ice cream today, but I really want more. And I don't have any in my flat."

"There are a few half-eaten tubs of ice cream in my freezer. Let's talk there."

Ted nodded. He removed the glasses and then shoved them into a pocket. "I'd take off the wig, but I'd hate to think what my hair looks like underneath. On balance, I'd rather be in public in the wig than risk it."

"Aren't you worried about someone seeing us together and recognizing you? You might have trouble using that disguise again."

"I don't plan to use it again. I don't expect to have to work undercover again. And if I do, I have several other disguises. This one is just the quickest and easiest to put together."

No one paid any attention to them as they walked back along the promenade to Margaret's building. She used her keycard to get them into the building and then into her apartment. Katie ran straight to Ted as they entered.

"She recognizes you, then," Margaret said.

Ted picked up the cat and snuggled her close. "I'm glad of that."

Margaret walked into the kitchen and opened the freezer. "Chocolate or vanilla?"

Ted laughed. "Is that it? No fancy flavors with chunks of something yummy mixed inside?"

"Sorry. I don't buy ice cream very often, but when I do, I usually buy fancier flavors. I'm not actually sure where these two tubs came from."

Margaret thought for a minute, trying to remember if the ice cream had been there the last time she'd looked in the freezer. It seemed unlikely that Mona was magically filling the freezer, but so many things in Margaret's life on the island seemed unlikely that she'd mostly stopped questioning them.

"I think I'll skip the ice cream, then," Ted said. "Let's just sit and talk. You can tell me everything that Karina said."

Margaret sighed. "I feel really sorry for her. Her parents kept her really sheltered. It sounded as if Oliver was her only friend. And then he broke her heart."

"Start at the beginning."

Margaret nodded. She sat down next to Ted on one of the couches and waited for a moment, hoping that Mona would appear. She really didn't want to have to repeat herself.

"The first thing that she told me was that her parents never really wanted children," Margaret began.

A bright flash of light made her jump. Ted gave her a curious look as Mona appeared in front of Margaret. She was hovering a few feet above the ground and frowning.

"Are you okay?" Ted asked.

Margaret nodded. "I thought that car was going to crash into those pedestrians," Margaret said, pointing to the zebra crossing that was visible below them.

"It stopped, though, didn't it?"

"Yes, it stopped." Margaret glared at Mona.

Mona shrugged and then took a step toward the chair next to Ted. She was still several inches off the ground. When she reached the chair, she sat down. Margaret stared as Mona settled into the chair, floating at least an inch above the cushion.

"Don't mind me," Mona said, waving a hand. "Carry on."

"Where was I?" Margaret asked.

"Karina's parents didn't want children," Ted replied.

Margaret nodded. She leaned her head on Ted's shoulder and then did her best to repeat the conversation she'd had with Karina. When she was finished, she wiped away a stray tear.

"That poor woman," Mona said. "I never cared for Howard or Doris, but I never imagined that they were treating their daughter so badly."

"Interesting," Ted said.

"Interesting?" Margaret repeated.

He shrugged. "She told you a few things that she didn't tell Michael, but that's to be expected, really. Michael asked questions that he thought were relevant to the murder investigation. He didn't ask for the woman's entire life story."

"But her life story could be relevant to the murder."

"Maybe. If Oliver was killed because he divorced Karina."

"That's one possible motive. I'm sure there are others."

Ted sighed. "I'm going to have to ring Michael and tell him about the conversation you had with Karina. I already told him about our brunch conversation."

"Is that a polite way of telling me that you're leaving?"

"Sadly, yes. It's Sunday night. We both have to work in the morning, and I don't expect my conversation with Michael to be short. I'd better go."

Margaret walked him to the door. After they kissed, she frowned at him.

"Kissing you while you're wearing a disguise is weird."

"I'm sorry. One of my former girlfriends used to like it. She said she felt as if she were cheating, but without the guilt."

"I don't want to cheat on you."

Ted nodded. "I really should have seen that as a red flag, shouldn't I? She did end up cheating on me – several times, in fact. I only found out when one of the other inspectors at the station spotted her with another man while I was on an undercover assignment. He spent some time investigating her on my behalf and then brought me a stack of photos of her with other men."

"I'm sorry."

He shrugged. "Two of the other men were me in disguise, which I found quite amusing, but the other three were not. We'd been talking about moving in together – or rather, she'd been talking about moving in with me. She already had a key to my flat. I packed up the things she'd left in my flat and had someone drop the box off to her. Then I had the locks changed on my flat. When she tracked me down and demanded an explanation, I just handed her copies of the pictures."

"Where is she now?"

"Married with three kids. They all have different fathers, but the third is her husband's. They've been married for a few years now and they seem happy together."

"And you need sleep."

"We both need sleep."

"Yes, but only one of us needs to call Michael."

Ted sighed. "That would be me. I'm going."

He kissed her again, just quickly, and then let himself out. Margaret watched as he walked to the elevators at the end of the corridor. When the doors opened on one of the elevators, Elaine walked out. She frowned at Ted and then walked past him without saying a word.

Elaine was halfway down the hall before she spotted Margaret. She flushed and then quickly opened her handbag. Margaret frowned as Elaine kept her nose buried in her bag as she walked past her.

"Good evening," Margaret said as Elaine reached her.

"Oh, I didn't see you there," Elaine said. "I can't find my key."

She rushed past Margaret and then pulled out her key and let herself into her apartment without saying another word. Margaret frowned and then slowly shut the door.

"What is wrong with Elaine?" Margaret asked Mona as she walked back across the living room.

"Is there something wrong with Elaine?"

"She seems to be avoiding me. I just saw her in the hallway, and she didn't say one word about Oliver's murder. Elaine always wants to talk about murder investigations."

"Indeed. Interesting. I shall see what I can learn if I can find time to investigate with everything else that's happening."

"Michael is investigating the murder. You can focus on Elaine."

"Perhaps," Mona said. "After your conversation with Karina, I think you need to meet Drake next."

"Don't interfere," Margaret said.

Mona simply smiled before slowly fading away. Margaret frowned as Mona disappeared, leaving behind a single, shimmering, ghostly shoe in the middle of the living room floor.

"That isn't going to stay for long, is it?" Margaret asked, staring at the sliver stiletto.

"Merroow," Katie said. She swiped a paw at the shoe, knocking it over.

Margaret blinked several times. "But it isn't really there," she muttered as she walked closer. "How did you knock it over?"

She bent down and reached for the shoe. Her hand passed right through it.

"Hit it again," Margaret said to Katie.

Katie yawned and then ran out of the room, heading for Fenella's bedroom. Margaret tried to touch the shoe again. As she put her hand over it, the shoe suddenly popped like a bubble and disappeared.

"Weird," Margaret said as she stood up. "My life is really weird."

In the kitchen, she refilled Katie's water bowl. Then she peeked into the freezer. The two tubs of ice cream were still in the same place. Shaking her head, she took herself off to bed.

"I love my job," she said loudly the next morning when Katie began tapping on her nose. "But I'd very much rather sleep for another hour or two," she added as she rolled out of bed.

An hour later, she was ready for the day ahead.

"Mrs. Jacobson will be here around noon," Margaret told Katie. "Have a good day."

Mrs. Jacobson lived across the hall and came over every afternoon to get Katie her lunch while Margaret was at work. Mrs. Jacobson adored cats but was living with her daughter, who was allergic to them. The arrangement suited both women, and Katie, who got a great deal of love and attention from Mrs. Jacobson along with her midday meal.

Margaret left her car in her usual spot in the lot outside of Park's Cleaning Supplies. Joney Caine, the office manager, was already at her desk when Margaret walked inside the building.

"Good morning," Margaret said.

"Good morning. I hope you have lots of skeet on the island's latest murder," Joney said.

Margaret shook her head. "No skeet here," she said, using the Manx word for gossip.

Joney frowned. "I suspect you actually know a lot, but I do understand that you aren't supposed to talk about it. You are involved with a police inspector, though. He must tell you things."

"If he did, and I'm not saying he does, I couldn't repeat them."

"I know. I'm just frustrated because I want to know everything."

"You want to know everything?" Rachel Bass asked as she walked in behind Margaret. "I actually know one of the suspects, so I'm really curious."

Rachel was the small company's business manager.

"Which suspect do you know?" Joney demanded.

"Drake Livergood. We actually went out a few times, years ago," Rachel replied.

"And now you're going to tell us everything you know about him," Joney said.

Rachel laughed. "I can do that."

Margaret glanced at the clock. While she was eager to hear what Rachel was going to say, she was supposed to start work in three minutes.

"Don't talk about the good stuff without me," Arthur Park said as he rushed into the foyer from the back of the building.

"Did I ever mention that that door isn't soundproof?" Joney asked, winking at Margaret.

Arthur laughed. "I think we need to have a meeting in the conference room. I brought donuts this morning. We can have donuts and coffee and talk about the murder."

Margaret wasn't about to argue with the man who owned the business and employed her. Joney locked the front door and then they all made their way to the rarely used conference room. Arthur put the box of donuts in the center of the table while everyone else quickly headed to the break room to get themselves cups of coffee.

"I'll start," Arthur said when they were all sitting together around the table. "I know just about everyone involved, although I don't know any of them well."

"You play golf with Howard Stone," Joney said.

Arthur nodded. "We belong to the same golf club. And we play together occasionally. Howard uses the golf course as a place to hold meetings as much as anything else. We've made more than one deal between holes."

"More's the pity," Joney muttered.

Arthur laughed. "I know. I know. He's a difficult customer."

"Is he?" Margaret asked.

Joney nodded. "We get a lot of complaints from his team. He doesn't complain himself, of course. He has people for that."

"And most of the complaints are ridiculous," Rachel added. "Some junior assistant rang once to complain that one bottle out of a shipment of two thousand bottles was slightly less full than the others. I really wanted to demand that she measure exactly how much liquid was in the bottle before I would do anything about it, because I know we overfill our bottles by at least five percent, but in the end it seemed easier to simply send her another bottle."

"And Rachel isn't even supposed to have to deal with complaints," Joney said. "But that doesn't stop some people from ringing her."

"Have you ever met Doris?" Margaret asked Arthur.

"Oh, yes. Howard often brings her to the club for meals. He sometimes brings Karina, too. She's lovely, but very shy."

"She's shy because her parents never let her go anywhere or do anything," Joney said. "I've met her a few times, when Arthur has taken me to the club. She always used to sit silently at the table while her father held court with whatever unfortunate souls were dining with him that evening."

"I read all about her online," Rachel said. "Apparently, her parents and Oliver's decided that they should get married when they were babies. Poor Karina was raised to be Oliver's wife and nothing else. And then, after a year of marriage, he left her."

Joney nodded. "He got a nice big lump sum of money for staying with her until their first wedding anniversary. If I were Karina, I would have killed him before he could cash that check."

"But she didn't," Rachel said. "And it's been a few years since the divorce. That suggests to me that someone else killed him."

"Maybe. Probably," Joney said.

"What about Howard?" Rachel asked Arthur.

Arthur looked surprised. He frowned and then reached for a donut. "Howard is a businessman," he said as he put his donut down on the small paper plate that had held his first donut. "I can't imagine him killing anyone. I suppose it depends on how the man was murdered. If Howard could have simply waved a hand and that would have killed him, I can see him doing so. But I think he would have done that when Oliver filed for divorce, not now."

"He could have paid someone to kill Oliver," Joney said.

"Yes, I suppose so," Arthur said as if the idea had never occurred to him. "If Howard had anything to do with the murder, that must be what happened. Because, of course, you can't simply wave a hand and kill anyone."

"What about poison?" Rachel asked.

"Poison?" Arthur echoed. "I can imagine Howard poisoning someone, yes. And I suppose he has the necessary connections to find a poison that would kill."

"Anyone can find that these days," Joney said. "There are recipes online and places where you can order poisons."

Everyone looked at her.

She laughed. "I've been thinking about writing a book," she explained. "I want to write a murder mystery, so I was doing some research. It's shocking what you can find online these days."

"Where does Doris fall on your list of suspects?" Rachel asked Arthur.

"Oh, she's at the very bottom," Arthur said. "I can't imagine her killing anyone. She's incredibly careful with her money, too, so I can't see her paying to have Oliver killed. Not unless there was some financial advantage to her in doing so. I can't see her having him killed just because he broke Karina's heart. As much as I hate to say it, I don't think she cares that much about Karina."

"Ouch," Rachel said.

"What about Karina, then?" Joney asked. "He broke her heart. Maybe her anger has been growing ever since and she finally snapped."

"Or maybe she was upset all over again because Oliver had just started seeing someone else" Rachel said. "Maybe, up to that point, she thought that he'd be coming back to her one day."

"I can see that," Joney said. "It would be really helpful if we knew how Oliver died. The method used could be quite telling."

Everyone looked at Margaret.

She laughed. "I have no idea how he died. Ted isn't part of the investigation and even if he was, I'm sure the police are keeping that information confidential."

"Karina has plenty of money," Joney said after a moment. "Maybe she paid someone to kill Oliver. Maybe she'd been wanting to kill him for years, but it took her this long to find an assassin."

"Don't tell me that you can find them online, too," Rachel said.

Joney shrugged. "I haven't gone looking, but I suspect that they're there if you know exactly where to look."

"There are plenty of other suspects," Arthur said. "I know Glen and Caroline Walton, and they aren't on my list at all. They both loved their son dearly."

"He cost the company a lot of money when he divorced Karina," Joney said. "And from what I've seen, his father loves the company a great deal, too."

Arthur nodded. "He and Donald Livergood worked incredibly hard to build Livergood and Walton into the island's best accountancy firm. And they're good at what they do, too. They're the accountants for Park's Cleaning Supplies, and they take care of my personal finances as well."

"And then Oliver lost them their biggest client," Joney said.

"Which was unfortunate," Arthur admitted. "But I know that Oliver worked really hard to find the company new clients to help replace the lost business."

"And all of that happened years ago," Rachel added. "If Glen was upset enough to kill Oliver over it, surely he would have killed him when it happened."

"Unless," Joney said, holding up the hand that held her half-eaten donut. "Unless the killer has been angry since the divorce, but deliberately waited to make his or her motive less obvious."

"What about Oliver's new girlfriend?" Rachel asked. "Does anyone know anything about her? Her name is Leia or something similar."

"It's Lelia. I've met her," Margaret said. "She came to the pub with Mark and Ashley the night the body was found. Ashley is her room, er, flatmate."

"She was in the pub the same day the body was found?" Joney asked. "It sounds as if she was celebrating."

Margaret quickly shook her head. "She was only there because Ashley didn't think she should stay at home alone. She wasn't drinking, and she was clearly very upset."

"So upset that you're certain she didn't kill Oliver?" Joney asked.

Margaret frowned. "I don't know her well enough to answer that.

She seemed like an incredibly nice young woman. She had a difficult childhood."

"It sounds as if Oliver was attracted to women who'd had difficult childhoods," Rachel said.

Joney laughed. "He was attracted to Karina because she had money. Does Lelia have money?" she asked Margaret.

"Quite the contrary. She works for the *Isle of Man Times* in the subscriptions office and lives in a small apartment with a roommate," Margaret replied.

"I wonder what Oliver saw in her," Joney said.

"She seems very nice," Margaret said. "And she's quite pretty, in an understated way."

"Can we think of any motive for her?" Rachel asked.

"Maybe Oliver rewrote his will, naming her as his heir," Joney suggested. "He was already worth quite a bit before he got the big payout from Howard Stone. If she is his heir, she won't be sharing a flat and working for the local paper for long."

"I doubt Oliver would rewrite his will after just a few months with someone," Arthur said. "That's the sort of thing you do after you get married, or at least engaged."

"Maybe they were engaged," Joney said. "Maybe they secretly got engaged and then Oliver redid his will in her favor. Then she stabbed him to death at Dreeym Gorrym Point and left him there to die."

Margaret shuddered. "What a horrible thought."

Arthur reached for another donut. "You mentioned Ashley, Lelia's flatmate. She's on the list of suspects, too. The article I read online suggested that she'd fallen in love with Oliver and that he'd rejected her."

"She's currently involved with Mark Hammersmith," Margaret told them.

"The police inspector? That explains why he isn't in charge of the investigation," Joney said. "I was surprised that Ted wasn't put in charge, but I suppose his friendship with Mark was a concern."

Margaret bit her lip and then decided it made more sense to bite into a donut. She picked one at random and took a large bite.

"How well do you know Ashley?" Rachel asked.

Margaret shrugged. "I met her for the first time this weekend. She and Mark spent some time with me and Ted." She stopped herself before she mentioned hiking.

"Did you get any hint as to why she might have decided to murder her flatmate's boyfriend?" Joney asked.

"Not at all. She did mention Lelia, but only in passing."

"Did she talk about Oliver at all?" Joney wondered.

Margaret slowly shook her head. "Not really. She might have mentioned him, but only in the context of him being Lelia's boyfriend."

"Maybe that's suspicious," Joney said. "Maybe she was avoiding talking about him because she was in love with him. Or maybe she secretly hated him for some reason. Maybe she'd already murdered him before you met her. Did she seem as if she was hiding something?"

"She didn't do or say anything that made me think that she'd just murdered a man," Margaret said.

"Is that everyone on the list of suspects?" Arthur asked as he wiped his fingers on a napkin.

Rachel shook her head. "Drake Livergood is on the list."

Arthur frowned. "He handles our account. I'd hate to think that he killed someone."

"Tell me about Drake," Margaret said.

Arthur picked out another donut. "He's Donald's son. Donald was the other founder of the company, with Glen Walton. Sadly, Donald died some years ago now. I thought the world of Donald. He's the main reason why we have our accounts with Livergood and Walton. Glen was the brains behind the company, but Donald was the personality. He attended all of the charity events and belonged to all of the clubs. He used to golf with me and Howard once in a while, in fact."

"And does Drake do all of that now?" Margaret asked.

Arthur shook his head. "Drake doesn't golf. He does go to some charity events, but he seems to prefer going out clubbing with friends to them. I will admit that most charity events are incredibly dull, but being seen at them is an important part of life on the island when you own a small business."

"Except Livergood and Walton isn't a small business," Joney said.

"That's very true," Arthur said after a sip of coffee. "But I would argue that attending those kinds of events is even more important for companies like Livergood and Walton. I would suggest that more deals are made at special events and on golf courses than in boardrooms."

"Does that mean that Livergood and Walton have been losing business?" Margaret asked.

Arthur thought for a minute. "I don't believe so, aside, of course, from the big one. Most of their clients have had their accounts with the company since the earliest days when Donald and Glen were just starting out. They might have lost a bit more than just Howard's business when he pulled his accounts, but not much. A few people might have moved their business elsewhere in an effort to show solidarity with Howard, but his decision to move his business was strictly personal and as far as I know, most people opted not to take sides."

"And Oliver didn't do any socializing on behalf of the business?" Margaret asked.

"He did more than his father ever did, but it still wasn't much," Arthur said. "I'm certain I saw him at a few charity events over the years, but only a few. I believe the last one that I saw him at was during his marriage. It would have been the annual ball that Doris holds for her charity. Oliver was there with Karina."

Margaret ate her last bite of donut. Arthur wiped his fingers again.

"But you know more about Drake, don't you?" Joney asked Rachel.

Rachel shrugged as everyone looked at her. "We went out a few times, years ago."

"Before or after his father died?"

Rachel thought for a minute. "After, but not much after. I should point out that I'm almost a decade older than Drake. I was shocked when he asked me out."

"You don't look your age," Joney said.

Rachel nodded. "He thought I was only a few years older than him. We didn't discuss age until after we'd gone out a few times. When he found out how old I actually was, he seemed to find it funny."

"So that isn't why you broke up?" Margaret asked.

"We broke up because he didn't want anything serious, and I didn't want to keep going out with a guy who was seeing other women every second that he wasn't with me. I'll admit that some of it might have been my insecurities, too. All of the other women in his life were much closer to his age."

"How did you meet him?" Margaret asked.

Rachel laughed. "I met him when he came here to meet with Arthur when he first took over our business accounts. That's why I know it wasn't long after his father had died. When his father died, Drake took over some of his accounts. Glen took over the rest."

Margaret frowned. "He came here to talk to Arthur and then asked you out?"

"Arthur had me speak with him. We talked for about an hour about the business. Drake took a lot of notes and was nothing but professional for the entire time. When we were finished, he gave me his card. He'd written his personal mobile number on the back, and he suggested that I should ring him sometime. He said he wanted to take me out and get to know me better. As I said before, I was shocked."

"But you went anyway," Joney said with a laugh.

Rachel grinned. "Do you remember the year that I decided that I was going to say yes to every man who asked me out, no matter what?"

Joney made a face. "I remember it very well. It was a very long and difficult year."

"It was indeed," Arthur said.

"What happened?" Margaret asked.

"It was as if someone announced to the universe that Rachel had made that decision," Joney said. "She started getting asked out by every man she met, from grocery store clerks to insurance salesmen to, well, our company accountant."

Rachel nodded. "It was a bit odd. I used to get asked out now and again, but that year I started to feel as if I couldn't leave my house without some stranger asking me to have coffee with him. I went out with a lot of guys who I would never have said yes to any other time."

"And Drake was one of those guys?" Margaret asked.

"He was, although I might have said yes to him anyway. He's gorgeous," Rachel said.

"He is very attractive," Joney agreed. "But is he a killer?"

Rachel frowned. "I hope not. Even though we only went out a few times, I liked him a lot."

"What motive did he have?" Margaret asked.

Joney frowned. "If he did it, maybe it was something to do with work. Maybe Oliver kept getting all of the good clients. Or maybe Oliver was stealing from the company and Drake found out."

"It seems more likely that Drake is the one stealing," Arthur said. "If Oliver was stealing, Drake could have had him arrested. If Drake is stealing and Oliver found out, though, maybe he killed Oliver."

Rachel grimaced. "I hate that idea."

"Or maybe Drake is in love with Lelia," Joney said.

"Or Karina," Margaret added.

"But Oliver and Karina were divorced," Joney said.

Margaret nodded. "But maybe Karina is still in love with Oliver."

Rachel nodded. "I can see that being the case."

Joney glanced at her watch. "You have an appointment in ten minutes," she told Arthur as she got to her feet.

"And I have formulas to work on," Margaret said. She got up and followed Joney to the door.

"Does anyone want to get lunch later?" Rachel asked before they left the room.

"I wish I could," Arthur said. "But I'm going to have lunch with our new clients. I'm assuming they're going to sign a deal with us today. If they don't, I'll join you for lunch."

Rachel laughed. "And now I have to hope that you can't join us for lunch."

He shrugged. "I hope I can't join you for lunch, even though I'd much rather eat with you than them."

"And I'll be joining Arthur for lunch so that he doesn't have to suffer alone," Joney said.

"I'll meet you at noon in the lobby," Margaret told Rachel.

"Excellent," Rachel said.

10

Margaret spent her morning working on several formulas. One of the reasons she'd been hired was to help the company move toward making household cleaning products instead of just commercial ones. Margaret had already reformulated a few of the many products that the company sold into products that could safely be used at home, but there were still a large number for her to work through. Meanwhile, the very first bottles of her new products were going to start being produced soon in the production facility in the back of the building, They would be extensively tested before they would be made available to the public, but it would be a huge step forward.

"I ate two donuts," Rachel said when Margaret joined her in the foyer just after noon. "I shouldn't be this hungry."

Margaret laughed. "I only had one, and I'm starving."

"Which way should we go?" Rachel asked as they walked out of the building together.

There were two cafés within an easy walking distance of the building, but they were in opposite directions. Margaret looked back and forth and then shrugged.

"How about left today," she suggested. "We went right the last time we had lunch together."

Rachel nodded. "I was hoping you'd have an opinion, because I want something from both places, and I'm not sure which one I want more."

Margaret laughed. "They both have great food."

"Yeah, and I'm always hungry."

"Maybe we should have gone the other way," Margaret said as they approached the small café. "It looks really busy."

"I've never seen the car park full before," Rachel said. "I wonder what's going on."

Mona, Margaret thought. *What has she done now?* She sighed and then tried to guess which of the suspects from the murder investigation she was about to bump into.

She and Rachel walked into the restaurant. Margaret looked around.

"There isn't an empty table anywhere," she said.

Rachel nodded. "There are a few empty chairs here and there, but we'd have to join strangers, which wouldn't necessarily be fun."

"Rachel?" a voice called.

She looked around and then waved to the handsome man who was sitting alone at a table for four. "Or we could join Drake," she said to Margaret.

"That's Drake Livergood?" Margaret asked. "We were just talking about him."

Rachel nodded. "That's life on a small island. I'll probably see him everywhere I go for the next month and a half and then not see him again for another five years."

"You and your friend are welcome to join me," Drake said.

Margaret jumped. She hadn't realized that the man had walked over to join them near the door.

"But you're working," Rachel said as they walked back towards Drake's table with him.

"I was working," Drake said. "But I'd much rather talk to you."

He quickly gathered up the papers that were spread across the table. Then he slipped them into a large briefcase. He shut his laptop and slid that into the case as well before spreading out both hands and smiling at Rachel and Margaret.

"Please, join me," he said.

Margaret and Rachel exchanged glances before taking seats on either side of the man. He waited until they were seated to sit back down.

"I'm Drake Livergood," he said to Margaret, holding out a hand.

She took it. "Margaret Woods."

He nodded. "Fenella's niece. Everyone on the island knows who you are." He made a face. "And after the events of this weekend, I'm afraid a lot more people know who I am, too."

Rachel laughed. "Everyone on the island knew who you were well before this weekend," she said.

Drake shrugged. "It's a small island," he said to Margaret. "And my father did everything he could to meet everyone who lives here."

"As I understand it, he was working to build a business," Margaret said.

"Yes, of course," Drake said, tipping his head sideways in acknowledgement. "And I'm incredibly grateful to him for all of the hard work that he did. He and Glen Walton built a business that is still successful today. Sometimes I worry that we're too successful," he added, waving a hand at his briefcase.

"I'm surprised to find you working in a café," Rachel said.

"It started out as a business meeting with the café's owners and then, well, circumstances meant that I decided to stay here for longer than I'd planned," Drake replied.

"Ah, menus," the passing waitress said. "I didn't realize people had joined you," she told Drake. "And I took the menus off your table when you started working. I'll get you some right away."

"Thanks," Drake said.

"The café uses Livergood and Walton for their accounts?" Rachel asked as the waitress walked away.

Drake nodded. "They were one of Oliver's accounts. I'm doing my best to meet with all of his accounts as quickly as I can. I need to reassure everyone that nothing significant is going to change at Livergood and Walton in spite of the tragic happening over the weekend. I have a stack of account paperwork for a dozen different clients in my briefcase. This café was my sixth stop today."

"Here you are," the waitress said, handing them each a menu. "What about drinks while you're looking at the menus?"

Margaret ordered a soft drink. Rachel asked for tea while Drake requested coffee.

"I haven't slept properly since I heard about Oliver," he said as the waitress rushed away again. "I don't feel as if I'll ever sleep properly again."

"I'm sorry for your loss," Margaret said.

Drake gave her a small, sad smile. "Thank you," he said, staring into her eyes. "I could talk all day about Oliver, but I'm afraid to say anything. I'm doing my best to hold myself together when I'm in public."

"I still don't understand why you were working here," Rachel said.

"As I said, this was my sixth stop. I've discovered a great many interesting things while visiting Oliver's former clients. After our discussion, I asked the owners of the café if I could use a table for a short while to go through some of my notes from the morning. I would have gone back to my office, but the police are there."

"The police?" Rachel echoed.

Drake nodded. "Glen gave them permission to go through Oliver's office. We removed all of the client files before they were allowed in, of course. I couldn't even imagine trying to get any work done there, though, not while the police were searching through Oliver's things."

"What sorts of interesting things have you discovered?" Rachel asked.

"Nothing that I can talk about," Drake said, his expression apologetic. "I should make it clear that nothing that I've found suggests in any way that Oliver was doing anything inappropriate. I didn't find an interesting motive for his murder or anything dramatic like that. The things I found were more procedural than anything else and are of no interest to anyone other than another accountant."

"Are you ready to order?" the waitress asked as she dropped off their drinks.

"It's weirdly busy in here today," Rachel said.

The waitress nodded. "I don't understand it, but I won't complain. It's been too quiet for the last few months."

They all ordered sandwiches.

"It shouldn't take long," she told them. "Except the kitchen is a bit backed up, so it might."

Drake laughed. "We aren't going anywhere," he assured the woman.

She grinned at him. "That's good to know."

As she walked away, Drake looked at Margaret.

"I know a fair bit about you because you're the topic of a good deal of gossip. I know you haven't been on the island for long. How are you finding it?"

"I love it here," Margaret said. "It feels like home in a way that nowhere else ever has, which is odd, because I wasn't born here."

"But your ancestors came from the island. And sometimes we have more in common with our ancestors than we realize," Drake said. "I believe I was told that you're involved with Ted Hart, one of the island's most highly regarded police inspectors."

Margaret nodded. "We've been seeing each other for a while now."

"All of the most beautiful woman are already taken," Drake said. He turned his attention to Rachel. "Are you madly in love with someone, too?"

She laughed. "I'm so single I can't even remember why I ever wanted a man in my life."

"We had a great deal of fun together years ago," Drake said. "Maybe we should try again."

Rachel raised an eyebrow. "I don't think so."

He sighed. "I was an idiot in those days." He looked at Margaret. "I was young and stupid. My father had just died. His death frightened me. I started chasing excitement, mostly by chasing after beautiful women. I had this idea that going out with lots of different women would somehow protect me from dying. Or something. Or maybe I was just behaving badly because I could. I've been told I'm not bad-looking. And I had some money to spare. I set myself a goal of asking out every single woman I met. Most of them said yes, to at least one night out anyway. And that was all that most of them got. A single night out. Some of them, though, were special."

He looked over at Rachel.

"I never meant to hurt you," he said. "You were exactly the sort of woman I knew I wanted to marry one day. I wasn't ready to settle down, though. I was afraid that if I settled down and got married and had a child or two that my life would be over in a heartbeat. That was the last thing that my father said to me. He'd had a heart attack. They were about to take him back for surgery. He grabbed my hand and told me that I needed to pay attention to time, that it passed far too quickly. He told me that he'd worked too hard and that he'd married the first woman he'd ever fallen in love with. And then he told me not to make the same mistakes he'd made. He said that time just went faster and faster every year and that I needed to fit every bit of excitement into my years. And then they wheeled him away. He died on the operating table."

"I'm sorry," Margaret said as Drake pulled an old-fashioned handkerchief out of his pocket and wiped his eyes.

As he carefully folded the cloth so that the wet section was on the inside, he smiled ruefully.

"My father always carried a handkerchief. I inherited dozens of them, in unopened boxes. I'm fairly certain I gave him a box of them every year for Christmas for decades. After he was gone, I started tucking one into my pocket when I had a business meeting. It made me feel as if my father was with me in some way. I've been carrying one with me every day for years now. And today is the very first time I've ever needed to use one."

"I'm sure Oliver's death was a huge shock," Rachel said.

Drake nodded. "I feel as if a rug has been pulled out from under me. It's a very similar feeling to when my father died, but in a different way, which probably doesn't make sense."

"You don't have to make sense," Rachel said.

Drake laughed. "You were always too nice to me," he said. "After my father's death, I wanted to chase after every woman on the island. Now, after Oliver's death, I find myself wanting to find one special woman, one who will be too nice to me and can help me get through my grief and come out the other side."

"There are a lot of lovely women on the island who I'm certain would love to help you," Rachel said.

Drake frowned. "Does that mean you aren't interested in the position?"

Rachel laughed. "We had some fun together, but no, I'm not interested."

"Here we are," the waitress said, putting a plate down in front of Rachel. She quickly distributed the rest of the plates. "Do you need anything else?" she asked.

"We're good," Rachel replied.

"Shout if you need anything," she said before she walked away.

"I'm not going to try to change your mind," Drake said after a short pause. "But if you ever do, please ring me."

"I'm not going to change my mind," Rachel said before taking a bite of her sandwich.

"I suppose I'm making a terrible first impression," Drake said to Margaret. "It's difficult for me to even try to explain just how upside down my life feels right now."

"In that case, now isn't the time to try making any serious decisions," Margaret said.

"I know you're right, but it seemed too wonderful of a coincidence when Rachel walked in the door today. I'd just been thinking about her. I know I treated her badly. At least I've been given the chance to apologize."

He looked at Rachel. "And I am sorry," he said. "I wish we'd just met today. I'm in a very different place now."

"You need time to get over Oliver's death," Rachel said.

Drake sighed deeply. "I don't even know where to start with that. I can't really process what happened. Oliver was ten years younger than me. It was bad enough, losing my father unexpectedly. Losing Oliver in this way has been, in many respects, more difficult."

"You'd been working together for the last few years," Rachel said.

Drake nodded. "But our relationship goes back so much farther than that. I want to call it a friendship, but it was more like a brotherhood than a friendship. We grew up together, as much as you can grow up with someone ten years your junior. The thing is, though, we had a lot in common. The big thing was that neither of us was allowed to have any of our own dreams."

Margaret raised an eyebrow. "What do you mean?" she asked.

"Our fathers started Livergood and Walton before either of us was born. And they poured every bit of their blood, sweat, and tears into building the company. They both believed very strongly that Oliver and I should be grateful to them for what they had built. And we were, to some extent, anyway. I'll never forget the conversation I had with Oliver when I was home from uni on a break the summer he was ten. Our parents used to have dinner together every week, and by that point I was included in the plans when I was on the island. This was the first time Oliver was included, though."

"What about pudding?" the waitress asked. "It's quieter now. You don't need to rush away if you want pudding."

Margaret looked around the room. While they'd been talking and eating, the room had mostly emptied.

"The chef made a chocolate cake this morning," the waitress added. "And we've only sold one piece because most people didn't want to stay for pudding."

"I'll have a slice of cake, then," Rachel said.

"Me too," Margaret said.

"Just more coffee for me," Drake said.

As she walked away, Margaret looked at Drake. "You were telling us about a conversation that you had with Oliver when he was ten."

Drake's smile was sad. "He asked me about uni. He wanted to know all about studying accounting. I gave him a quick summary. Then he asked me if I was happy. I didn't know how to answer that. He said he'd been reading a lot of books lately, biographies and autobiographies. And he said he wasn't certain that he wanted to be an accountant on the Isle of Man for the rest of his life. He wanted to travel. And he thought he wanted to be a doctor."

"Wow," Rachel said.

Drake nodded. "I told him that I wished him luck, but that I didn't think his parents would approve. He told me that he'd already tried talking to them about his dreams, but that they'd told him that his life was already planned for him and that he was going to be an accountant and marry Karina Stone. For what it's worth, I told him that I thought he was lucky to have Karina. It was already clear that she was going to be beautiful, even at the age of ten. And she was heir to a fortune. I told him it could be worse. He could be me. I wanted to be an engineer, but instead, I was going to be an accountant, and I didn't even get a millionaire bride out of it."

Margaret sighed. "Did you tell your parents that you wanted to be an engineer?"

"A few times, when I was younger. I loved nothing more than taking things apart and then putting them back together again. I fixed a lot of things around the house and improved a few others. And I blew up a toaster, but I don't want to talk about that," he said with a chuckle.

"What did Oliver say to all of that?" Margaret asked.

"He just shrugged and told me that he was going to hold on to hope for a little while longer. The next summer, I had an internship in London. By the time I came home the following summer, I could tell that Oliver had given up hope and fallen into line with his parents' expectations."

"I feel sorry for both of you," Rachel said.

"I appreciate that," Drake said. "I spent the next decade watching Oliver grow up. He used to ring me once in a while for advice. Neither of us ever spoke again about what we really wanted out of life. He rang me every week from uni to ask for help with assignments. I was happy to help. Sometimes he'd mention that he was seeing someone, but we both knew that he was never going to get serious about anyone, not while Karina was here, waiting for him."

"And then he came home and married her," Rachel said.

"I tried to warn him," Drake said. "I didn't hear much, but I heard enough to know that his mother and Karina's were planning a wedding. I rang him at uni and warned him. He just laughed. He didn't believe me. And then when he got home he rang me and asked me to be his best man. I couldn't say no."

"He did divorce her, though," Margaret said. "That seems like a huge act of rebellion after everything you've said."

"It was a huge act of rebellion. I was shocked when he told me that he was filing for divorce." Drake sighed. "That isn't entirely true. I knew they were having problems. Oliver confided in me. That doesn't mean that I approved of what he did, though."

"You thought he should have stayed with Karina?"

Drake shook his head. "I don't want to speak ill of the dead, but Oliver did a lot of things over the years that I didn't feel were right."

"You can't stop there," Rachel said. "What things?"

"Two slices of chocolate cake," the waitress said. She put huge slices of cake in front of Margaret and Rachel. "Are you certain you don't want anything?" she asked Drake.

He shook his head. "I'm fine with just coffee."

As she walked away, Drake sighed. "Look, Oliver was like a brother to me. We were close. Very close. But Oliver had his own agenda. He did everything that was expected of him, but he wasn't planning on being a dutiful son forever. I knew about some of his plans, and he knew that I didn't approve of them."

"What sort of plans?" Rachel asked.

"Mostly they had to do with making money. He wanted to save enough money so that he could quit his job and travel the world. And I very strongly believe that was the only reason why he married Karina."

Rachel frowned. "You think he married her for her money?"

Drake nodded. "Oh, I know he cared about her. They'd been friends since infancy, but I also know he never loved her the way a man should love his wife. We talked about it a lot. He wondered if that sort of thing could develop over time. I told him that if it hadn't developed over all of the years they'd known each other, I doubted anything would change after they got married."

"So you didn't think he should have married Karina?"

"Not really, but I also knew how much pressure he was under to do so. And then her father dangled a huge check in front of his face. Once the money was offered to him, he was never going to say no."

"Karina must have had some idea that their marriage was in trouble," Margaret suggested, remembering what Karina had said about having to talk Oliver into staying with her until after their anniversary. She wasn't going to repeat any of that conversation to Drake, though.

Drake nodded. "Oliver was very smart. He was also very manipulative. And he knew exactly how to get Karina to do what he wanted. He used to laugh about how easy she was to control. He wanted out of his marriage, but he didn't want to upset Karina too much. I believe very strongly that he was planning on getting back together with her eventually."

"Surely she hates him after the way he treated her," Rachel said.

"Not at all. They were still friends. And the reason they were still friends is because Oliver very carefully controlled the entire situation. He went to Karina and asked for a divorce after six months of marriage. He told her that he loved her, but he thought they were too young to be married. He said that he just wanted a few years on his own before he took on the responsibilities of marriage and fatherhood. While she was crying her eyes out, he casually mentioned that he wanted to get through the divorce before their anniversary, that he knew he'd be penniless and alone if they separated before he got the check from Karina's father, but that he would rather be penniless and alone than continue to keep Karina from finding true happiness."

"What a creep," Rachel said.

Drake nodded. "Of course, Karina then suggested that they stay together until after their anniversary so that Oliver could get the check from her father to help fund his new start. From what Oliver told me, she spent the next six months doing everything in her power to make him happy, hoping that he'd change his mind about the divorce."

"That poor girl," Rachel said.

"It didn't work, of course. He filed for divorce right after he got the check. Karina was devastated, but she couldn't say much because she'd been warned. Again, Oliver told her that he just thought that he needed a break, that he knew that one day they'd be together again. That was exactly what Karina wanted to hear, of course."

"Of course," Rachel murmured. She took a big bite of cake and frowned at Drake.

"And the pair remained friends right up until Oliver's death," Drake added. "Although they hit a rough patch when Oliver started seeing someone else."

"Where did Lelia fit into Oliver's plans?" Rachel asked.

Drake shrugged. "I'm not entirely certain about that. Perhaps the house she inherited from her mother sits on land that some developer has an eye on. Or maybe her mother left her some stocks or bonds that Oliver realized have great value, stocks or bonds that Lelia is unaware are worth anything. I do know that Oliver seemed to think that he was going to make money out of his relationship with Lelia. I'm just not certain how he was expecting to do so."

"What makes you so certain of that?" Rachel asked.

Drake chuckled. "He told me. He rang me a while back and told me that he'd finally met someone who was worth his time. I said something about how she must be incredibly special. He just laughed and said that she had the potential to be valuable, if he played his cards right."

Rachel sighed. "Poor Lelia."

"I asked him to tell me more, but he said he wasn't going to tell me anything until he had the situation in hand. Then I asked him if his new girlfriend was worth risking his relationship with Karina over. He said he knew Karina wasn't going to be happy, but that he wasn't worried, that he knew he could win her back once he'd profited as much as he could from his new relationship."

"You should have stopped him," Rachel said angrily.

Drake looked surprised. "What could I have done? He didn't tell me anything about his new girlfriend. I only learned her name when I saw it in the newspaper after Oliver's murder. As for Karina, I've tried talking to her in the past. She always absolutely refused to believe anything negative about Oliver."

"Can I get you anything else today?" the waitress asked as she took away their empty dessert plates.

"Just the check," Margaret said. "We're going to be late back to work if we don't hurry."

"Lunch is on us today," the waitress replied. "We always used to give Oliver a meal when he visited, either breakfast or lunch. Under the circumstances, we're happy to give our new accountant and his friends some lunch today."

"I wouldn't have had dessert if I'd known," Margaret said.

The waitress laughed. "I'm glad you had some cake. We were worried that we'd have to throw some out, but everyone who was still here when I brought out your cake saw it and ordered it for themselves. We have one slice left, and the kitchen staff are going to fight over it if it's still around after the dinner rush."

"We do need to go," Rachel said, checking her watch. "I have a couple of client meetings this afternoon."

"It was really good to see you again," Drake said. "And I meant what I said. I'd love to go out with you again, even if it's just once for old time's sake."

"Thanks, but I'm going to pass," Rachel said.

Drake frowned. "I feel as if I need to apologize for saying as much as I did about Oliver. I've been trying not to talk about him with anyone, and then I started babbling and couldn't shut up. Our relationship was complicated. We were friends and we were work colleagues, but I don't know that I actually liked him as a person. I definitely didn't like a lot of the choices he made in his life."

"It was nice meeting you," Margaret said as she got to her feet.

"The pleasure was all mine," Drake said. "I hope you find great happiness here on the island. And if you ever need an accountant, please think of me."

He reached into his pocket and pulled out a silver card case. As he handed Margaret his card, he spoke again.

"As a US citizen living abroad, your tax filing status is complicated. If you need a bit of help putting together your US and island tax returns, please ring me. I can help with those, and I won't charge you for my time. I'd just hate to see you in trouble with your IRS. They terrify me."

Margaret laughed. "They terrify everyone. But I think your firm is already taking care of me. Aunt Fenella made arrangements with Doncan Quayle to make sure that my tax returns are filed correctly."

Drake nodded. "Glen handles various accounts for Doncan's clients. I'm glad someone is looking out for you."

Margaret and Rachel walked out of the restaurant a minute later.

"That was weird," Rachel said as they walked back toward the office. "I can't believe he asked me out again."

"I'm surprised you turned him down, really."

Rachel laughed. "He is gorgeous and very successful and everything

I look for in a man. Except he's also a suspect in a murder investigation, which is what put me off. Maybe once the killer is behind bars – assuming it isn't Drake – I'll ring him and let him buy me dinner."

Back at Park's, Margaret went into her office and shut the door. She needed to call Ted and tell him about her lunch conversation before she could get back to work.

11

Margaret kept the conversation with Ted as short as she could. He was eating lunch at his desk when she called. After she finished repeating what she could remember of the talk with Drake, he had only a few questions.

"Thanks for ringing. I'll pass this along to Michael. He might ring you back with some questions of his own," Ted said after she'd answered them.

"I'll be here, but I'll be working."

"Understood. In other news, I should finish on time tonight unless something comes up between now and six o'clock. Do you want to get dinner somewhere?"

"Yes, please."

"I'll meet you at your flat around half six."

"Sounds good."

"Love you."

"Love you, too."

Margaret put the phone down and then spent the rest of the afternoon working hard. Joney stopped her as she was leaving.

"Rachel told me that you had lunch with Drake Livergood."

"We did."

"Did you ask him probing questions to try to find out if he killed Oliver?"

"No, but he did talk about Oliver a great deal."

"I always wondered if they were friends in spite of the large age gap. Okay, that isn't true. I never gave either of them a single thought until Oliver's murder. Earlier today, though, I found myself wondering if they were friends or just work colleagues."

"From what Drake said, I think they were both."

"How weird would it be to grow up knowing that you were going to work with someone who was ten years younger than you one day? I mean, I suppose it's possible that one or the other of them might have decided to study medicine or chemistry or something else other than accounting, but I assume they were both strongly encouraged to follow in their fathers' footsteps."

Margaret nodded. "Drake said something about how he and Oliver weren't allowed to have dreams."

Joney frowned. "That's very sad. But don't let me keep you. You probably have exciting plans for the evening. I'm just waiting for Arthur to wrap up his last meeting so that I can go home."

"I hope he pays you overtime."

Joney laughed. "I own enough of the company that I don't want to get overtime pay. I'd rather just enjoy my share of the profits, thanks."

Margaret grinned. "As long as you're happy."

The drive back to her apartment was a fairly short one. As Margaret drove around a small roundabout, she looked at the tiny circle of grass at the center of the traffic circle. "Who starts a charity to make the island more beautiful? There are so many good causes out there. I really don't understand it," she said. "And now I'm talking to myself, which is a terrible habit."

She shut her mouth and turned up the radio. As she pulled in to the parking garage under the building, she was singing along to an eighties classic. Ted was waiting for her in the corridor outside her door.

"You have a key," she reminded him after he'd greeted her with a kiss.

"I know, but I worried that if I let myself in, I'd scare you when you got home."

"You could have texted me and told me that you were here," she said as she let them into the apartment.

"I could have, but it seemed more polite to wait for you. I knew you'd be home soon."

Katie ran out of Margaret's bedroom, straight to Ted. He picked her up and gave her a cuddle as he headed for the nearest couch.

"You look tired," Margaret said as she kicked off her shoes.

"I am tired. I didn't sleep well last night. I kept having dreams about hiking in different places around the island. Every place I went, I found another dead body."

Margaret shuddered. She sat down next to him and put her arm around him. "I'm sorry," she said. "That sounds dreadful."

"It was pretty awful."

"Why don't we stay here, and I'll cook something," she suggested. "You can just rest and snuggle with Katie while I throw something together."

Ted yawned before he replied. "I promised you dinner."

"And I'll get dinner, just one that I prepared instead of a restaurant meal. I eat far too many restaurant meals these days anyway. Let me see what I have in the fridge and then we'll talk again."

"I have a few slices of deli meat and three cans of lager in my fridge," Ted said with a laugh.

Margaret went into the kitchen. When she returned, she gave Ted three options for dinner.

"The stir-fry will be the fastest, right?" he asked.

"It will be."

"Then that. I'm tired, but I'm also starving. The sandwich I had for lunch was a long time ago."

"I'll get everything started."

"I'll come and help," Ted offered. As he started to get up, Katie "mewed" angrily.

Margaret laughed. "You stay and snuggle with Katie while I cook. It won't take long."

Twenty minutes later, she spooned rice onto plates and then

topped it with stir-fried chicken and vegetables. After putting the plates on the table, she filled Katie's food bowl and then looked over at Ted and Katie. It looked as if they were both fast asleep.

"I don't want dinner to go to waste," she muttered as she walked over and kissed Ted's forehead.

He opened one eye and sighed. "I was going to help, just as soon as Katie got down."

"She's still there, and she's sleeping. You're going to have to wake her and put her down."

"Sorry, Katie," Ted said. He patted her gently until she opened her eyes. "You need to get down. It's time for dinner."

When Katie heard the word "dinner," she sat straight up and then jumped off Ted's lap. She was in the kitchen, emptying her bowl, when Ted and Margaret followed.

"This is really good," Ted said after a few bites. "Thank you for making me dinner. I'll take you out somewhere nice tomorrow night to make up for tonight."

"I don't mind cooking. It's better for us, and I have a lot of quick and easy recipes from my single days. Besides, I end up going out for lunch on a lot of my working days. I'm going to gain weight if I keep eating out multiple times a day."

"Maybe I should start grocery shopping a bit more often. Then I could cook dinner for both of us once in a while."

"That would be nice. Are you a good cook?"

Ted laughed. "I'm an adequate cook in that I can more or less follow a recipe, and I rarely burn things, but I don't necessarily enjoy cooking. I cook because I need to eat, mostly."

"Maybe we should do more cooking together."

"I'd really like that."

They talked about favorite foods and recipes that they wanted to try while they finished their dinner. By the time Ted put their plates in the dishwasher, Margaret had a list of meals that she and Ted were planning to make together.

"I'll give you some money towards the shopping," Ted said. "Or we can go shopping together on the weekend and buy what we need for a few of the meals."

"Let's plan to go shopping over the weekend, assuming you don't end up having to work."

Ted nodded. "There was something else I wanted to talk to you about."

Margaret frowned. "That sounds ominous."

Ted laughed. "It wasn't meant to, not at all. The crime rate on the island is still lower than average, aside from the current murder investigation, of course. I've been talking to the chief constable about taking a fortnight's holiday. He suggested that September might be the perfect time for me to take time off."

"This September? Like next month?"

"Yes, this September. Obviously, I want you to come with me. I thought we'd go across with a car and do some sightseeing in England and Wales, but the itinerary can be mostly up to you. Where do you want to go?"

"I don't even know if I can take any vacation time, let alone two weeks."

"You should have at least twenty days of annual leave. Whether Arthur will let you take ten days of it at one time is another matter, but we can just go away for a week if that's all you can take off."

"Next month," Margaret said thoughtfully.

Ted nodded. "I know it's short notice, but I could really use a holiday."

"I can talk to Arthur tomorrow and see what he says," Margaret said.

"Unless you'd rather not go on holiday with me?"

Margaret laughed. "I'd love to take a vacation with you. Spending all that time together should tell us both a lot about the future of our relationship."

Ted laughed. "That's very true. I went on holiday with my girlfriend when I was eighteen. We broke up halfway through the trip, but neither one of us could afford to fly home early or pay for another hotel room, so we were stuck together in a small hotel room in Portugal for four very long days after the relationship ended."

"I have a similar story, although after the huge fight and messy breakup, I did fly home early from my vacation in Florida. My parents were kind enough to foot the bill to change my flight because they'd always hated the guy I was dating."

Ted laughed. "My mother wasn't disappointed that the relationship ended, but she wasn't about to spend her hard-earned money on flying me home just because I'd been dumb enough to go on holiday with one of the most unpleasant women on the planet."

"I think I want to know more about your ex-girlfriend."

"I'd rather not even think about her, really."

The pair settled together on one of the couches.

"What did you think of Drake?" Ted asked as he put his arm around her.

"He was charming. Too charming, really. He's very handsome, but I didn't trust a single thing that he said."

"Does that mean that you don't think that Oliver manipulated Karina into staying in the marriage until he got his check?"

Margaret sighed. "I don't know what to believe. I didn't trust Drake, but what he said made a lot of sense. After talking to Karina, it seems obvious that she would be fairly easily influenced by someone she trusted. And she trusted Oliver."

"You heard Karina's version of events. In your opinion, does it match with what Drake told you?"

"Karina told me that she was the one who talked Oliver into staying with her until after their anniversary. Now that I've spoken to Drake, I can see how Oliver might have put the idea into her head, though. I don't want to believe that Oliver was a horrible person, but everything Drake said seemed sadly possible. Except I didn't trust him in the slightest."

Ted shook his head. "I'm lost."

Margaret laughed. "I'm lost, too. I hope Michael is doing better than I am with the investigation."

"He's doing his best, but I think he's a bit frustrated because people keep telling you more than they are telling him."

"I don't go out of my way to find them and talk to them."

"I know, but you do seem to have a knack for crossing paths with the suspects."

"Tomorrow I'll take a packed lunch and stay in my office all day."

"I'd rather you didn't."

Maragaret frowned at him. "What do you mean?"

"I mean, I think we might only solve this case if someone says something to you that he or she hasn't told Michael. Michael is a good investigator, but this is his first murder. Back in Derby he'd been working in their cybercrime unit for the past several years. It's been a long time since he's been out in the field actively investigating anything."

"I think I've spoken to just about everyone already."

"Except the grieving parents."

"I don't want to meet the grieving parents. I'm sure they must be devastated."

Ted shrugged. "It might be helpful if you talked to them."

"I don't know that I can do anything aside from going out to lunch with anyone who suggests it," Margaret said. "If that doesn't work, maybe we should go out for dinner tomorrow night."

"Maybe. I don't mean to put any pressure on you. And I really don't want you going out looking for anyone. It just seems as if you often have good luck getting people to tell you things that end up being relevant to the investigation."

"Or maybe I just got lucky a few times and now you're hoping I'll get lucky again."

Ted chuckled. "I think you'd be surprised if you knew how many crimes get solved due to a lucky break."

"I'm sure I don't want to know. I'd much rather believe that all crimes are being solved due to the incredibly smart and amazingly handsome inspectors who work for the Isle of Man Constabulary."

"Mark *is* pretty handsome."

Margaret laughed. "I've never noticed."

"I don't believe that."

"You are also quite handsome. And you're smart."

"And I have excellent taste in girlfriends."

Margaret laughed before he kissed her.

"I should go," Ted said a short while later. "As much as I love being with you, I'm exhausted."

"And I need to get some sleep so that I can dream up a way to meet Glen and Caroline Walton tomorrow."

"Good luck with that."

Margaret walked Ted to the door. He kissed her one last time before making his way down the corridor to the elevators. She waved as the elevator doors slid shut before closing her door and checking that it was locked.

"I need sleep," she told Katie, who was prowling around the living room.

"Meroww," Katie said, nodding toward her telephone.

It rang a moment later.

"Hello, Little Sister," she answered the call.

"Hello, Big Sister," Megan replied. "How is my favorite big sister today?"

"Tired. It's late here."

"I'm sorry. I know there's a time difference, but I always forget about it when I want to talk to you."

"How are you?"

"I'm feeling guilty because I called you so late."

Margaret laughed. "Ted just left. We can talk for a few minutes, anyway."

"How is Ted?"

"He's fine. We might be taking a vacation together next month."

"Ah, that's one of the things I was calling about, actually."

"Don't tell me that you're finally planning to come and visit me after all this time? Next month?"

"Yes, I'm planning to come and visit, but not next month. We want to come and visit in October."

"We?" Margaret echoed.

Megan giggled. "Me and Carter, of course. We're still deliriously happy together. I can't wait for you to meet him."

"I can't wait to meet him, either."

Megan sighed. "I can hear disapproval in your voice. He's really wonderful. You're going to be sorry that you were so horrible about him."

"I didn't say a word. And I've never been horrible about him. I simply want you to be very careful, that's all."

"I am being careful. We're still taking things slowly, even though he tells me every day that he wants to propose."

"Is he still living with you?"

"He's staying with me, which isn't the same thing. Except he's in New York City right now. I told you that he flies back and forth regularly for work. Something came up late yesterday and he flew back very early this morning. I'm expecting him to call any minute now, though."

"Which made it the perfect time to call me?"

Megan laughed. "Okay, I'm exaggerating. Carter probably won't call until nine or ten tonight. My time, that is. Or he might not get a chance to call me until tomorrow. When he's working, he's very focused."

"Uh huh."

"I know. I know. And if I were you, I'd probably feel the same way, but I'm not you. I know Carter. And I know he's every bit as wonderful as I think he is."

"And you're coming to visit me in October?"

"We are. Carter is working on making the travel arrangements now. Or rather, he was working on them before whatever went wrong at work went wrong. Now he's working, but once he gets back here, he'll get our travel plans finalized."

"I wish I could offer to let you stay here, but it isn't my apartment."

"Oh, I know. And if it were just me coming, I'd stay with you, of course, but Carter is looking at bed and breakfast places or maybe a small cottage. We need four bedrooms, though, so a cottage might be hard to find."

"Four bedrooms?"

"Because Carter loves to travel with his friends. He's treating a whole group of friends to a vacation on the island."

"A whole group of friends? Have you met them all?"

"Nope," Megan said. "But we'll have the long flight from the US to the UK to get to know each other. And then an entire two weeks of lovely vacation time together."

"That is a long time to spend with a bunch of strangers."

"We won't be strangers for long."

"Sure."

Megan laughed. "I know that for my introverted big sister that sounds like the stuff of nightmares, but I love meeting new people. I'm really excited to meet some of Carter's friends and to show them the island."

"How are you going to get around on the island?"

"We're still working out the details. Carter is looking into lots of different options. The last I heard, he was talking about flying into London and then renting at least two cars there. Then we'd drive to the ferry and take that across to the island. That would give us transportation on the island while we're there."

"Or you could fly to the island and rent cars from here."

"Yeah, but I kind of liked the idea of driving up from London to catch the ferry in Liverpool. I've never spent any time in the UK."

"I'm looking forward to seeing some of it with Ted next month, assuming I can get the time off work."

"Don't use up all of your vacation time traveling with Ted. I'm coming to visit!"

"It sounds as if you're going to have a crowd with you."

"That's true. Maybe you don't need time off while I'm there. We'll have evenings and weekends at least."

"Do you have any idea on dates yet?"

"Not yet. Just October. But I will let you know as soon as Carter starts booking things."

"I'm excited that you're coming."

"I'm excited to get back to the island. Obviously, I miss you, but I also miss the island. It's such a unique place."

"Does Carter know much about it?"

"Not a single thing. When I told him where my sister lives, he thought I was making up the name. None of his friends had ever heard of it either, at least according to Carter."

"I'm not sure how many of the tourist sites are open in October."

"It doesn't matter. If we can't tour everywhere we'll just have an excuse to visit again."

The pair chatted for a few more minutes about Megan's upcoming visit before Margaret found herself yawning every few minutes.

"Yes, okay, I know," Megan said after Margaret had to stop mid sentence to yawn. "It's late. You need sleep. I'll call you again soon."

"Love you and miss you," Margaret replied.

"Same, same," Megan said before the line went dead.

Margaret put her phone down. "I didn't even get to mention Oliver Walton," she said as she walked into the kitchen. "Not that Megan needs to hear about him, but I was with Ted when he found the body. How odd is my life that my boyfriend finds a dead body and don't even mention it to my own sister? How odd is my life that I now talk to myself regularly? And how odd is it that I haven't seen my resident ghost today?"

She filled Katie's water bowl and then made sure the kitchen was tidy before switching off the lights. Now she found herself worrying about Mona. It wasn't like her ghostly roommate to stay away when Ted was visiting, not during a murder investigation, anyway.

Half an hour later, Margaret crawled into bed. Katie was already asleep on the spare pillow next to Margaret's.

"Night night," she whispered to Katie. "And good night, Mona," she added a bit more loudly.

"Good night."

The ghostly whisper made Margaret shiver, but she felt better knowing that Mona had heard her and replied. She shut her eyes and fell into a deep sleep almost immediately.

"What are the odds of me having lunch with Glen and Caroline Walton today?" Margaret asked Katie as she got ready for work the next morning.

"Meewww," Katie said.

"Yeah, that's what I thought," Margaret replied. She looked around the apartment. "I don't think Mona can pull this one off, but if she does, I'll be impressed."

Half an hour later, she headed out of her apartment. As she walked down the corridor toward the elevator, the door next to hers opened. Elaine stuck her head out and looked up and down the hall. When she spotted Margaret, she pulled her head back and shut her door.

"And what is going on with her?" Margaret said loudly as she got into the elevator. "I must see if Mona can find out."

In the parking garage, Margaret hesitated in front of the two cars in Aunt Fenella's parking spaces. She nearly always drove the very sensible car that Fenella had purchased when she'd first moved to the island. But Margaret had promised her aunt that she'd occasionally drive the very fancy and very valuable sports car that had formerly belonged to Mona. And it had been at least a week since she'd taken the sleek red machine for a spin. She dug around in her handbag and pulled out the first keyring she touched.

"Ah, well, it looks as if fate wants me to drive Mona's car today," she said with a chuckle as she unlocked the little red sports car.

She climbed behind the wheel and sighed happily. While she didn't typically pay much attention to cars, seeing them as simply a very convenient form of transportation, even she had to admit that Mona's car was fun to drive. She started the engine and smiled as the car began to purr softly. As she touched the accelerator, the engine growled and the car rushed toward the garage's exit. The drive to work felt as if it took only seconds that morning. Margaret parked the car and gave it a friendly pat before she walked inside the building.

"Good morning," Joney greeted her. "Arthur wants a word with you when you have the time."

Margaret frowned. "I hope I'm not in trouble."

Joney laughed. "You aren't in trouble. Honestly, you work incredibly hard and you're good at your job. Why would you even think that you might be in trouble?"

"Rachel and I were a bit late back from lunch yesterday."

"Arthur doesn't pay any attention to such things. He's happy if the work is getting done. And he's delighted with the work you've been doing since you got here. We're already three months ahead of where he thought we'd be on your project. He's busy dreaming up what he's going to have you do next, even though you still have at least a year of work to do on the current project."

"I'm glad he's happy with my work. I'm also glad that we're ahead of his targets. I might want to take some vacation time next month."

"Oh, he'll be really glad to hear that. He was concerned that you're about to hit a stopping point on the project. You've developed the formulas, but we aren't ready to start manufacturing trial batches yet. The production facility is working all-out to fill a few large orders that we got rather unexpectedly. But why am I telling you all of this? Go and talk to Arthur."

Margaret laughed. "Thanks for the heads-up, anyway. I'll just throw my bag in my office and then see if Arthur is free."

"Grab some coffee, too. You know Arthur is going to want to talk."

"That's very true."

Margaret walked to her office and unlocked the door. She slipped her handbag into the bottom desk drawer and then checked that she didn't have any phone messages. She would have been shocked if there had been any. No one ever called her office number. But she still checked every morning. Then she walked to the break room and poured herself a cup of coffee before continuing to Arthur's door. He was sitting behind his computer, frowning at the screen.

"Good morning," Margaret said. "Is this a good time for a chat? Joney said you wanted to talk to me about something."

"It's a great time for a chat," he replied. "I've been playing this same stupid card game for the last half hour. I keep restarting and trying different approaches, but I can't win. And the game tells me that it can be won, if you play your cards just right."

"That doesn't sound fun."

Arthur chuckled. "I let myself play one round of solitaire every morning before I start work. There are five different games on here, and I rotate through them. I only play games that are supposed to able to be won, and I let myself play until I've managed it. Except every once in a while, I can't manage it. Then I get frustrated and snap at Joney."

"Oh dear."

"But you didn't come in to listen to me complain about cards. Have a seat. Let's talk."

Margaret sat down in one of the comfortable chairs in front of Arthur's desk. He sat back and smiled at her.

"How are you?"

"I'm fine, thank you."

"And how are you finding the island? I hope you're happy here."

"I am happy here."

"Excellent. You should know that I'm very happy with your work. I went through your last report and then mixed up one of your formulas for myself. I was quite impressed with the results."

Margaret flushed. She'd always rather assumed that Arthur didn't really read the reports that she sent. It was a surprise to hear that he not only read them, but that he'd tried one of her formulas. "Thank you," she said.

He nodded. "You're a few months ahead of schedule, which I also appreciate, but we might have an issue soon because the production facility is working at capacity at the moment. While we can start doing some testing with hand-mixed versions of your formulas, we can't test anything fully until we can run limited production runs of each of them."

"I still have a lot of formulas to create."

"I know, but as I said, you're quite far ahead of where I thought you'd be at this point. And it's August. I was wondering if you had any plans for a summer holiday?"

"I'm glad you asked," Margaret said with a grin. "Ted and I were just talking last night about going away for a vacation, er, holiday in September. That's assuming he can get the time off, of course."

"Next month? For how long?"

Margaret frowned. "Ted was talking about two weeks, but I don't know that I can be away for that long."

"You absolutely can be away for that long. My wife and I are planning a fortnight's holiday in Portugal next month and Joney is going to be away for the last week of August and the first week of September. As long as production continues at a steady pace, no one will miss any of us. And I need to send Rachel away for at least a fortnight, because she keeps selling our products to new customers, which is why production is so overworked."

"I don't know what dates I'll be away yet."

Arthur waved a hand. "Just give them to me when you get them. Or give them to Joney. She'll put them on the master calendar. I'm just happy that you're going to use some of your leave entitlement. It's important to have a nice work-life balance, after all."

"My sister is coming to visit in October. I don't know how much more leave I'll have, but I might want to take a few days off while she's here."

"You're entitled to twenty days a year under Manx law, but that seems inadequate to me, so I give everyone, from the production staff to the cleaning team to myself, thirty days a year. Technically, I could prorate that because you didn't start in January, but I'm not that bothered about that detail. It's more important to me that my staff are happy and healthy and that they love their jobs."

"I do love my job. I can't imagine that I'll use thirty days of vacation before the end of the year, but I might."

"I want you to use it. If you don't, you'll get paid for the days you didn't use rather than being allowed to carry them over into next year. Unless you have a good reason for wanting to carry them over, like say you're getting married or having a baby or something. I try to be really flexible about such things. That's assuming that the work is getting done, of course."

"Thank you." Margaret remembered that Arthur had said something similar when he'd interviewed her for the job. She hadn't wanted to push him on exactly how many days of vacation she'd get during the interview and the subject hadn't really come up again until today.

"There was one other thing," Arthur said as Margaret started to get up from her chair.

"Oh?"

"I'm having lunch at my club today with a few friends. I'd very much appreciate it if you'd join us. Joney and Rachel both have other plans. And you know that I have to eat there a certain number of times each month."

Margaret laughed. "I remember that from the last time I went there with you. Will you please let me pay for my lunch today?"

He shook his head. "It all gets added to my account, but the prices are quite reasonable, really. Belonging to the club is expensive, but dining there is quite affordable."

"What time?"

"We'll leave from the lobby about quarter to twelve. We're meeting Glen and Caroline at midday."

Margaret nodded and then walked back to her office, feeling slightly dazed. It was possible that there was another couple on the island with the same names, but that seemed incredibly unlikely. Pushing all thoughts about the Waltons out of her head, she sat down at her desk and got to work.

12

"Ready to go?" Arthur asked when Margaret joined him in the lobby at eleven forty-five.

"I am. And I'm happy to get away from chemicals and formulas for an hour," she said with a laugh.

"I know what you mean," Arthur said. "I was the one who developed the original formulas that we used back when I first started the company. And after I was finished, I swore I'd never do it again. That's why we hired a company in the UK to do all of our chemistry before we hired you."

"I didn't realize that you developed the original formulas," Margaret said.

"I have a degree in chemistry. And one in business management. And I very much prefer business management on a day-to-day basis. I still love a bit of chemistry now and then, though. But we're going to be late for lunch if we don't get moving."

They walked out to Arthur's car. He stopped next to it.

"You drove Mona's car today," he said.

Margaret smiled. "Do you want me to drive us to lunch so you can ride in it?"

"I'd much rather drive it, but riding in it is a very close second. And honestly, I don't think I'm brave enough to drive it. I know how much it's worth. I'd be terrified of scratching the paint or dinging the door or something."

"You'll have to give me directions."

"I can do that."

Margaret unlocked the car and then got behind the wheel. Arthur climbed in and clapped his hands.

"This is the most amazing car in the world."

"It is pretty awesome," Margaret agreed. "Left or right?"

"Oh, sorry. Left and then take the second right. I'll tell you more as we go."

A short while later, Margaret pulled the car into the parking lot at Arthur's golf club. She parked in one of the large spaces and then switched off the car.

"Your car is going to draw a crowd," Arthur told her as they got out. "I'd be willing to bet that every man here has always wanted one of these. They only made a very small number of them and as I understand it, there aren't very many of them still running."

"Well, Aunt Fenella's runs like a dream. And it doesn't use very much gas, either. I don't think I've put any gas in it since Aunt Fenella left."

"You must not drive it very much."

"I try to drive it at least once a week. I really hope the gas gauge isn't broken. I'd hate to run out of gas somewhere."

"You can always try topping it up one day, just to see how much it needs. That will give you a good idea of whether the gauge is accurate or not."

Margaret nodded. "I should do that." She patted the car and then followed Arthur into the building.

"Ah, good afternoon," the man behind the small host stand near the restaurant's entrance said. "Mr. and Mrs. Walton are awaiting your arrival."

He led them across the room to a table for four in the corner. Margaret smiled at the couple, who were sipping wine as she and Arthur approached.

"Good afternoon," Arthur said.

"Yes, good afternoon," the man replied.

"This is Margaret Woods," Arthur said. "Margaret, I'd like you to meet Glen and Caroline Walton. Glen is our company accountant, but he and his wife are also my friends."

"Thank you," Glen said. He smiled at Margaret, but the expression looked forced. He looked as if he hadn't slept in days.

"It's nice to meet you," Caroline said flatly. She also looked exhausted. Her smile consisted of nothing more than slightly upturned corners of her lips. It certainly never reached her eyes.

Margaret smiled at her. "It's nice to meet you both," she said as she took the seat next to Caroline.

"We ordered a bottle of wine," Glen said, identifying the bottle.

Margaret shrugged. "I'm going back to the office to work all afternoon. I think I'll stick to soft drinks."

"I have to work this afternoon, too," Arthur said. "So I'd better limit myself to a single glass of whiskey."

"I have to work this afternoon, too," Glen said. "But I realized earlier in the day that I no longer care if the numbers add up correctly or not."

"That's a bit worrying, considering you do our accounting," Arthur said with a chuckle.

Glen shrugged. "I think I might retire."

"I'm very sorry for your loss," Margaret said after a short awkward silence.

Glen and Caroline both looked at her.

"Thank you," Caroline said. "We both made a lot of mistakes as parents, but we both loved our son. Our lives have been irrevocably broken."

"He should have stayed with Karina," Glen said after emptying his wine glass. "Then we'd have a grandchild or two. That would help."

Caroline pressed a tissue to her eyes. "We aren't going to talk about that," she said tightly.

Glen nodded.

"Let me tell you about today's specials," the waiter said as he delivered drinks for Margaret and Arthur.

Everything sounded wonderful to Margaret. Glen and Caroline

ordered while she quickly read through the menu. Then she selected one of the specials. Arthur chose a different one.

"Do you have children?" Glen asked Margaret.

She shook her head. "Not yet. I would like them one day, though."

"Have at least two," he told her. "I wish we'd had a second child."

Caroline shook her head. "Neither of us wanted a second child, not during those difficult years. You were busy starting and then building a business. I could barely manage one child on my own. A second would have been impossible for me."

"Other people manage," Glen said.

Caroline looked at him for several seconds. "No," she said firmly.

Glen sighed. "I'm sorry," he said to Arthur and Margaret. "We aren't ourselves. We should have stayed at home and annoyed one another there rather than coming out in public and annoying other people."

"You've no need to apologize to us," Arthur said. "We're all friends here."

"I think it would be easier if he'd died in a car crash or some other accident," Glen said. "The idea that he was murdered, that another person chose to end his life, is an incredibly difficult thing to try to understand."

"I know he wasn't always perfect, but he never did anything that should have made someone want to murder him," Caroline said.

"And now I'm going to start talking about all of the possible suspects," Glen said. "We've talked about all of them, over and over again, trying to work out who might have wanted to kill him, but we keep reaching the same point. No one had any reason to kill him."

"Karina had reason to hate him," Caroline said.

Glen nodded. "Karina was his ex-wife. They'd been promised to each other since infancy. Maybe that was a mistake on our part."

Caroline shrugged. "Karina's parents are wealthy beyond belief. Glen and Karina's father became friends when Howard hired Livergood and Walton to handle his accounts. I was stunned when Doris and I met, and she seemed to want to pursue a friendship. When we both fell pregnant just a few months apart, she began to joke that one day our babies should get married. When I had a boy and she had a girl, the joke somehow started to get repeated far more seriously."

"And marrying Karina was a wonderful opportunity for Oliver," Glen said. "Not only is she lovely, but she's the sole heir to two considerable fortunes. If Oliver had simply stayed with her, he probably could have retired as soon as Karina's father died and then simply sat back and lived a life of luxurious leisure."

"Not that he married Karina for her money," Caroline said quickly. "The two of them grew up together. And they loved each other very much."

"She was crazy about Oliver," Glen said. "I do think Oliver was more guarded with his heart."

"He worried that they were getting married too young," Caroline said. "And I suppose Doris and I must share the blame for that. We were so excited to see our dreams coming to fruition that we planned their wedding, perhaps a bit prematurely."

"They didn't tell Oliver that he was getting married at all until just a few weeks before the ceremony," Glen told Margaret.

She nodded. "I'm surprised he went through with it."

"Karina's father offered him a great deal of money to go through with it," Glen said flatly. "And Oliver loved Karina. He simply wasn't ready for marriage. He was too young, and it all happened too quickly."

"And then he divorced her and cost the company a great deal of money," Caroline said.

Glen waved a hand. "The money wasn't the issue. I was more concerned that he'd broken poor Karina's heart."

"Here we are," the waiter said. He began putting plates of food in front of each of them. "Does anyone need anything else right now?" he asked when he was finished.

"I think we have everything," Arthur said.

"Very good," the man said with a bow.

As he walked away, Glen picked up his fork.

"Howard was angry. Oliver filed for divorce immediately after he'd been given a very generous anniversary present from Howard. I never blamed Howard for taking his business elsewhere. He had every right to be angry," Glen said before taking his first bite.

"And we've been able to rebuild our friendship with Howard and Doris since the divorce," Caroline said. "I know we were all hoping that Karina and Oliver would find their way back to one another one day."

"But then Oliver started seeing someone else," Glen said. "She seemed lovely, but she wasn't Karina."

Caroline sighed. "We should have been nicer to Lisa," she said.

"Lelia," Margaret blurted out.

Caroline frowned at her. "I'm sorry?"

"Oliver's new girlfriend is Lelia, not Lisa," Margaret said.

"Is that right?" Caroline looked at Glen. "Does that sound right to you?"

He shrugged. "I can't remember the girl's name. It hardly seemed worth worrying about. At the time, I assumed that they'd only be together for a short while."

"Why?" Margaret asked.

Glen stared at her. "One of the reasons that Oliver ended things with Karina was because he felt as if he was too young to be tied down. He wasn't looking to replace his marriage with another serious relationship. He simply wanted to have some fun. I truly believe that he fully intended to go back to Karina eventually."

"Maybe she wouldn't have wanted him back," Margaret said.

Caroline and Glen both frowned.

"Of course she would have wanted him back," Caroline said eventually. "She understood that she and Oliver belonged together."

"But what if she'd found someone else while Oliver was off having his fun?" Margaret asked.

"You obviously don't know Karina," Caroline said. "It would never have occurred to her to find someone else. She's been in love with Oliver for her entire life. And Oliver loved her, too, even if he did behave a bit badly."

Margaret took a bite of her lunch and realized that she'd been so focused on the conversation that she hadn't really been tasting what she was eating. After a couple additional bites, she decided that being distracted might be better than her lunch.

"I had lunch with Drake yesterday," she said.

Glen looked surprised. "Drake Livergood?"

Margaret nodded. "He was visiting clients. A work colleague and I went to lunch at the café he was visiting. It was very busy, so he was kind enough to invite us to join him at his table."

"He invited random strangers to join him for lunch?" Caroline asked.

"Ah, I should have said that my work colleague went out with Drake a few times years ago," Margaret added.

Glen chuckled. "That makes sense. Drake spent quite a few years trying to go out with every single woman on the island. He's calmed down a bit now, but there was a time when his parents worried a great deal about him."

"They're both gone now, of course," Caroline said. "We do our best to support Drake, though. In some ways, he's been like a second son to us, although he's quite a bit older than Oliver was."

"He's also a good accountant," Glen added. "And we work well together. We're going to miss Oliver at work, though, too. He handled quite a few accounts for the company."

"All of the smallest and least important, according to Oliver," Caroline said. "He used to complain to me all the time about how Drake got all of the interesting new clients and how he only got the small boring accounts."

Glen shrugged. "Drake and I had been discussing reallocating a few of our larger accounts. But Oliver hadn't been working with us for long, really. I wasn't completely convinced that he was ready to deal with the bigger customers."

"Drake seemed very upset about Oliver's death," Margaret said after she'd finished her last bite.

"They were like brothers, or nearly," Glen said. "Even if they did disagree from time to time."

"I keep wondering if Drake killed Oliver," Caroline said. "Not because I think he had any reason to kill Oliver, but because I can't think of any reason why anyone would have wanted to kill Oliver."

"Maybe Karina was upset because he was seeing someone else," Glen said.

"Karina wouldn't hurt a fly," Caroline said.

"Maybe Howard was upset because Oliver was seeing someone else, someone who was so clearly inferior to his beloved daughter," Glen said.

Caroline slowly shook her head. "I can't imagine that Howard knew anything about the new woman in Oliver's life. He never let us say a single thing about Oliver in front of him, and Doris told me that he never let her or Karina discuss him, either. And even if he had known about Lisa, I can't see him caring. He'd have known that it wasn't anything serious."

Lelia, Margaret thought, biting her tongue this time.

"And maybe that's the answer," Glen said. "Maybe Oliver's new girlfriend realized that she didn't really matter to him, so she killed him."

Caroline nodded. "That seems the most likely solution."

Glen sighed. "I'm tired of talking. I don't want pudding."

He got up and slowly walked out of the room. Caroline watched him go.

"I want pudding," she said. "I'm doing everything I can to pretend that everything is fine, even though it is so far away from fine that I can't imagine ever actually feeling fine again."

"I'm sorry," Margaret said.

The waiter brought them dessert menus when he came over to clear away their empty plates. After they'd ordered, Caroline sat back in her seat and sighed.

"I'm just going through the motions while my mind desperately tries to work out who killed my son," she said. "Although I believe I'm supposed to say that the police have yet to determine if it was murder or not. Except they have determined that it was murder. They rang us last night to tell us. But we aren't supposed to be telling other people. And now I'm babbling because you are the first *other people* we've seen since Oliver's death."

While Margaret tried to think of a polite response, the waiter arrived with their desserts.

"That looks good," Margaret told Caroline, who was staring at her Victoria sponge with a frown on her face.

"This was Oliver's favorite pudding," she said. "I don't really care for Victoria sponge, but Oliver loved it. I don't know why I ordered it. I don't want it."

She pushed her plate away and then wiped her eyes. Glen walked back over and sat down in his seat without saying a word.

"We could trade," Arthur said. "If you'd prefer jam roly-poly."

Caroline looked at his plate and then shrugged. "I suppose we could trade. Or you could just eat both puddings."

"We'd better trade," Arthur said. "I don't dare go home and tell my wife that I had two puddings with lunch."

He handed her his plate and then pulled hers into place in front of him. Margaret took a bite of her crème brûlée while Caroline simply stared into space.

"Someone murdered our son," Caroline said suddenly. She blinked and then looked around the table. "Did I say that out loud? It's a thought that keeps whirling around in my head. I don't know that it will ever make sense to me."

"The police will find the killer," Glen said. He looked at Margaret. "I hope the police will find the killer."

"They're working on it twenty-four seven," Margaret replied.

He nodded. "The police will find the killer. Once they do, maybe everything will start to make sense."

Caroline shook her head. "Oliver's murder will never make sense. No one had any reason to kill him."

She picked up her fork and stabbed at the jam roly-poly.

"It had to have been a stranger," Glen said. "Oliver was in the wrong place at the wrong time."

"Except Oliver had no reason to be there," Caroline said. "He never went hiking." She took a bite of her dessert.

"Someone must have asked him to meet them there," Glen said. "Maybe it was a potential client. You know as well as I do that Oliver would go to great lengths to acquire new clients for the business."

"If it was a business meeting, surely someone in the office knew where he was going," Arthur said.

Glen shrugged. "We have a pair of administrators who handle appointments for all of the accountants, but Oliver often did his own thing. Not during business hours, of course. On a typical workday, he was nearly always at his desk from eight to five or even six. But that left his nights and weekends free for what he called 'client hunting.' He didn't like to socialize, but he had a talent for finding new clients while grocery shopping or at the petrol station."

Caroline smiled. "I was with him at ShopFast one day when he started taking to the man queuing in front of us. By the time we all left the shop, Oliver had persuaded him to move his business to Livergood and Walton."

I wonder if anyone has mentioned any of this to Michael, Margaret thought.

"We need to go," Glen said. "I have to go back to the office and sit at my desk and pretend to work for the rest of the afternoon." He looked at Arthur and sighed. "I promise you that my inability to focus is only temporary. Your accounts are completely safe."

"I'm not worried about my accounts, but I am worried about my friend," Arthur said, putting a hand on Glen's shoulder.

"Thank you. I appreciate that," Glen said.

"And I have a memorial service to plan," Caroline said. She pushed her half-eaten dessert away and picked up her handbag. "You both should come. I want the building as full as it can be with the right people."

She flushed. "And that sounded quite terrible. What I meant was that I want the building full of people who knew Oliver or at least knows someone connected to Oliver. I know that there will be a crowd of people who turn up simply to be nosy because Oliver was murdered. I want them to have to stand at the very back, if they can get in at all."

"That still sounds quite terrible," Glen said.

Caroline shrugged. "I won't apologize for wanting my son's memorial service to be filled with people who actually care about me and my family. I can understand why people are curious about Oliver's death, but that doesn't give them the right to impose on our grief."

"When and where is the service?" Arthur asked.

"Thursday afternoon at one at the Onchan Community Centre," Caroline replied. "Oliver wasn't religious. A service in a church didn't feel right. We're still discussing where we'll have the actual funeral, but the police haven't yet released the, er, uhm..."

"We'll be there," Arthur told Caroline. "Everyone from Park's will be there."

"I appreciate that," Caroline said. "I hadn't really thought about it, but I suppose I should expect a lot of Oliver's clients to attend, shouldn't I? I wonder if the community center will be large enough to accommodate everyone who truly should be there."

"We'll make it work," Glen said. "I'll hire a few security guards to stand at the door and turn away anyone who didn't have an actual connection to Oliver and our family."

"Can they also turn away Lisa?" Caroline asked.

Glen frowned. "I don't think that would be a smart thing to do."

"I would imagine Lelia is going to want to be there," Margaret said. "She loved Oliver."

Caroline nodded. "I hope she'll understand if Karina sits in the front row with us. I feel very strongly that Karina's loss is greater than Lisa's."

"Let's not worry about the details now," Glen said. "We need to go."

"We'll see you at the service," Caroline said. "Thank you for lunch."

"Yes, thank you," Glen said.

Margaret watched as the pair walked away.

"They're both very upset," Arthur said. "I rang Glen yesterday to offer my condolences and he suggested that we meet for lunch today. Since I already had the booking here, I invited them. I don't know what I was expecting, but I'm rather surprised by how badly shaken they both are."

"I can't imagine what they're going through."

"No, neither can I. When I spoke to Glen, he said that he was doing everything he could to keep Caroline busy. That was why he'd suggested lunch in the first place. He didn't want Caroline simply sitting around the house on her own all day."

"I hope Michael finds the killer quickly."

"I agree, although finding out who killed Oliver might be even more upsetting for Glen and Caroline. Most of the suspects are people they consider friends."

Margaret finished the last of her dessert and then sat back in her chair. "I suppose we need to get back to the office, too."

"We do. Remind me to tell everyone about the memorial service. We'll close up the office and go together, unless you're going to be attending with Ted?"

"Oh, that's a good point. I assume Ted is going to be there. I'm sure Mark and Michael will also attend. I'll have to talk to Ted and let you know."

"It doesn't really matter. I was just thinking that we'll probably want to take only one car. There isn't a lot of parking at the community center."

"Maybe I'll ride with you and then sit with Ted."

"That would work."

Arthur signed the check and then they walked out of the club together. As they approached the car, Margaret sighed. Three or four men were standing around it, pointing and talking excitedly.

"Oh, hi," one of them said as Margaret and Arthur reached them.

"Hey," another said.

"I'll give you five thousand pounds if you let me drive the car around the car park once," a third said.

Margaret shook her head. "I'm sorry, but it isn't my car. My aunt gave me permission to drive it, but I can't let anyone else drive it. The insurance company was very clear on that."

"Ten thousand," the man said.

"Sorry, no," Margaret replied.

"Fifteen? Twenty? What will it take?" he demanded.

"I'm sorry, but I can't take the risk. If something happened to the car, I can't afford to replace it," Margaret said.

"I could afford to replace it if there were cars available to be purchased. I have requests in at specialist car dealerships around the world. If one of these cars ever comes on the market, I'll buy it, no matter the price," the man said. "This is the closest I've ever come to one."

"It's beautiful," one of the men said.

The others nodded in agreement.

"I used to see Mona driving around the island in it," another said. "This car suited her."

Everyone looked at Margaret. She was sure none of them felt that the fancy sports car suited her. But she was the one with the key, so it didn't really matter what they thought. Feeling slightly smug, she hit the button to unlock the doors. The car chirped. The men all seemed to lean closer to the vehicle.

"Ready to go?" Margaret asked Arthur.

He nodded and then opened the passenger door. As he climbed inside, Margaret walked to the driver's door.

"Can I just take a peek?" the man who'd offered her money to let him drive asked as Margaret opened the door.

She nodded reluctantly. The man stuck his head inside the car and inhaled deeply.

"I want to bottle that smell," he said.

"Thanks," Arthur said with a laugh. "But it already comes in a bottle." He named the expensive aftershave that he wore.

The man shook his head. "The car smells of leather seats and premium motor oil. I'm also getting a hint of the perfume that Mona always wore."

"Her perfume was something special," someone said.

"It was indeed," another man said.

"I need to get back to work," Margaret said to the man who was standing in the car's open door.

"Just let me take a picture," he said.

Margaret watched as he snapped a few pictures of the car's interior. Arthur smiled brightly for every photo, even though he had to know that he was going to be cropped out of any that he appeared in. The man put his phone away and slowly stepped backward. Margaret quickly got into the car before anyone else could ask for pictures. She shut the driver's door and then turned the key.

"I'm going to hit someone," she muttered as she slowly began to pull forward.

"I think a few of them would be quite happy to be run over by this car," Arthur said.

Margaret laughed. "You might be right about that."

She could feel everyone watching as she slowly drove out of the parking lot and onto the drive that led back to the main road. It wasn't until she was nearly back at the office that she finally relaxed.

"I don't think I'll be driving Mona's car again in a hurry," she said to Arthur.

He frowned. "That's a shame, because you can tell she loves being out and about."

Margaret nodded. "She really does seem to love being driven."

"And you shouldn't let those guys put you off driving her. They're just rich idiots."

Margaret laughed. "They certainly seemed that way."

"If it makes you feel any better, the guy who kept offering you money to let him drive definitely can't afford a car like this. I don't think he could have afforded to give you five thousand pounds to take the car for a drive, either. He was mostly just showing off."

"I'm glad I didn't take him up on the offer, then."

"Oh, he'd have given you a check if you had. Whether the check would have been honored is a different matter."

Margaret sighed. "It's a great car, but I really don't understand why so many people are so obsessed with it."

"I do. I'm rather obsessed with it myself, but I count myself incredibly lucky that I'm getting to ride in it. As I said before, I'd be afraid to drive it."

Margaret turned in to the parking lot at Park's and pulled back into her usual space. "I try not to think about how much the car is worth when I drive it," she said. "And I remind myself that it is insured. Driving it very occasionally seems the lesser of two evils. It wouldn't be good for it just to sit in the garage all the time."

"I hope you'll let me ride in it again one day," Arthur said.

"Thank you for lunch," Margaret said as they got out of the car.

"Thank you for coming with me. I didn't want to eat with Glen and Caroline on my own."

Back in her office, Margaret quickly called Ted.

"Tell me that you had lunch with Glen and Caroline," he said.

"I did, actually. Arthur arranged it."

Ted chuckled. "I hope you learned something interesting, because Michael is really struggling."

"I don't think I learned anything. The conversation was difficult."

Margaret did her best to repeat the conversation from lunch. When she was done, Ted asked her a few questions.

"You cooked last night. Let's go out tonight," Ted said when she'd answered them. "Maybe something quick. I really want to go to the pub and sit with a cat on my lap and a drink in my hand tonight."

"That does sound quite nice."

Margaret put her phone away and went back to work.

13

Ted was waiting at her door when she got home from work.

"Here we are again," she said before they kissed.

"I like it here," Ted said with a grin when he released her several minutes later.

"It's a good place to be," she agreed.

She opened her door and then stepped into the apartment. Mona was sitting on one of the couches. Katie was sleeping on Mona's lap. The small animal opened her eyes and then jumped to the floor as Ted followed Margaret into the living room.

"Hello, baby," Margaret said to Katie.

"Meroooooooowwww," Katie replied.

"Good afternoon," Mona said. "I know I've missed a few things. Please go over the entire case with Ted while I take notes."

Margaret very nearly replied, stopping herself just in time. *We're going out for dinner*, she thought.

"Yes, of course, but before you go, you can have a quick chat about the case," Mona replied.

Margaret sighed. "Glen and Caroline seemed very upset at lunch," she said to Ted. "Although sad might be a better word. They were both very sad."

"They're still on the short list of suspects," Ted told her. "Although Glen is higher on the list than Caroline."

"I can't imagine either of them being involved, but then I'm still not clear on the killer's motive. Is it possible that Oliver was meeting a potential client out there?"

Ted shrugged. "Anything is possible. Michael hasn't been able to find anyone who knew where Oliver was supposed to be on Saturday morning. I should say anyone who will admit to knowing where Oliver was going to be on Saturday morning."

"His parents said that he never went hiking."

Ted shrugged. "There's certainly no evidence that the body was moved at any point after the man's death. And that information has already been released to the press. The chief constable is looking for people who might have seen Oliver that morning, either somewhere near Dreeym Gorrym Point or maybe driving in that direction."

"Which of the suspects would he have been willing to meet there?" Mona asked.

Margaret nodded and then frowned. Ted obviously hadn't heard the question. "He must have arranged to meet someone there," she said. "Which of the suspects could have talked him into a short hike?"

"I can see him meeting Karina out there," Ted said after a moment's thought. "Especially if he was doing his best to keep her on the hook while also chasing Lelia."

Margaret frowned. "I feel as if they're both going to be better off without him."

"I suspect the killer would agree with that."

"He'd have met Lelia there," Margaret said. "And I would imagine he would have met Drake there."

Ted nodded. "Actually, I can see him agreeing to meet just about anyone there, assuming the person had a good enough reason for the request. Karina could have just said she wanted to meet him somewhere private. I can't imagine any of the others would have had to work too hard to come up with an excuse to get him there, though."

"Was the location significant?" Mona asked.

"I wonder why the killer chose that location," Margaret said.

Ted hesitated. "I think there were reasons, but I can't discuss them."

"You think there were reasons?"

Ted shrugged. "I'm starving. Let's go and get something to eat."

"That was very frustrating," Mona said.

Margaret nodded. "Give me five minutes to get ready," she told Ted before disappearing into her bedroom.

When she emerged a few minutes later, Ted was just walking out of the kitchen.

"I gave Katie her dinner and a treat," he said. "And I refilled her water bowl with fresh water."

"Thanks. That almost makes up for you withholding information from me." Margaret did her best to keep her tone light.

Ted frowned. "You know there are always things I can't talk about during murder investigations."

She nodded. "It's fine. It comes with the territory. I still love you."

"You're too easy on him," Mona said. "Fenella was the same with Daniel. If I were in your position, I'd insist on being told everything."

Margaret just shook her head and then put on her shoes and grabbed her handbag. "Let's go," she said.

They walked out of the building hand in hand.

"What sounds good?" Ted asked.

"Anything. I ate way too much at Arthur's club, so wherever we go, I'm not going to get much."

"Let's try the new sandwich shop," Ted suggested. "They're supposed to be a lot like the big American franchise place, but nicer."

"That sounds good."

The shop was only a short walk away. They stood in line behind another couple while the man at the counter built his sandwich. When he was done, the next couple took their turn. Margaret paid close attention to the process so that when it was her turn, she knew what to do. Ted did the same. A few minutes later, they walked out of the restaurant together, each carrying a small bag containing a sandwich, some chips, and a can of soda.

"Let's sit on the promenade and eat," Ted suggested.

"This is delicious," Margaret said after a few bites. "Everything tastes fresh, and the turkey is wonderful."

"Mine is good, too."

While they watched the waves lapping on the shore, Margaret told Ted about her incident in the golf club's parking lot.

"It is a really special car," Ted said when she was done. "But that doesn't give people the right to make you feel uncomfortable."

"It wasn't deliberate, though. And only one guy was really obnoxious about it."

"Hello, hello," a familiar voice said.

Margaret frowned. She kept her eyes on the water, hoping that Heather Bryant would just keep walking.

"How are you both tonight?" Heather asked as she sat down next to Ted.

"We're fine," Ted replied. "How are you?"

Heather shrugged. "Frustrated. There's a killer walking around the island and the police don't seem to be doing anything to find him. Or her."

"The police are working very hard to find the killer," Ted countered. "Inspector Madison has been working incredibly long hours since the body was found."

"And why exactly is Inspector Madison the one investigating?" Heather asked. "It seems odd to me that a visiting inspector would be asked to investigate a murder the day after he arrived on the island. Especially considering there are a number of other inspectors who were already here and who have significant experience with investigating homicides."

Ted shrugged. "You'd have to ask the chief constable about that."

"Oh, I have," Heather said darkly.

Margaret swallowed a laugh.

"I knew Oliver," Heather said.

Ted gave her a curious look. "I didn't realize that."

She shrugged. "I went out with Drake Livergood a few times. We went out with Oliver and Lelia on a couple of occasions, too."

"Do you want to talk to Inspector Madison?" Ted asked. "He'd be happy to speak with you if you think you can add anything to the investigation."

Heather sighed. "Oliver seemed like a really nice guy. That's about all I can add. Oh, and when I told Drake that Oliver seemed really nice, he laughed and told me that appearances can be deceiving. When I asked him what he meant, he just shook his head and changed the subject."

"Maybe Inspector Madison needs to have another talk with Drake," Ted said.

"Lelia is sweet," Heather added. "But I did wonder what Oliver saw in her. Let's just say I can't imagine that anyone would consider Lelia an upgrade over Karina."

"Anything else?" Ted asked.

Heather shook her head. "It's different when you know the victim," she said. "I wouldn't have said that Oliver and I were friends, but we were friendly. I find myself not wanting to talk about him. I've actually been letting Dan Ross write the stories for the paper and the website. I don't want to do that, but I can't seem to write them myself."

"Are you still friendly with Drake?" Margaret asked.

Heather stared at her. "I suppose so. He ended things, but I'd known it was coming. He doesn't really do commitment. I knew we were just having some fun together, so I wasn't surprised when he stopped ringing. He was kind enough to give me a statement for the paper."

Margaret finished the last of her sandwich and then washed it down with a drink of soda. Ted crumpled up the bag from his chips and stuck it inside his now-empty sandwich bag.

"I hope Inspector Madison finds the killer soon," Heather said. "I'll sleep better when I know he or she is behind bars."

Before either of them could reply, Heather got up and walked away.

"That was weird," Margaret said.

Ted nodded. "It was odd. She wasn't at all herself."

"Maybe she's having to reconsider her past behavior when it came to dealing with witnesses in murder investigations. She's always been pushy and rude. Maybe knowing a victim will teach her to be nicer in the future."

"I doubt it," Ted said. "But we can hope."

They threw away their trash and then strolled for a short while along the promenade.

"Is it time for the pub?" Ted asked eventually.

Margaret nodded. "A cold glass of wine and a warm kitten are just what I need."

Ted laughed. "I'm hoping that Asparagus is in the mood for another cuddle."

They crossed the street and walked into the pub. After getting their drinks, they headed up the stairs. The upstairs was all but empty. Margaret nodded at the young man who was reading in one corner of the room. She and Ted settled on a couch as far from him as they could be.

"Now I just need a friend," Margaret said.

A moment later, she spotted Asparagus. He and another cat seemed to be prowling around the room together. When they got closer to Margaret and Ted, the cats exchanged glances.

"They seem to be trying to decide if we are worthy," Ted said.

Margaret laughed. "It does seem that way."

A moment later, Asparagus jumped into Ted's lap. His feline friend climbed carefully onto the couch and then into Margaret's lap. She rubbed his back once he was settled.

"This is just about perfect," Ted said.

"Hello, hello," a voice called from the stairs.

Margaret forced herself to smile as Ashley waved at them.

"So much for perfect," Ted whispered in Margaret's ear.

Margaret's smile was more genuine for Mark and then Lelia, who'd both followed Ashley to the upper level. The trio walked over and joined Margaret and Ted.

"Good evening," Ted said.

"It is a good evening," Ashley replied. "We've been invited to Oliver's memorial service, which was a huge shock."

Margaret looked at Lelia. "How are you?" she asked.

Lelia shrugged. "I'm doing better. I'm almost ready to have you burn that box. I will admit that it did make me feel a tiny bit better when Caroline rang and invited me to Oliver's memorial service. She'll probably expect me to sit at the back and keep quiet, but just being there is going to help bring me some peace."

"I'm glad she's including you. You were clearly important to Oliver."

"I'm sure Karina won't be happy that I'm there."

Margaret shrugged. "They were divorced. She understands that."

"Have you met Karina, then?" Lelia asked.

Margaret nodded.

"I hope she didn't say horrible things about me," Lelia said with a frown.

"She did not."

Lelia sighed. "I'm sorry. I'm kind of a mess right now. I probably should have stayed at home."

"But you need to get out," Ashley said. "You need to meet more people. You need to meet another man."

Lelia shook her head. "I'm not interested in meeting another man, not right now. Maybe one day."

"From what you were saying, there's at least one guy waiting in the wings for you," Ashley said teasingly.

Lelia's cheeks turned bright red. "I think you're misreading the situation."

"And I'm certain that I'm not," Ashley countered.

Lelia shook her head.

Ashley looked at Margaret. "What would you think if a man came to see you to offer his condolences and then gave you his card and told you to ring him anytime you needed a friend?"

Margaret shrugged. "I suppose that would depend on a number of factors. Is it a man I already knew or a stranger? Is he single? And a lot would probably come down to how he said the words, his tone and whatnot."

"His tone was clearly flirtatious," Ashley said. "And he's someone that Lelia met through Oliver. And he's very, very single, although he did tell Lelia that he's starting to feel as if he's ready to start looking for the person he wants to spend forever with."

"That sounds like a line," Margaret said flatly.

Ashley laughed. "Yeah, it does, but I'm not suggesting that Lelia should fall in love with Drake. I just think she should let him buy her dinner a few times and see where things go from there. At least she'll get a few free meals out of it."

Margaret raised an eyebrow. "It was Drake?"

Ashley nodded. "He seemed very concerned about Lelia. They sat and talked for hours."

"It wasn't hours," Lelia said. "And he was very nice and not at all flirtatious."

"He was flirting so hard I could feel it in the other room," Ashley countered. "And he was doing everything he could to play on your sympathies, telling you all about his childhood and all of his broken dreams."

Lelia flushed. "I think it was quite sad that his parents more or less forced him to become an accountant, especially when he knew exactly what he wanted to do with his life, and it wasn't accounting."

Margaret nodded. "He told me something similar. He said that he'd wanted to be an engineer, and that Oliver had wanted to be a doctor."

Lelia shrugged. "Oliver wanted to be a doctor very briefly, but then he found out about all the science he'd have to study and decided that he didn't want to be a doctor after all. He changed his mind fairly regularly throughout his childhood, or so he told me. According to Drake, *he* always wanted to be an engineer. He told me that he still wishes he'd studied engineering instead of accountancy."

"He could always go back to school," Margaret said.

Lelia nodded. "We talked about that. He told me that he's been trying to save some money so that he can at least take a few Open University courses in the future, but he's worried that he'll struggle to find the time to take classes and work full-time."

Margaret looked at Ted. He had an odd expression on his face. Mark noticed it too.

"I know what you're thinking," Mark said to Ted.

Ted nodded. "We need another round," he said.

"I'll help you get it," Mark replied.

The two men got up and walked to the elevator together. Margaret watched as they started whispering to each other as they walked into the elevator car.

"That's odd," Ashley said. "One of us must have said something interesting."

"Or they both just remembered that they were supposed to do something before they left work for the day," Margaret said. "Now they'll be arguing over which one of them should go back to the station and do whatever it is."

"Does that happen often?" Ashley asked.

Margaret shrugged. "I wouldn't say often." *Because it's never happened, but I don't want you thinking too hard about what we've just been discussing in case something someone said solves the murder,* she added silently.

"I've been thinking a lot about my box," Lelia said. "I told Ashley about it. She thinks I should open it and see what's inside."

"You have to be the one to make that decision," Margaret said.

"I told her that *I* could open the box and see what's inside," Ashley said. "I'd only tell her if I found something good."

Lelia frowned. "I almost feel as if I need to know if there is something bad in there more than if there's something good in there."

"There probably isn't anything that's at all interesting," Ashley said. "Your mother probably burned all of the interesting stuff when she first moved to the island."

Lelia nodded. "You're probably right. I should just burn the box."

"You should have someone check the contents first, just in case," Ashley said.

"I'll think about it," Lelia replied.

"How are you doing otherwise?" Margaret asked the woman.

She shrugged. "Sometimes I feel pretty okay. Other times I just want to sit and cry. Work has been weird, too. I took a few days off, but I had to go back. The other girls were struggling to cover my shift for me, but that meant that they were both working extra hours and on their own for a lot of the time. I couldn't leave them doing that for long."

"The paper should have hired a temp," Ashley said.

"They tried that the last time one of the other girls took some time off," Lelia told her. "I spent so much time trying to train the temp that I couldn't get any work done. My supervisor keeps talking about cross-training a few of the other admin staff to help out in our department when someone is poorly or on holiday, but he's been talking about that for over a year and nothing has been done yet."

"And now you're going to have to take Thursday afternoon off," Ashley said.

Lelia shrugged. "I'm just moving my lunch hour. I hope the service won't take longer than an hour."

"Do you really think you'll feel up to going back to work after the service?" Margaret asked her.

"I don't know. I just know I can't really afford to take any more time off right now. My supervisor has been hinting that I could easily be replaced. I need my job."

"Yeah, you do," Ashley said. "I can't afford the rent on our place by myself."

Lelia nodded. "If I lost my job, I'd have to move back into my mother's house, but I'd have to kick the tenants out first. I don't want to do that to them. They seem to love the house."

"You could let them buy it," Ashley suggested. "That would give you some money to live off of while you're job hunting."

"It might come to that, but I hope not. I'm doing everything I can to keep my job."

Mark and Ted returned a moment later. Ted was carrying a small tray with drinks for everyone. When he'd stood up, Asparagus had stepped off his lap and then curled up on the couch where Ted had been sitting. Now Ted stared at the animal.

"That's my seat," he said.

The cat opened one eye and then squeezed both eyes tightly closed.

Margaret laughed. "It looks as if Asparagus doesn't agree."

Ted put the tray of drinks on the table and then walked over and sat on the opposite end of the couch. He picked up his drink and then sat back and slid his arm around Margaret.

"It looks as if it might rain later," Mark said.

"We want to know what you two were talking about when you went downstairs," Ashley said.

Mark shrugged. "Nothing important. Probably the rugby score."

Ashley frowned. "Now you're lying to us. We know you were

talking about the investigation. Someone said something that made you both think of something. We want to know what all of those things were."

Mark shook his head. "You know there are things I can't talk about. You can assume this is one of them, or believe me that we were talking about the rugby."

"This isn't going to work," Ashley snapped. "I can't be involved with a man who keeps secrets from me."

"A lot of my work needs to be confidential. You knew that when we started seeing each other," Mark said calmly.

"I knew it, but I didn't understand what that actually meant. And now I do understand, and I don't like it. I don't like it one bit," Ashley said, her volume rising with every word.

"I'm not interested in changing jobs," Mark said.

"Then I'm not interested in continuing this relationship," Ashley shot back.

She got to her feet, grabbed her bag, picked up her drink and drained it and then headed for the elevator. After a few steps, she stopped and looked back.

"Lelia? Aren't you coming?" she demanded.

"I suppose I should," Lelia said. "Neither of us should be walking home alone."

As she reached for her bag, Ashley spoke again.

"I'll wait for you downstairs," she said loudly.

"I think she's hoping that you're going to go after her," Lelia said to Mark as she picked up her bag.

"There seems little point," Mark said. "I'm not changing jobs in the foreseeable future."

Lelia nodded. "For what it's worth, I've always thought you were too good for her," she told Mark before blushing.

"Call me when you're ready to do something with the box," Margaret said.

"Yeah, I will," Lelia replied. She frowned. "Although, actually, I'm pretty happy with the current situation. I know the box is safe, but getting access to it would take some effort. I can almost forget all about it, which feels really good."

"The box will continue to be safe with me for however long you need it to be," Margaret assured her. "I am going to be away for a few weeks next month, though, just so you know."

Lelia laughed. "Ah, that's a complication. I was imagining that I could just ring you out of the blue one day and get the box back the next. I never thought about you going on holiday or anything. I'll have to think about that little wrinkle."

"Lelia!!" Ashley was standing at the top of the stairs, glaring at them.

"Sorry, I'm coming," she said quickly.

"We'll see you at the memorial service," Ted told her.

She nodded. "I'll be there," she said grimly.

She walked over to the stairs and then she and Ashley disappeared down them.

"Phew," Mark said a moment later. "I've been trying to find a way to end things with her since the first time we went out."

Margaret shook her head. "You should have just told her that you didn't think it was working and ended things immediately."

He shrugged. "I was exaggerating. The first few times that we went out were actually really nice. We had fun and Ashley was quite good company. It wasn't until the morning of our hike that I started to question the relationship. She was quite rude to you."

"She was," Margaret agreed.

"And then we found the body and it didn't seem to be the right time to end things. But I've never been good at ending relationships. I usually just start behaving badly until the woman dumps me."

"That's a terrible thing to do," Margaret said.

He nodded. "My very first serious girlfriend, back when I was sixteen, threw herself down a cliff when I told her that I didn't want to see her any longer. It took me a long time to even think about getting into another relationship after that, and it's made it almost impossible for me to end them, too."

Margaret stared at him. "She threw herself off a cliff?"

"Yeah, although to be fair, it was only a small cliff and she really just rolled herself to the bottom. She was always overly dramatic. That was one of the reasons why I'd wanted to end things."

"So she was okay?" Margaret asked.

Mark laughed. "Sorry, yeah, she was fine. A bit dizzy more than anything else. And still very, very angry with me."

"You can't let that one incident all those years ago impact your relationships now," Margaret said. "The women you date deserve better."

"She's very smart," Mark said to Ted. "I hate that she's right."

"She's usually right. And she's very beautiful," Ted replied.

"And she's just as eager as Ashley to know what you both suddenly realized at the same time," Margaret said. "We were talking about Drake, which makes me think that you've both realized that he killed Oliver."

Ted chuckled. "I wish it were that simple, but when is a murder investigation that simple? You're right, we did both realize something about Drake, but there's no guarantee that it has anything to do with the murder."

"But I think it does," Mark said. "And I'll be sitting next to Drake at the memorial service, just in case."

"Just in case what?" Margaret asked. "You don't think he's planning to kill anyone else, do you?"

Mark shook his head. "I'm just hoping that someone might say something at the service that leads Drake to let something slip. It could happen."

Ted nodded. "Emotions run high at these kinds of events. People often say things they shouldn't when they're feeling emotional."

"If it was Drake, what do you think was his motive?" Margaret asked.

Ted shrugged. "I don't know, but I do find it interesting that he's already made a play for Lelia."

"I would have expected him to go after Karina, really," Margaret said.

"And maybe he's done that as well," Mark said.

Margaret frowned. "Yeah, okay, I can see him going after both women, but only if Lelia is secretly worth a fortune."

Mark shook his head. "Maybe he simply thinks that she's worth a fortune. Who knows what Oliver told him?"

"What if Oliver lied about Lelia's worth and then Drake killed

Oliver to get his hands on a fortune that doesn't even exist?" Margaret said.

"That's definitely one possibility," Ted said.

Margaret shook her head. "I need to go home and get some sleep, but I don't think I'll sleep."

"It's been an interesting evening," Ted said as Margaret woke the cat who'd been sleeping on her lap.

They all stood up and walked to the elevators together.

"You say that," Mark said, "but I got very publicly dumped."

"And you aren't the least bit sorry," Ted said.

"Margaret, do you know any nice single women?" Ted asked.

Margaret laughed. "I'll think about it." As they walked out of the elevator she sighed. "Too bad Megan thinks she's in love with someone else. She'd be perfect for you."

"Your younger sister? Doesn't she live in the US?" Mark asked.

"Yes, but she's coming to visit me in October. Sadly, she's bringing her boyfriend, a man I do not trust, and some of his friends with her."

Mark frowned. "Do you want me to investigate the boyfriend?"

"No, but thank you for offering. I'm trying hard to reserve judgement until I actually meet him. It's very remotely possible that he's everything Megan seems to think he is."

They walked out of the pub together. Mark turned left.

"Good night," he called over his shoulder as Margaret and Ted turned right.

"You know I'd be happy to take a look at Megan's boyfriend if you want more information about him," Ted said.

She nodded. "Like I said, I'm trying to reserve judgement. I'd feel better about it if Megan had a better track record when it comes to choosing men, though."

"If she hadn't chosen one who got himself murdered, we might never have met."

"Let's hope that never happens again."

Ted walked her to her door.

"Do you want to come in for a minute?" she asked.

He shook his head. "I need some sleep. Tomorrow is going to be a busy day and so is Thursday."

After their kiss, Ted smiled at her.

"Thank you for not asking," he said.

"I respect the fact that you aren't supposed to talk about certain parts of your work and that doing so might compromise the investigation."

Ted nodded. Then he leaned closer to her. "The murderer used a fairly simple, but unusual contraption, to kill Oliver," he whispered in her ear. "It's possible that he or she bought the device somewhere, or maybe he or she did their own engineering."

Margaret frowned. "A contraption?"

He shrugged. "Imagine a device that could tighten a rope around something very quickly and easily with little effort."

"Oh dear," Margaret said with a shudder.

"As I said, the device might have been purchased somewhere. But Mark and I both found it interesting that Drake used to want to be an engineer."

"I told you that when I told you about my conversation with him," Margaret said.

Ted nodded. "But I didn't make the connection at the time. I was talking to you. You're an engineer, but if you wanted to murder someone, you'd mix up some poison to do it. I didn't really think about what sort of engineering Drake might have wanted to study."

"He did say something about taking things apart and putting them back together again," Margaret said. "And I probably didn't mention that when we talked because it didn't seem relevant."

"Because you didn't know about the contraption."

"I did not."

"And now you can't tell anyone about it."

"I won't."

He kissed her again. "I'll see you tomorrow. I think you've talked to everyone involved in the case now, so maybe you'll have a boring day tomorrow."

"I think I'd quite like a boring day tomorrow. Thursday might not be boring."

"I'm really hoping it won't be."

Margaret walked into her apartment and sat down in the chair nearest the door.

"It sounds as if Ted is convinced that Drake killed Oliver," Mona said as she appeared next to Margaret.

Margaret nodded. "I hope he's right and he can get Drake to say the wrong thing on Thursday. I really want Oliver's killer found."

"You might get a hint as to the motive if you open Lelia's box."

"I might, but I'm still not opening it."

Mona sighed. "I didn't think you would. I'll be back on Thursday afternoon to hear how the memorial service went."

Margaret stared as Mona started to sparkle brightly. A sudden explosion of small fireworks made Margaret blink. When she opened her eyes, Mona was gone.

"It's bedtime," Margaret said as she got to her feet.

14

Wednesday was fairly uneventful for Margaret. She went to work with a packed lunch that she ate while sitting in the lobby chatting with Joney, who had her own packed lunch. After work, she cooked dinner for herself and Ted. They watched some television before having an early night.

When Margaret woke up on Thursday, she felt an odd sense of foreboding.

"You're being silly," she told herself as she got Katie her breakfast. "Everything is going to be fine."

She chose her outfit with care, opting for a pair of black trousers and a lightweight grey sweater. The outfit felt appropriate for work and for a memorial service. When she got to the office, she found Joney similarly attired.

"I had to dig these trousers out from the back of the wardrobe," Joney said. "They're really too heavy for summer, but they're the only black trousers I could find."

"Whereas I have a wardrobe full of little black dresses," Rachel said as she joined them. "But none of them are appropriate for a memorial service. Does this look too bad?" she asked.

Margaret looked at the black dress. Rachel had paired it with a dark grey jacket that made it look more formal and less like it belonged at a cocktail party.

"You look fine," Joney told her. "No one is going to be looking at you, anyway."

Rachel laughed. "I know that's true. Everyone is going to want to see what Karina is wearing. I'm certain she's going to go full widow-mode, even though she isn't actually a widow."

"I think it's quite sad that she was still in love with Oliver," Joney said. "And I really hope that she and Oliver's new girlfriend don't come to blows during the service."

"They won't," Margaret said confidently. "They're both really nice women. Under different circumstances, I think they would be friends."

She spent the morning working and then ate her sandwich at her desk while continuing to work in order to make up for the time that she was going to be spending at the memorial service. They all met in the building's lobby at twelve-thirty.

"I hope it won't be too difficult to find a parking space," Arthur said as he drove them toward Onchan.

A short while later, he stopped at the entrance to the community center's parking lot. A man in a black uniform with "Security" printed across it held up a hand. Arthur put his window down.

"The Community Centre is closed for a private function," the man said.

"Yes, we're here for the memorial service," Arthur told him.

He nodded and then held up his phone. "Your name?"

"Arthur Park."

The man scrolled down his screen. "Yes, okay. You can park anywhere," he told Arthur, stepping back to let Arthur drive into the parking lot.

"I wasn't expecting that much security," Rachel said.

"I believe Caroline is worried that some people might just come to gawk because Oliver was murdered," Arthur said.

"She's not wrong," Rachel replied.

The parking lot was already about half full. Arthur pulled into a spot and turned off the ignition.

"Ready?" he asked.

They all got out of the car and walked toward the building. Two more men in security uniforms were standing in front of the entrance. They checked each person's name in turn before finally allowing them all to enter.

"I don't know if I should feel flattered to be allowed in or just weirded out about the whole thing," Rachel whispered to Margaret as they walked down the short corridor inside.

"Thank you for coming," Glen said when they reached the entrance to the large community room.

"You know we want to do what we can to support you and Caroline," Arthur said.

"Please sit near the front," Glen replied. "It's a bit of a mess in there, really. People are mostly sitting near the back. They're mostly clients, so I understand why, but Caroline will be upset if the front rows are empty."

"We'll sit near the front," Arthur promised.

Glen nodded and then turned his attention to the next group of people who were walking toward him.

Margaret followed Arthur into the room. Rows of chairs had been set up and filled nearly the entire room. A small lectern stood in front of the rows of chairs. The back half of the room was mostly full of small groups of people, many of whom looked uncomfortable in their Sunday best sitting on folding chairs. The rows from there to the front of the room were either empty or had only a few people sitting in them. The chairs in the front row had small "Reserved" signs on each seat.

"How close do we need to be?" Arthur asked.

"Glen asked us to sit near the front," Joney said. "How about the third row?"

"We could sit in the second row," Rachel suggested. "Then we won't miss anything."

Arthur chuckled and then led the little group down the makeshift aisle between the rows of chairs. He stopped three rows from the front and then filed into the row. The others followed. Margaret sat at the end of the row with an empty seat next to her on the aisle for Ted. He arrived a few minutes later, while Margaret and Rachel were chatting about the large bouquets of flowers on either side of the lecture.

"Hi," he said as he sat down next to Margaret. "Thanks for saving me a seat. I'll be right back."

Margaret laughed as he got up and walked away. A moment later, Drake dropped into the seat next to hers.

"I'm not staying," he said. "I know this is Inspector Hart's seat. I just wanted to thank you for coming." He leaned around Margaret. "Thank you all for coming," he said.

"We wanted to be here for Glen and Caroline," Arthur said.

Drake nodded. "That's why we're all here. They need our support." He sat back in the chair. "Are the police getting close to finding the killer?" he asked Margaret in a low voice.

She shrugged. "Ted isn't involved in the investigation. I'm sure Michael is doing everything he can, though."

Drake nodded. "And here's Karina. I need to go. Thanks again for coming."

He walked to the back of the room and then escorted Karina down the aisle. She gave Margaret a small smile as she walked past her to the front row. Glen and Caroline were standing near the lectern. They rushed over to greet Karina before they all sat down together near the center of the row. Drake almost immediately stood back up. Margaret watched him as he scanned the room.

"Who do you think he's looking for?" Rachel whispered.

Margaret shrugged. "It could be anyone. Maybe Karina's parents?"

A minute later, Howard and Doris made their entrance. They very quickly walked down to the front row and took seats next to Karina.

"And then things got interesting," Rachel whispered.

Margaret looked at the back of the room. Lelia and Ashley had just walked in. They stood together, looking uncomfortable. Drake quickly walked back to join them. He said something to Lelia that made her smile and then he escorted them both to the front of the room. Margaret watched as he guided them into the chairs on the other side of the aisle from the others. Ashley said something to Drake, but it didn't look as if he replied.

As Ted returned to his seat, Margaret noticed that both Mark and

Michael were sitting in the second row behind Lelia and Ashley. The room was mostly full by the time a man in a dark suit walked behind the lectern. He nodded at the crowd, his expression somber.

"Good afternoon," he said. "And welcome. We're here today to celebrate the life of a wonderful young man who was taken from us far too soon: Oliver Donald Walton. Let's all take a minute to reflect on our very personal and individual relationships with Oliver."

Ted took Margaret's hand and gave it a squeeze. She squeezed back as Karina started to cry quietly.

"Glen and Caroline, Oliver's devoted parents, want today to be a celebration. While we are all mourning, they want us to rejoice in how very fortunate we were to have had the chance to get to know Oliver during his time with us. With that in mind, I would like to invite anyone and everyone to come forward and say a few words about Oliver," the man said.

The silence started to get awkward after a minute. Margaret looked at Ted. He shrugged.

"I'll start, then," the man said with a small chuckle. "I do appreciate that this is difficult, but your memories of Oliver will help his dear friends and family members in the long and complex healing process. Please don't feel shy or uncomfortable. You are among friends here."

"I don't know that Lelia would agree with that," Rachel whispered.

"As for myself, I was fortunate enough to know Oliver through Glen. Glen has been handling the accounts for my business for many years now. I'm fairly certain that Oliver was not much more than a toddler when I started working with Glen, which means I was able to watch young Oliver grow up into a smart, interesting, and professional young man. Glen and I had been talking recently about him turning my account over to Oliver, something that I would have been more than happy to accept. And now I once again invite you all to consider coming forward and sharing your memories of Oliver with his family and friends."

After another short pause, Glen stood up and walked to the lectern.

"I was going to speak at the end, but I don't suppose it matters.

Oliver was my son. I was incredibly proud of him. We had our differences, of course, but he was my legacy. He was going to carry on the family business and the family name. I'm devastated to have lost him."

He shook his head and then walked back to his seat. There, he had a whispered conversation with Caroline, who kept shaking her head. After a minute, Karina stood up. As she walked toward the lectern, her parents got up and followed her. When she turned to face the room, they stood on either side of her.

"Oliver was my ex-husband," Karina said softly. "And even though we divorced some time ago, I never got used to thinking of him in that way. But you all know that Oliver and I grew up together. I never knew a life without him in it, and I can't imagine what my life is going to be like now that he's gone. We were divorced, but we were still friends. He was my closest friend. My confidant. My world."

She burst into tears. Her mother pulled her into an awkward embrace, patting her back as Karina sobbed.

"I always liked Oliver," Howard said. "Until he broke my daughter's heart. I think we all believed that he and Karina would end up together again at some point. I know that Doris and I hoped that would be the case. We're both very sorry that he was taken from us before that could happen."

Howard led Doris and Karina back to their seats. As they sat down, a man walked up from the back of the room.

"I'm Jake Clucas," he said from the lectern. "I went to school with Oliver. He was a good guy with big dreams. I remember him telling me that he was going to be retired and rich before he turned thirty. I think we were around ten when he said that. We all just laughed. None of us could really imagine adulthood, so it was impossible to imagine retirement. But Oliver always seemed older and smarter than the rest of us. And he had a beautiful girlfriend when most of us were struggling to get girls to even notice us." He nodded at Karina. "We all thought he was crazy when he divorced you."

Karina seemed to freeze in her seat. After a moment, she nodded back at him.

"Anyway, we were friends, even though our lives moved in different directions. I hadn't really thought about him since I left school, but weirdly I bumped into him a week or so ago at the DIY store. I asked him how close he was to retiring. He laughed and said he had things well in hand. When I said I didn't think there was any way he'd be able to retire by thirty, he said it simply took careful planning and clever marrying." As soon as the words left the man's mouth, he flushed. "Er, I mean, that is, uhm."

"Wow," Rachel whispered.

"He should have cut that anecdote short," Ted said quietly.

Margaret nodded. The man took a deep breath.

"I'm sure he was just kidding," he said quickly. "Oliver used to make jokes all the time. We all know that he loved you very much," he told Karina.

"Thank you," the man in the suit said. "We all appreciate you sharing your story with us. And how very fortunate for you that you were able to spend some time with Oliver recently."

"Yeah," the man said. "We grabbed a pint and talked for a short while. He was a good guy."

As the man quickly walked back to his seat, Drake stood up and walked to the lectern.

"You all know who I am," he said. "Oliver and I worked together. The age gap between us made it difficult for us to be friends when we were younger, but we'd developed a friendship in the years since Oliver started working with me. Jake was right. Oliver was ambitious. He often talked to me about his desire to retire early, although I don't remember him ever suggesting that he wanted to do so before the age of thirty. I don't suppose it really matters now, though. He will be missed."

Drake sat back down and passed a hand over his eyes.

After a moment, Lelia stood up and walked to the lectern. The entire room went silent.

"Oliver and I were seeing each other at the time of his death," she said. "He told me that he loved me. I know I was falling in love with him. He was charming and sweet and kind and wonderful and I'm going to miss him terribly."

She made it back to her seat before she started crying. Ashley sat next to her, handing her tissues as the man in the suit stepped back up to the lectern.

"Does anyone else have anything to add?" he asked. "If you don't feel comfortable coming to the front of the room, you can speak from your seats."

That got a handful of Oliver's clients to stand up and talk briefly about how much they'd enjoyed working with him. When they were finished, the man in the suit spoke again.

"The family would like to invite everyone to enjoy coffee or tea and biscuits together as a part of the celebration," he said. "I believe that's ready now?"

A voice from the back of the room said "Yes" loudly.

The man nodded. "Then, if no one else has anything to add, please stay and talk amongst yourselves. You are all more than welcome to share additional memories with Glen and Caroline while you enjoy your tea."

"That was boring," Rachel said.

Ted looked at Margaret. "Stick close to Drake. He'll be more careful in front of me," he told her.

She nodded and then got to her feet. Drake was still sitting, but he stood up as Margaret bent down to get her handbag. As he headed toward Lelia, Margaret followed.

"Are you okay?" Drake asked Lelia when he reached her.

She wiped her eyes and then stood up. "I'm fine," she said. "Or as fine as I can be, under the circumstances."

Drake nodded. "I know Oliver cared about you, but he never did anything without the expectation of financial gain. We need to talk about your inheritance."

Lelia shook her head. "I don't have an inheritance, unless you mean what I inherited from my mother, which was a small and run-down house and about a thousand pounds in a savings account."

"We can talk another time," Drake said. "Please ring me."

She shrugged. "I can't see that we have anything to discuss."

He frowned and then took a step closer to her. "I know that you need time to recover from your loss, but I also know that I will treat you better than Oliver ever did. Please give me a chance to prove that to you," he said.

"She's going to need some time," Margaret interjected as Lelia just stared wordlessly at the man.

Drake gave Margaret a broad smile. "Yes, of course, it just pains me to see her mourning for a man who was really just using her. But I shouldn't speak ill of the dead." He looked back at Lelia. "Please ring me," he said before he walked away.

"Are you okay?" Margaret asked Lelia.

She nodded. "What did he mean by that? How was Oliver using me?"

Margaret shrugged. "I'll see if I can get him to explain himself," she said before she walked after Drake, who'd now joined Karina and her parents, who were still standing in front of their chairs.

"...home and cry myself to sleep," Karina was saying when Margaret joined them.

"He did treat you very badly," Drake said.

Karina shook her head. "He needed time, that's all. We would have ended up together again."

Drake shrugged. "Maybe, one day, after he'd married and divorced a few other women for their money."

"*She* doesn't have any money," Karina said, looking over at Lelia.

"Oliver seemed to think that she does," Drake replied.

"I can't do this right now," Karina said. She took a step toward the door. Her parents were quick to follow her.

"You were far too young for me when I met you," Drake said. "But now the age gap seems less significant. You know I'll do everything I can to support you through your loss. If I happen to fall in love with you along the way, don't be surprised."

"She needs to rest," Howard said.

Doris and Karina started to walk back down the aisle. As they went, Howard put his hand on Drake's arm.

"I'll talk to her," he said. "I think you could be very good for Karina."

"Thank you, sir," Drake replied.

Howard nodded and then strode away after his wife and daughter.

As Drake looked around the rapidly emptying room, Margaret wondered if there were more women he was planning to hit on that afternoon. A moment later, Drake walked away. Margaret did her best to try walking in the same direction without it looking as if she were following him. When he stopped to talk to Ted, she chuckled to herself and then joined them.

"...the killer during the service," Drake was saying when Margaret reached them.

"We don't typically announce the results of our investigations at things like funerals or memorial services," Ted replied.

Drake shrugged. "I keep hoping to hear that you've arrested someone."

"I'm fairly confident that you'll be hearing about an arrest soon," Ted told him.

Margaret thought she saw fear flash over Drake's face for just a second before he smiled at Ted.

"That's good to hear. I know everyone will feel better when the killer is behind bars."

"I'm sure Karina and Lelia will," Margaret said.

Drake nodded. "They're both very upset."

"But at least they both know that you want to go out with them when they're feeling better," Margaret said flatly.

Drake chuckled. "They're both beautiful women. I love beautiful women. I believe most men do."

"Most men don't try to pick up women at a memorial service," Margaret said.

"It might not have been my best idea ever," Drake admitted with a shrug. "But I'm not certain when I'm going to see either of them again. And I really want to get to know them both better."

"It seems as if you have a lot in common with Karina," Margaret said. "She never really got to chase her dreams, either."

Drake shrugged. "She has enough money. She can start chasing them anytime."

"And you're saving money so that you can go back to school and study engineering," Margaret said.

"Maybe. Maybe not. Maybe I'll get married and start a family instead."

Margaret frowned. She really wanted to push Drake a little bit, but she wasn't certain Ted would approve. "I can tell you from experience that engineering is a fascinating field in which to work," she said.

"I'm sure it is," Drake said. "I need to go and talk to..." He trailed off as Mark and Michael joined them.

"We were just talking about engineering," Ted told the new arrivals.

Michael raised an eyebrow. "Really?"

Margaret nodded. "Drake told me the other day that he used to spend a lot of time taking things apart and putting them back together again."

Drake flushed. "When I was a child. I haven't done anything like that in a long time."

"Really?" Michael asked. "Then I hope you won't mind if I search your house."

"Search my house?" Drake echoed. "I would mind very much, actually." He chuckled, a nervous sound to Margaret's ears. "It's a mess, that's all. Give me the weekend to tidy up and then you can have a look around on Monday. Although I can't even begin to imagine what you could possibly be looking for."

"We're going to be getting search warrants for a few houses," Michael told him. "We're looking for a few very specific things."

"I really need to go," Drake said, taking a step toward the door.

"I'll go with you," Michael said. "The warrant should be coming through any minute now."

Drake stood very still for a second and then slowly shook his head. "You don't need a warrant," he said. "You can search my house without one. I'll even tell you in advance what you're going to find. You're going to find devices just like the one that killed Oliver."

Michael nodded. "Let's move this conversation down to the station," he said.

"It was an accident," Drake said. "I've been working on this clamping system for years. I thought, once it was perfected, I could sell it and make a fortune."

"Did you really?" Ted asked.

Drake nodded. "It's designed to help people move things. You know how annoying it is to try to strap something to the top of your car or onto a hand truck. My system is designed to automatically tighten the strap to just the right point. And it has a quick-release mechanism, too."

"That doesn't explain how the strap got around Oliver's neck," Michael said.

"He put it there. We were talking and he was laughing at me. He said I'd become obsessed with the device and that there were so many easier ways to make money than with some stupid invention."

"Why were you at Dreeym Gorrym Point?" Ted asked.

"I wanted to test my device on a few of the trees out there," Drake replied. "I've been testing it on boxes for ages, but I needed to test it on something irregularly shaped and delicate."

"And why did Oliver agree to meet you there?" Mark asked.

"I invited him to meet me there. I wanted to show him the device. I was hoping he would be interested in investing in it. I told him that the potential was there for us both to make a fortune. He just laughed and said that he was already about to make a fortune, just as soon as he married Lelia."

"And then you killed him," Mark said.

"It wasn't supposed to kill him. The whole thing with my mechanism is that it's supposed to tighten until it gets resistance and then stop. You can manually adjust it tighter from there, if you need to, but it's really designed to tighten perfectly, automatically.

"I can't believe that Oliver was dumb enough to put it around his neck, regardless," Mark said.

Drake shrugged. "I suggested it. I even demonstrated it on my own neck. I thought it was an impressive way to show off just how perfectly calibrated my device was. And then it all went terribly wrong. Obviously, I didn't want to kill Oliver. His death was simply a horrible accident."

"What happened? Mark asked.

"He put the strap around his throat and then hit the button to tighten the strap. It tightened automatically but somehow when it started to get resistance, instead of stopping, it kept tightening. Oliver hit the quick-release mechanism, but something got jammed somewhere. I pushed him to the ground and did everything I could to get the strap off, but I simply couldn't manage it."

"So you left him there," Margaret said.

"I wasn't planning to leave him there. I didn't know what to do. I sat next to him on the ground for ages, unable to believe what had just happened. And then I wandered back to my car. I had this idea that I could drive down the path and load the body into the back so that I could take it, well, I don't know where I was going to take it, but I wasn't just going to leave him there. But when I got back to my car, there were people around, and I'm afraid I just panicked and drove away. I thought I'd ring the police when I got home and tell them the whole story, but by the time I got home, the body had already been found."

"You've had plenty of time to tell us the story now," Mark said.

"Yeah, and every time I started trying to talk about it, I got scared," Drake said. "It was just a horrible accident, but I don't know if anyone will believe that."

"Let's go down to the station for now," Michael said. "I'll take your statement and then we can search your house. We'll go from there."

Drake nodded. "I never meant to kill anyone," he said. "It was just a horrible accident."

Michael led the man out of the room. Mark and Ted exchanged glances.

"How much of that did you believe?" Mark asked Ted.

"Not much," Ted said. "But I've seen the toxicology reports."

Mark nodded.

"What toxicology reports?" Margaret asked.

Ted looked around the room. There were only a handful people still there and they were all clustered around the table near the door that held the refreshments.

"Oliver was drugged before he was killed," Ted told Margaret in a low voice. "The report suggests that he would have barely been able to stand up in the minutes before his death."

Margaret frowned. "Drake forgot to mention that part," she said dryly.

Ted nodded. "I'm fairly certain Drake forgot to mention quite a few things," he said.

"Has Drake gone?" Glen asked as he approached them.

Ted nodded. "He realized that he had some additional information to share with Inspector Madison."

Glen frowned. "But he drove us here," he said.

"I can give you a ride wherever you need to go," Mark said. "Whenever you're ready."

"What could Drake have realized that was that important?" Glen demanded. "What aren't you telling me?"

"Let's talk in the car," Mark said, taking the man's arm and steering him back toward Caroline, who was standing near the door.

Margaret looked around the room. Rachel waved from her spot next to a large plate of cookies.

"I need to get down to the station to help Michael," Ted said. "I should take a statement from you before I do anything else, though."

"Arthur and the others need to get back to the office. So do I, for that matter."

"They can go. I'll drive you back there after I take your statement. And then I'll probably meet Michael at Drake's house and help him with the search."

Margaret told the others that they could go, and apologized to Arthur for the fact that she was going to be late getting back to the office. Then she sat with Ted in his car and gave him her statement. He took notes and recorded the conversation.

"I can't believe he tried to get both Karina and Lelia to go out with him at a memorial service," Ted said when she was finished.

"That's pretty awful, but as it turns out, not the most awful thing he's ever done."

Ted nodded. "I'll drive you back to the office now. I hope we'll learn more when we search Drake's house."

"I hope you'll be able to tell me what you learn."

"I think someone needs to talk to Lelia, too. Both Oliver and Drake seemed convinced that she's wealthy or maybe the heir to some wealth. She needs to think very carefully about what she does with that box."

"I'll ring her in a day or two, after the dust has settled once you announce that an arrest has been made."

Ted nodded. "Let's get you back to work."

15

Margaret was happy that she needed to spend the afternoon in her lab, doing very precise measuring and mixing. That not only kept her focused so that she couldn't think too much about Drake, but it also meant that no one could question her about what had happened at the memorial service. By the time she finished her last test of the day, the police had announced Drake's arrest.

"I can't believe it," Joney said when Margaret walked into the lobby on her way home for the day. "Drake is so handsome, and he seemed so charming when he came over to thank us for coming to the service."

"He was also charming when he tried to get Lelia and Karina to go out with him," Margaret said.

"He asked them out at the memorial service? That's quite tacky. Okay, maybe he is a murderer."

"According to his advocate, it was all just a tragic accident," Rachel said as she joined them. "He said more details would be released soon and that he was confident that his client would be absolved of all responsibility for the tragedy."

"I hope he's wrong," Margaret said.

"You don't think it was an accident?" Joney asked.

"No, I don't, but I can't say anything more than that," Margaret said apologetically.

"I'm certain we'll hear the whole story soon," Rachel said. "And in the meantime, at least we now know who was responsible for Oliver's death, whether it was an accident or not."

Margaret nodded. The three women walked out of the building together. Ted called her a few minutes after she arrived home.

"I'm going to be tied up for a few more hours here. There's a lot going on. Let's talk about it all over dinner tomorrow night," he told her.

"That sounds good," Margaret agreed.

She made herself something to eat and watched some television before having an early night.

※

The next day was a blur of formulas and tests. She ate lunch at her desk and then drove home, eager to see Ted and find out what was happening with the investigation. Once again, she found Ted waiting for her in the corridor.

"Hello," he said, pulling her close. He hugged her tightly for several seconds.

"Are you okay?" she asked without letting go.

He sighed. "Sometimes I don't love my job."

"Come on inside and cuddle with Katie. She'll make you feel better."

She opened her door. Katie came running and quickly snuggled into Ted's arms. He sat down on the couch and stared out at the sea.

"Do you want to talk about it?"

"Yes. And no. And maybe. Drake has brought in a team of solicitors from London. They're going to be doing everything they can to portray Oliver as the villain in the piece."

"Even if Oliver was a horrible person, that doesn't justify murder."

"No, of course not, but Drake is still insisting that Oliver's death was a tragic accident while testing his invention. Michael confiscated an entire workroom full of stuff while we were searching. Interestingly, his initial impression when he went through everything is that it had all been purchased in the last six months."

"Which suggests that he only started working on his device quite recently."

Ted nodded. "Drake told Michael that he'd thrown away dozens upon dozens of prototypes before he landed on his most recent design. He also said that he always bought new materials before he started on a new prototype. He said he could afford the best, so why not?"

"Surely you'd keep some of your earlier designs so you could look back at what worked and what didn't?"

"You'd think so. Drake insists that he did not. He's also been talking a lot more about Oliver."

"What else did he have to say?"

"He said that Oliver never cared about Karina at all, but that he knew that he was going to have to marry her one day. According to Drake, Oliver didn't mind marrying her right after he'd finished uni. Drake reckons he was just planning on cheating after the first year or two. According to Drake, Oliver told him that he could do whatever he wanted, and Karina would never leave him."

"Sadly, that might be true."

Ted nodded. "Drake said that Oliver only changed his mind when he met a rich widow and realized that he could make a lot more money if he divorced Karina after his big payday and then married someone else who was equally wealthy. Drake said that Oliver told him that he'd figured out that he needed to get married and divorced about five times in order to end up with enough money to retire. Apparently, he also said that he'd probably remarry Karina at that point because by that time she'd most likely have inherited a ton from her parents."

"She's so much better off without him."

"Indeed, and so is Lelia, I believe."

Margaret glanced toward her aunt's bedroom where the safe was hidden. "What's the story with Lelia?"

"Drake claims he doesn't know. Apparently, Oliver found out something about her that led him to believe that she would be a good second wife. I should add that he did chase after the rich widow that he'd originally left Karina for, but in spite of his best efforts, she refused to go out with him."

"And Karina never knew."

"No one knew, aside from Drake, who stated that he felt as if Oliver was behaving very badly."

"I wonder what Oliver discovered about Lelia."

"Maybe you'll be able to find out if you can talk Lelia into opening that box."

Margaret sighed. "I'll call her on Sunday and try to talk to her."

Ted nodded. "For now, let's worry about ourselves. I'm starving."

"I am, too. And I want pizza."

"That does sound good."

They walked to the nearest pizza place and split a pizza covered in vegetables before sharing a small apple pie pizza.

"That was different, but delicious," Margaret said as they walked out of the restaurant together.

"I'd have never thought to put apple slices on a pizza, but a pizza crust isn't that different to a pie crust."

They talked about different approaches to desserts as they walked to the pub. There, they had a round of drinks and a lengthy conversation about all of the things they wanted to do on their upcoming vacation. Ted walked Margaret home a few hours later.

"I need to stay close to Douglas tomorrow in case anything else comes up with the investigation," Ted told Margaret at her door. "We could wander around the Manx Museum for a change, if that sounds fun?"

"Sure, let's do that."

Arrangements made, Margaret let herself into her apartment and got ready for bed. She crawled under the covers and slept well.

It was only six thirty when Margaret woke up the next morning. Katie looked startled when Margaret suddenly sat up and got out of bed. The small animal watched as Margaret slid her feet into her slippers and pulled on her bathrobe. Then Katie shut her eyes again and snuggled into her pillow.

Margaret laughed. "Your breakfast will be in the kitchen," she told Katie.

Half an hour later, Margaret was ready for the day, even though she wasn't expecting Ted to arrive until closer to ten. She looked out the window and then decided to take a stroll along the promenade to fill the time. When she opened her door, she was surprised to see Elaine walking toward her, pulling a small suitcase.

"Hello," Margaret said.

Elaine blushed and then took several steps backward.

"Are you okay?" Margaret asked.

"I'm fine," Elaine said.

"Going on holiday?" Margaret asked, gesturing toward the suitcase.

"I was just, er, uhm, that is." The older woman blushed bright red before taking a deep breath and squaring her shoulders. She stared at Margaret. "I was just coming back from spending the night with Ernie," she said.

"Lovely," Margaret said. She walked into the corridor and shut her door. After checking that it was locked, she turned back to Elaine. "I'm glad you found someone who makes you happy," she said.

Elaine sighed. "You don't even care," she said.

"I'm sorry?"

"I've been sneaking around so that no one would know that I've been staying with Ernie, but now that you know, you don't even care."

"You and Ernie are both adults. What you're doing isn't any of my business."

"I know, but I thought people would at least tut a little bit," Elaine said.

Margaret laughed. "I can pretend to tut if that will make you feel better."

"I don't know what will make me feel better. Ernie wants to get married."

"Congratulations?" Margaret made the word a question.

"Yeah, exactly. I don't know if I want to get married or not. I thought maybe, if a few people were scandalized by the idea of us spending nights together without being married, that I would feel as if I had to marry him. I'd marry him before I'd stop seeing him."

Margaret nodded. "It sounds very much like you're just looking for an excuse to accept Ernie's proposal. Would you like me to act scandalized?"

"Would you?"

Margaret laughed. "Does Shelly know? Maybe she and/or Tim could pretend to be upset about the situation."

Shelly was Elaine's niece. She owned the apartment that Elaine was currently calling home. Shelly had fairly recently married Tim, and they usually spent their time at his house in Douglas rather than in Shelly's apartment, anyway.

"Maybe you could ring her and tell her," Elaine suggested. "You could tell her that the entire building is talking about us."

"I'll call her when I get back from my walk," Margaret said. "If I call now, I might wake her."

Elaine nodded. "You might need to buy a hat," she muttered as she walked past Margaret.

Margaret smiled. She knew that was a very British way of saying that she should expect to be invited to a wedding soon.

After a brisk walk on the promenade, Margaret went back to her apartment and called Shelly. They had a long conversation about Elaine and Ernie that ended with Shelly promising to pretend to be unhappy about the situation.

"Thanks for ringing," Shelly said eventually.

"Good luck with Elaine," Margaret replied.

Ted knocked on the door a few minutes later. She was still telling him about Elaine when her phone rang.

"Hello?"

"Margaret, it's Lelia. I think I need to, well, talk to you at least."

"Do you want to come here, to my apartment?"

"Yes, I think that might be for the best."

"Do you mind if Ted is also here?"

"No, at least I don't think so."

"We can kick him out if you decide you'd rather have more privacy."

Lelia laughed. "I hope it won't come to that."

Margaret told her how to use the intercom system to get into the building. She'd only just finished giving her the instructions when the intercom buzzed.

"I was standing outside when I rang," Lelia said apologetically.

"Come on up. We'll talk," Margaret said.

While she waited for Lelia to arrive, she filled the kettle and then put some cookies on a plate. Ted answered the door to Lelia's knock.

"I don't have to stay," he told her as a greeting.

She laughed. "You can stay for now, but I reserve the right to change my mind at any time."

Margaret made tea and then they sat together in the kitchen sipping their drinks. Mona appeared, perched on the counter, before Lelia began to speak.

"Everyone seems to think that I'm the heir to a fortune or something," Lelia said. "I think Oliver must have misunderstood something that someone said. Maybe someone was talking about a rich heiress and when they pointed the person out, Oliver thought they were pointing at me."

"Maybe," Margaret said. "But there are a lot of question marks about your family."

Lelia laughed. "That is very true. And I've always told myself that I didn't mind the question marks. It was important to my mother that I not know anything about my past. And I've always wanted to honor her wishes."

"I think you deserve to know the truth," Margaret said.

"Ashley asked me last night if I'm certain that my mother actually had my best interests at heart. I've never questioned that before, but it got me thinking. Maybe she thought what she was doing was best, but maybe she was wrong."

"I think you should open the box," Margaret said.

"I'm going to open the box," Lelia replied. "And now that I've actually said that out loud, I'm terrified."

"I have whiskey," Margaret said.

Lelia seemed to give the offer some thought before she shook her head. "Let's just get it over with. How bad can it be?"

Margaret frowned. She could imagine a number of quite awful possibilities, but she wasn't about to share them with Lelia. Instead, she got up and went into Fenella's bedroom. When she returned to the kitchen, she was carrying Lelia's box. She put it down on the table in front of Lelia.

"Wow," Lelia said, putting her hand on the lid. "I really thought when I gave you the box that I was never going to see it again. I mean, that was my plan. I was going to ring you in a month or so and ask you to destroy the box and its contents. And instead, here we are."

"Would you like to be alone?" Margaret asked.

"Oh, goodness, no."

Lelia took a deep breath and then lifted the lid. She stared into the box for a minute and then slowly began removing items from it.

"That's my mother," she said, holding up a wedding photograph.

Margaret looked at the picture. "They look really happy together," she said.

"My mother always told me that she'd never been married," Lelia said softly.

She put the picture down and then looked at the next item in her hand. "They look happy here, too," she said, showing Margaret another picture of the couple.

In this one, they were casually dressed and standing in front of the Eiffel Tower. Lelia's mother was beaming at the camera. The man was staring at her looking as if he couldn't believe how lucky he was to be there with her.

Lelia took out another half dozen photos of the pair. In every picture they were smiling together.

"I don't understand," Lelia said. "But maybe this will help." She held up a letter. "It's addressed to someone named Anne Lawson. I don't know who that is."

"Are there more letters?" Margaret asked. "Maybe you should read them in order by postmark?"

"I don't know that I should read them at all," Lelia said.

"What is the address on the letters?" Margaret asked.

Lelia read out the address. "That's somewhere in London, but I don't know where."

"What else is in the box?" Margaret asked.

"Just one more envelope," Lelia said. "But this one has my name on it."

"Your mother must have known that you'd open the box."

Lelia put the envelope down and burst into tears. "I'm sure she must say horrible things to me in that letter," she said. "And I deserve it. I should have burned the box."

"Do you want me to read the letter and summarize it?" Margaret asked.

Lelia took several deep breaths and then wiped her eyes. "Start with these letters," she said, handing the two letters with the London address on them to Margaret. "Just summarize them for me. If I need to, I'll read them later."

Margaret opened the first letter. She quickly skimmed it and then looked at Lelia. "It's from a man named George Lawson. It sounds very much like he was married to Anne. It starts with an apology for not being more excited about the baby and then he begs Anne to come back to him. That's all."

Lelia frowned. "I don't understand."

"Neither do I," Margaret said. "Maybe there will be more in the second letter."

She opened it and read through it. Then she looked up at Lelia. "In this one, George tells Anne that he doesn't understand why she left and that he'd do anything to get her back. And then he says that if she doesn't want to ever speak to him again for whatever reason, that maybe one day she'll tell his child about him. He also says that he hopes that the child will reach out and be a part of his life eventually."

Lelia frowned. "I don't understand. Why did my mother leave? Assuming Anne is my mother and George is my father." She shook her head. "I don't know what I was expecting, but it wasn't this."

"Do you want me to open the envelope from your mother?"

"You may as well."

Margaret carefully opened the envelope and pulled out a pile of paperwork. "I'm going to guess that was your mother's birth certificate," Margaret said, passing the document to Lelia. "And her passport."

Lelia read through the birth certificate and then flipped through the passport. She stopped when she reached the page with the photograph.

"That's my mother," she said.

"There's also a marriage certificate in here," Margaret said. "Between Anne Duncan, who we know was your mother, and George Lawson." She handed the paper to Lelia.

"I don't understand any of this," Lelia said.

"The last thing is a letter from your mother," Margaret said. She skimmed it quickly. "I'm just going to read it to you," she said.

"'Lelia, I knew you'd open the box eventually. And I suppose in a way I wanted you to have its contents. You deserve to know the truth. I was very much in love with your father and had only just discovered that we were expecting when someone knocked on the door and introduced herself as Mrs. George Lawson. She and your father had been married for ten years. I was devastated, of course. I packed my bags and moved out the same day.'"

"He was already married to someone else?" Lelia asked.

Margaret shrugged. "Your mother seemed to think so, anyway. Let me read the rest of the letter to you. 'When I'd told George that I was pregnant, he didn't seem very happy about the news. I suppose I should have suspected that something was wrong at that point. He didn't mind having two wives, but he wasn't happy about having two families, I would imagine. His wife told me that they had three children together, two boys and a girl. She even showed me pictures of the children. They all looked like George.'"

Lelia held up a hand. "I need a break. I think I'm going to cry."

She sat for several seconds with her head in her hands before looking back up. "I'm not going to cry, at least not right now."

"I'll read the rest, then," Margaret said. "'I moved back in with my parents for a short while, but left before they could realize that I was pregnant. When I left, I changed my name and moved to the Isle of Man, where I knew no one and no one knew me. You may, if you wish, reach out to your father and to my parents. I don't know if any of them will be interested in knowing you or not, but someone might. You also might be able to get some money from one of them. Always remember that I did what I thought was best. I may have made mistakes. Love, Mother.'"

Lelia sighed. "I don't even know where to start. My head is swimming."

"The letter from your mother also includes an address and telephone number for her parents. And the letter from George has his address and telephone number," Margaret said.

Lelia pulled out her phone. "What's George's number?" she demanded.

Margaret read out the number while Lelia dialed.

"If I stop to think, I'll never do this," Lelia said as she put the phone into speaker mode.

"I don't need double-glazing or insurance," the voice on the line said.

Lelia laughed. "Is that George Lawson?" she asked.

"If you aren't selling double-glazing, it might be."

"Ah, now things get awkward," Lelia said. "My name is Lelia Dodson. I think you might be my father."

There was a long silence from the other end of the phone. After a minute, another voice came down the line.

"I'm terribly sorry, but Mr. Lawson is temporarily indisposed," the voice said. "Please hold the line for a moment."

"What does that mean?" Lelia asked.

Margaret shrugged.

"It means I nearly had a heart attack," the first voice said. "It was a good thing I was sitting down. Even then, Piedmont had to remind me to breathe."

"Piedmont?" Lelia echoed.

"My butler, but never mind that. Say your name again."

"Lelia Dodson."

"She named you Lelia," he said. "That was my mother's name. I can't believe she named you Lelia."

"She told me she named me after a character in a book, but she could never remember the name of the book."

George chuckled. "That sounds like Anne. She could be creative with the truth. But did she ever tell you why she left me? I've spent the

225

last twenty-seven years, three months, and six days wondering why she left."

"She left because your wife turned up on her doorstep."

There was another long pause. "I don't understand," George said eventually.

"My mother never told me anything about you, but she left behind a box. She told me to burn the box, but I finally decided to open it after someone close to me was murdered. In the box, I found a letter from my mother where she talks about how your wife turned up on her doorstep."

"Anne was my wife."

"According to my mother, the woman also had a photograph of your three children. Two boys and a girl."

George sighed. "Isabel," he said.

"I'm sorry?"

"My sister-in-law. My brother's wife. He was my half-brother on my mother's side. Sadly for Isabel, the family money was all on my father's side. Before I met your mother, I was always very generous to my niece and nephews. Once we got married, however, I started to be more careful with my money in anticipation of welcoming children of my own."

"According to my mother, you weren't very pleased when she told you that she was pregnant."

"I was surprised, and I didn't react the way she'd expected me to react. I knew her well enough to know that she'd imagined the conversation a dozen or more times before we'd had it. I strayed badly from her imagined script and that upset her."

Lelia sighed. "I'd never thought about it that way, but that's exactly how every conversation with her went, all the time."

"We had a disagreement, and she slept in the spare bedroom that night. The next day, when I got home from work, she was gone."

"Because your wife turned up."

"Because Isabel got a friend to pretend to be my wife and show up on my doorstep," George said. "She could have given that friend any number of pictures of her children, all of whom looked like their father, who was my brother."

"You weren't married."

"I was married. To Anne. And no one else."

"And you didn't already have children."

"I only have one child. A child I've never met but that I've dreamt of meeting for a very long time."

Lelia wiped her eyes. "I don't even know what to say."

"Where are you?"

"The Isle of Man."

"The Isle..." He sighed. "I should have done more to try to find your mother, but I didn't know where to start, and it seemed as if she didn't want to be found. If I'd known that it was all just a misunderstanding, I'd have found your mother and explained."

"What happens now?" Lelia asked.

"Now you need to come to London. Your mother's parents will be delighted to hear that you are alive and well. Piedmont can make all of the arrangements. Can you come today?"

Lelia gasped. "I don't think so."

"I must ring your grandparents. My parents died years ago now, but your mother's parents still live in the same home in London. We've kept in touch over the years. In fact, your grandmother said something recently about trying to find you. She said she was working with a detective who was searching for you. Won't she be surprised when I tell her that I found you first?"

"I need to go," Lelia said. "I'm going to have to arrange for some annual leave and then I need to pack. Right now, I can't even think straight."

"I'll ring you back in an hour," George said. "That will give Piedmont time to make the necessary arrangements."

"What about a DNA test?" Ted asked.

Lelia nodded. "We should take DNA tests," she said.

George laughed. "We can, if you want to take them. I'm not going to ask you to take one, though. The number that you rang is one that I've only ever given to one person. That's why I answered it as I did. The only time it ever rings is when someone is dialing random numbers and trying to sell people things."

They talked for several more minutes before finally ending the call.

"I'm in shock," Lelia said after a minute. "That man is my father."

Margaret nodded. "What can I do to help?"

"You've already done everything that I needed you to do. I can't thank you enough for your help."

"Are you going to fly to London to meet George?" Ted asked.

Lelia smiled. "I have to go. But I'll make my own travel arrangements and meet George in a public place. And maybe my grandparents, too. I can't even imagine it."

She got up from the table and then put everything back in her box. Margaret walked her to the door.

"Thank you again," she said before she left.

Back in the kitchen, Ted was tidying away the teacups and leftover cookies.

"That was – something," Margaret said. "Just something."

Ted laughed. "It was indeed. And now I'm wondering if Lelia's grandmother found Lelia and somehow ended up talking to Oliver about her. Maybe that's how he knew that she came from a wealthy family."

"Maybe," Margaret said. "Is it too late to go to the Manx Museum?"

"Not if that's what you want to do."

Margaret nodded. "And while we're there, we can talk about anything other than Oliver and Lelia."

"That sounds like a plan."

Mona got up from the table and snapped her fingers. She disappeared in a huge puff of smoke. Ted frowned.

"Is something burning?" he asked.

MURDER AT EDGEWATER LANE
A MARGARET AND MONA GHOSTLY COZY

Release date: August 1, 2025

Margaret and Ted are excited to be taking a vacation together. Margaret has always wanted to see the sights the United Kingdom has to offer. They leave the island, planning for two weeks of adventure together. York is their first stop. In addition to enjoying their time in the historic city, Ted has a friend living there that they plan to see on their visit.

James Long is a police inspector in York. He's happy to see his friend, Ted, in part because he has a cold case he wants to discuss with another inspector. Margaret is happy to listen in while they talk about the case. And Mona somehow manages to hear all about the case as well.

While Margaret and Ted explore the city, they also revisit a few of the key locations from the cold case. And whether it's Mona's interference or just luck, they also find themselves bumping into some of the case's suspects.

They're only supposed to be in York for a week. Margaret wants to see all of the sights, but the more she learns about the death of Douglas Sims, the more she wants to help James and Ted find his killer before she and Ted move on to their next location.

A SNEAK PEEK AT MURDER AT EDGEWATER LANE
A MARGARET AND MONA GHOSTLY COZY

Release date: August 1, 2025

Please excuse any typos or minor errors. I have not yet completed final edits on this title.

Chapter One

"Good morning," Ted said when Margaret opened the door to his knock.

"Good morning," she replied.

He gave her a quick kiss. "Ready to go?"

"I think so. Of course, I'm worried that I've forgotten something essential."

"I promise there are shops in the UK," Ted said with a chuckle. "In fact, they have a lot of the same shops over there that we have here. If you did forget anything, you should be able to find it with little difficulty."

Margaret nodded. "Let's go quickly, before I open my suitcase and start checking for things."

Ted grabbed the suitcase she'd left near the door. She picked up her smaller bag and her handbag.

"Be a good girl," she told Katie, the small cat who was snoozing on the couch. "Mrs. Jacobson will be over every day to give you breakfast, lunch, and dinner and lots of extra snuggles."

Katie opened one eye and then shut it again.

"Don't miss me too much," Margaret said with a laugh.

"It is very early in the morning," Ted said.

"It is very early. Why does the ferry sail so early in the morning?"

"I have no idea. There is a later sailing, but when I went to buy a ticket, that sailing was sold out. For cars, anyway. There might have been tickets left for foot passengers, but we're going to need my car when we get across."

Margaret peeked into her handbag to make sure her wallet was inside and then shrugged. "Let's go. I've probably forgotten something, but hopefully it isn't anything too important."

They walked out into the corridor together. Margaret pulled the door shut and then checked that it had locked securely behind them.

"I hope you're looking forward to our fortnight away," Ted said as they headed toward the elevators.

"Oh, I am. Very much so. I'm excited to get to see parts of the UK."

"I'm excited to show them to you. And I'm happy that we're going to get to spend an entire fortnight together. We should learn a lot about each other over the next two weeks."

"Traveling with someone is definitely challenging, but I'm fairly certain that we've going to get along well."

"I wouldn't have suggested it if I didn't think we were going to get along well."

They took the elevator to the ground floor and then walked through the apartment building's lobby together. Ted had parked his car right outside the building. He loaded Margaret's bag into the car's trunk and then they both got into the car.

"Did you take anything to ward off seasickness?" Ted asked as he started the car.

Margaret shook her head. "I bought something, though. It's in my bag if I need it. I also bought these." She waved her wrist in the air, showing Ted the elastic band she was wearing. There was a matching one on her other wrist. They had small plastic buttons on the inside that were designed to apply pressure to a specific point in order to help alleviate nausea.

"I have friends who swear by those and other friends who say they do nothing at all."

"I thought it was worth trying them. I've never sailed anywhere before. I might not need anything, but the bands were inexpensive and they're supposed to work best if you put them on before you start sailing. As I said, I have some medication that I can take if I find myself feeling unwell once we're underway."

While they'd been talking, Ted had driven them to the end of the promenade to the Sea Terminal building. There, he joined a long line of cars that disappeared behind the building. The line moved slowly, but eventually Ted pulled up to a small booth and put his window down.

"Moghrey mie. Good morning," the woman in the booth said to Ted.

"Good morning," Ted replied. "Ted Hart and Margaret Woods. Or do you want my confirmation number?"

The woman shrugged. "I can use either, but I usually only need one name. Here we are, Ted Hart, one car and two passengers. And you've booked a cabin as well."

Ted nodded. "Just in case we need a bit of peace and quiet."

"Oh, aye, it's not so bad now that it's September. The kids are back in school and the ones going to uni have mostly gone, but the families with the really little ones do a lot of traveling in September. It's a good deal cheaper to travel after the school holidays and we all know the weather is going to get worse in the coming months."

"So maybe we'll need that cabin."

"Or maybe you'll just want a quiet cuppa. I shouldn't say it, but sailing across can get a bit boring after the first hour. Okay, you're all set. Safe travels." She handed Ted a piece of paper with a large number printed on it. He put the paper on the dashboard and then drove forward slowly.

"Now what?" Margaret asked as they turned into a huge parking lot that was about half full of cars in neat rows.

"Now we park in our row and wait until it's time to board."

A man in a dark uniform directed Ted where to park. He shut off the engine and then looked at Margaret.

"You can pop into the building if you want a snack or a drink or anything. Otherwise, we just sit here and wait. It shouldn't be too long before they start boarding the cars."

"We stay in the car, and you drive it onto the ship?"

"Yep. Once we're parked onboard, we leave the car on the car deck and go up to the passenger decks. The cabin was supposed to be a surprise. It's just a small private space for us to get away if we want to, nothing fancy or anything, but they are nice, especially if you feel a bit unwell."

"I can't wait to see it. I didn't even realize that the ship had cabins."

"As I said, they aren't anything fancy. They do have their own en suite facilities, though, which is nice, especially if the ship is busy."

Margaret sat back and looked around. "I never really thought about how many people must sail back and forth every day. Not that the same people are sailing back and forth every day, but that a lot of people are sailing. I don't think I'm making sense."

Ted laughed. "The ferries are larger than they seem when you simply see them from the promenade. They hold quite a lot of passengers. And they carry a great deal of cargo back and forth from the UK to the island. They're loading the lorries now."

Margaret looked where Ted was pointing and watched as several large trucks drove out of the parking area and onto the ship. This went on for several minutes, until the parking area was empty.

"Now it will be time for the cars," Ted said. "And the foot passengers are probably being allowed on now, too."

A short while later, the line of cars began to move. Ted waited until their row was actually moving to start his engine. They followed the car in front of them toward the ferry.

"The ramp is really narrow," Margaret said as Ted turned off the road and onto the ramp that led inside the boat.

"It isn't too bad," Ted replied.

They inched their way forward, following instructions from various crew members onto the boat's car deck. Margaret looked around as Ted drove slowly between two other rows of tightly packed cars. Eventually, he stopped the car and parked it.

"I don't know what I was expecting, but it wasn't this," Margaret said.

"They have to fit a lot of cars in here," Ted told her. "So the cars have to park very close together."

Margaret nodded and then carefully climbed out of the car. Getting out with her bags was a tight squeeze, but she managed it. Then she followed Ted between the parked cars toward the nearest staircase. The deck under her feet was uneven, so she walked carefully.

"I can feel the ship rocking ever so slightly," she said to Ted when they reached the stairwell.

"Just wait," the woman behind Margaret said. "We're supposed to have a fairly smooth crossing, but even so, you're going to feel a lot more movement."

Margaret smiled. "Maybe I should take something, just in case."

The woman laughed and named the medication that Margaret had in her bag. "I always take a tablet before I leave my house. That usually gets me across safely."

They climbed multiple flights of metal stairs. Eventually, Ted stopped at a door. The sign on the door said "Passenger Deck." Ted pushed the door open and then held it so that Margaret and the other woman could walk through.

"This is bigger than I was expecting," Margaret said as they walked into a large room full of couches, tables, and chairs.

"You need to grab chairs fast if you want two together," the other woman advised. "Although you might get lucky in the quiet area."

"Another reason for booking a cabin," Ted said in Margaret's ear.

Margaret looked around again. The room felt chaotic as groups of people were settling into the various clusters of tables and chairs

235

throughout the space. As they walked farther into the room, Margaret noticed the small play area off to one side. There were already at least ten children digging through the toys in the space.

Ted headed for the desk in the corner where a pair of crew members were working. Margaret followed him, taking note of the location of the quiet lounge off to one side of the main room, as she went.

"I have a cabin booked," Ted said when he reached the front of the short line in front of the desk. "Ted Hart."

The woman nodded and then flipped through a pile of envelopes on the desk in front of her.

"Cabin 119. The stairs are just behind me on the right or the left," she said. "Enjoy your sailing."

Ted took the envelope from her and then led Margaret away.

"Do you want to see anything else down here or do you want to check out the cabin first?"

"Is it going to get less crazy down here at any point?"

Ted chuckled. "Once the ship starts moving, it will get a lot less crazy down here. Most people will settle into seats and stay there until we reach Liverpool. There is a café and a gift shop to explore, but we can leave that until we're underway. Why don't we go up and take a look at our cabin? You might decide that you hate it in there and want to come back down here."

Margaret looked around the room again. Three different babies were crying in three different corners of the room. A large group of teenagers were shouting at each other across a large table. There seemed to be people everywhere trying to find spaces to settle into.

"Let's go find our cabin," she said to Ted.

Ted led her to a small door that had a very discreet sign saying "Passenger Cabins" on it. It opened into a narrow staircase. Margaret followed Ted up the stairs and then into a dimly lit hallway. Numbered doors were on one side of the corridor. Ted stopped in front of their cabin. He opened the envelope he'd been given and pulled out a key.

"Here we go," he said, turning the key in the lock.

He pulled the door open and then held it so that Margaret could walk in first. She walked into the small room and clapped her hands together.

"This is adorable," she said. "I had no idea what to expect, but this is really cute."

There were bunk beds on one wall with a small couch on the opposite wall. Margaret reckoned there wasn't any more than a foot of space between the end of the couch and edge of the bottom bunk. She made her way between them to look out the small porthole window.

"You probably can't see much yet," Ted said.

"Just Douglas," Margaret said with a laugh.

There was a small table under the window. It held a small kettle, and everything needed to make tea or coffee. Margaret picked up a wrapped packet of cookies and grinned.

"We have a snack," she said.

Ted laughed. "There will be two biscuits in there and they might be stale. If you're hungry, there is a café downstairs and they sell a lot of food in the gift shop, too."

"I brought breakfast with me," Margaret replied, patting her bag. "We should be in Liverpool before lunch, shouldn't we?"

"We should. I thought we'd drive outside the city and then find somewhere to stop."

"That works for me. I have emergency snacks if we get stuck in traffic."

"Emergency snacks for both of us?" Ted asked.

Margaret laughed. "I would never just bring enough for myself. Maybe because I grew up with a little sister. I always used to bring snacks for both of us, everywhere we went."

"And now you bring them for me, because you love me."

"I do love you," Margaret agreed before he kissed her.

"It is a little tight in here," Margaret said when he released her.

Ted had to back up to let her out of the narrow passageway between the bed and the couch. She walked back to the door and then peeked into the small bathroom.

"I wasn't expecting a shower," she said. "Do people actually take showers on the ferry?"

Ted shrugged. "I've never tried it, but I suppose if you became quite ill, you might want to clean up before you arrived at your destination."

"That makes sense."

She walked back out of the bathroom and looked at Ted. "Now what?"

"Now we wait. The crossing will take about four hours once we get underway."

A loud horn sounded as Ted finished speaking.

"And that should mean that we're underway," Ted added.

The horn blasted several more times over the next minute or so. Margaret walked over and looked out through the porthole.

"I still can't see much of anything, but I can feel that we're moving," she said.

"We can go back down and go out onto the outside deck if you want to see more."

She shook her head. "I think I'll be happier staying right here for now. I want to see how the movement is going to affect me before I do too much."

"Have a seat," Ted suggested, gesturing toward the couch. "We can watch some telly."

Margaret looked at the small television that was mounted on the wall near the ceiling. "I brought a book," she said. "Actually, I brought two books to read and also a few puzzle books to work through."

"That's good, because there isn't much on the telly on the ferry, anyway."

Ted sat down next to Margaret. A moment later, she got up and looked out through the porthole again.

"Anything?"

"Water."

Ted laughed. "You're going to see a lot of that for the next four hours."

Margaret looked at the view for a moment longer before sitting back down and pulling out one of her books. "Assuming I feel fine in half an hour or so, I'll make some coffee and have breakfast," she told Ted.

"Would you mind if I went for a walk while you're reading?" he asked. "I thought I saw someone I'd like a word with as we walked through the lounge downstairs."

"A friend?"

Ted grinned. "A constable from Castletown. We've only met a few times, but I thought it would be nice to say hello. He's traveling with his wife and their new baby. I haven't met the baby yet."

"You go and say hello, then. I'll be here."

"I'll leave the key with you, in case you decide to leave for any reason. I'll knock when I get back."

Ted put the key on a conveniently placed hook right inside the door and then let himself out. Margaret checked that the door had locked behind him and then settled back down with her book. Twenty minutes later, she decided that she was too hungry to wait any longer. It took her a minute to figure out how to get the kettle on, but once the water boiled, she made herself a cup of coffee and then opened her bag of food. She was halfway through her single-serving box of cereal when Ted returned.

"Ah, that coffee smells good," he said after Margaret let him into the cabin.

She made a face. "It's not good, though. Instant coffee is never very good, is it?"

Ted chuckled. "At this point, I'll take any coffee."

"In that case, the kettle shouldn't take long to boil. It should still be at least warm."

Margaret let Ted go first down the path between the bed and the couch before sitting back down and finishing her breakfast. Ted made himself a cup of tea and then they shared the packet of cookies on the table.

"That was good, anyway," Margaret said after she'd eaten her cookie. "Do you want anything else? I have cereal and apples and some crackers."

Ted shook his head. "I had a bowl of cereal before I left my flat. I'll be okay until we get out of Liverpool."

"Did you find your friend?"

"Yes, and I got to meet his wife and the baby."

They chatted about Ted's friend for a short while before the conversation moved on to other things. Margaret had Ted take her back through their plans for the next fourteen days. That led to a conversation about vacations that they'd taken in the past. Eventually, when Margaret looked out through the porthole, she could see land again.

"We're nearly to Liverpool," she said excitedly.

Ted looked out and then nodded. "It's going to take some time for the ship to dock, but we can walk downstairs now if you want to get a better view."

"I do want a better view. I haven't felt the least bit sick and now I'm sorry that I didn't explore the entire ship while we were at sea."

"You'll get another chance on the way back. But we have to be out of the cabin soon anyway, so let's go. You can explore a little bit of the ship, at least."

They walked back down the stairs. Margaret took a quick look in the gift shop and then followed Ted past the small café. She read through the menu in case they decided to eat on the ferry on their way back to the island. Then Ted led Margaret to the outside deck. From there, they watched as the ship was carefully steered into its dock.

"And now we go and sit in the car again," Ted said. "Eventually, the car in front of ours will move and we'll be on our way."

They walked back through the ship. Ted stopped to return the cabin's key and then they joined the long line of people trying to get back down the stairs to the car deck. Margaret glanced at the clusters of people who were still sitting around the lounge.

"Are they all foot passengers?" she asked Ted.

He shrugged. "They might have cars and are just waiting until the queue goes down a bit. Unloading takes time. There really isn't any rush."

Margaret nodded. "But there's always a chance that you might hold other people up if you wait too long."

"Some people don't care."

Margaret laughed. "I suppose that's true."

Eventually, they made their way down the stairs and then along the deck to Ted's car. Back in the passenger seat, Margaret looked around.

"So the driver of the car in front of ours isn't back yet," she said. "But the one behind us is there, and he looks to be in a hurry."

Ted glanced in his rearview mirror. "He does look as if he's eager to get off the ship. Too bad he's going to have to wait his turn."

A few minutes later, Margaret noticed that the cars a few rows over were starting to move. Over a dozen cars drove away before the driver of the car in front of theirs slowly sauntered over and climbed into his car. A short while later, the cars in their row began to creep forward.

Margaret shut her eyes as Ted drove across the narrow ramp from the ship to the dock. Then they followed the long line of cars driving away from the docks and toward the center of the city. Ted had their destination programmed into his phone. Margaret sat back and tried to take in as much of the scenery as she could as Ted drove them through Liverpool and then out of the city.

"Lunch?" he said a short while later.

"I could eat," Margaret said.

"There's a wonderful little pub just off the motorway a few miles from here. I used to drive out here to get lunch whenever I had a day off work. They do wonderful cottage pie and excellent puddings."

"And you'll be disappointed if we don't stop there."

Ted grinned. "Yeah, I will be."

The pub was everything that Ted had promised. Margaret and Ted both enjoyed servings of cottage pie and then they shared a thick slice of chocolate cake before returning to the car.

"And now we drive to York," Margaret said. "I'm really excited to see the city and meet your friend."

"We're about two hours away, assuming traffic is reasonable. I'm afraid there isn't much to see from the motorway, though."

"I don't mind. I'm in England. Two years ago, I never would have imagined that this would be my life right now."

Ted drove steadily along the three-lane motorway. Margaret read road signs as they went. Almost exactly two hours later, Ted took one of the exits for York.

"You should be able to see some of the city walls soon," he said as they made their way closer to the city.

"York has more miles of intact city walls than any other city in

England," Margaret said. "I also read that the walls are thirteen feet high and six feet across."

"In some places, anyway," Ted said. "We should have time to walk along much of their distance over the next week or so."

A short while later, Margaret got her first look at the famous walls. Ted kept driving and it wasn't long before she got a glimpse of York Minster, the city's cathedral.

"Wow," Margaret said.

"It is a gorgeous old cathedral," Ted said. "Built in the Middle Ages, it's one of the few churches in the UK that still retains its medieval stained glass."

"It was completed in 1472," Margaret said. "I remember that, because that's twenty years before Columbus set sail for America. It's hard to imagine such a spectacular building being built so long ago. And even harder to imagine that it's still standing."

Ted turned a corner and then pulled his car into the parking lot for a large hotel.

"Here we are. Our temporary home," he said.

Margaret looked up at the building. "It's lovely," she said.

"The building dates back to the eleventh century," Ted said casually as he opened his door.

Margaret stared at him for a moment before shaking her head then getting out of the car. Ted unloaded their suitcases and then they walked together into the building.

"Ah, good afternoon," the man behind the reception desk said. "Do you have a booking?"

Ted nodded. "Ted Hart."

The man opened the laptop on the desk and began tapping through screens.

"Check-in isn't for another few hours," he said. "But I do believe your room is ready. Let me just – ah – yes, that's right. Your room is ready. I just need to see some identification and the credit card that you used to book the room, please."

Ted handed him the cards.

The man checked them before returning them to Ted. "I'll just get you your keys," he said. "We use electronic keycards now for all of our rooms. The system was just installed about three months ago, and it can sometimes be a bit, uhm, challenging. If you have any difficulties, please don't hesitate to come back to the desk for assistance. There is someone here at all times, day or night."

The man inserted first one and then a second card into a small machine on the desk. He then slipped the cards into a folder and wrote something across it. When he looked up, he smiled at Ted.

"All of our rooms have names, rather than numbers. I've written your room on the folder. All of the rooms are on the second floor. The lifts are just behind me through the double doors. Is there anything else I can help you with right now?"

Ted looked at Margaret. She shrugged.

"Breakfast is served daily in our conservatory," the man added. "It is included in your stay. You are welcome to dine at any time between six and nine."

"Thank you," Ted said. He picked up the keycards and looked at Margaret. "Shall we?"

She nodded and then the pair walked through the double doors to the elevators. The car whisked them up to the second floor quickly and efficiently.

"The elevators aren't original," Ted said teasingly as the doors slid open.

Margaret laughed. "I can't wait to see the room. But this place must cost a fortune. I can't let you pay for everything."

"I told you that I was happy to pay for the ferry and for the hotels where we'll be staying while we're here. You can buy meals and drinks, at least some of the time."

"We should have had this conversation before you insisted on paying for lunch."

Ted shrugged. "I can afford to spoil you a little bit. You haven't been working on the island for all that long and you weren't working at all for some months before that."

"But I'm barely paying anything in rent to Aunt Fenella. I'm doing better financially now than I ever was before."

"Here we are," Ted said, stopping in front of one of the doors. "Let's hope the rooms are as nice as the rest of the place."

He waved one of the keycards in front of the lock. Margaret heard the mechanism disengage. Ted pushed the door open, and they stepped inside. Ted put the bags down as Margaret simply stared.

"Wow," she said. "This is stunning."

Ted nodded. "The furniture looks antique."

"I'm almost afraid to touch anything."

"Check out the view," Ted said as he walked farther into the room.

Margaret walked over and looked out the window. "York Minster," she said.

"And take a look at the en suite."

Margaret followed Ted into the large bathroom. There was a huge soaking tub in one corner and a large shower in another.

"This is absolutely wonderful," Margaret said, pulling Ted into a kiss.

"I'm glad. We won't be staying anywhere nearly this nice for the second half of our fortnight."

"I told you that I'm not particular. As long as the room is clean, I'm happy."

"But you're happier here?"

Margaret laughed. "I am happier here. This is really stunningly beautiful and completely unlike anywhere I could stay in the US. I can't believe the building is so old."

They walked back into the bedroom together. Ted picked up the large book that was on the table near the door.

"The entire history of the hotel is in here," he told Margaret. "Along with a brief history of York, a list of suggested places to visit while we're here, and other important things like a list of the available television channels."

Margaret looked around. "But where is the television?"

"I'm going to guess that it's in that wardrobe," Ted said, pointing to a large wardrobe on the wall across from the end of the bed.

Margaret crossed to it and opened the doors.

"There is a television in here," she said. "And a minibar."

"Ah, the price list for the minibar is also in this book," Ted said. "If you want to enjoy anything from the minibar, you can pay for that."

Margaret laughed as she shut the wardrobe doors and walked over to where Ted was standing. She glanced at the price list for the minibar and then quickly shook her head.

"I don't need a tiny and seriously overpriced bottle of wine," she said.

Ted nodded. "There are shops nearby. If we want to have a glass of wine in our room, we can buy a bottle and bring it back with us."

"We should unpack," Margaret suggested.

"We are here for a week, so it's probably worth unpacking."

Margaret looked at him. "Do you not unpack if you're staying for only a few nights?"

"I don't usually unpack everything unless I'm staying for several nights. It's just easier to live out of my suitcase if I'm only going to be there for a night or two."

"I prefer to unpack, regardless. I just feel more comfortable in a space if my things are ready to be used when I want them."

"See, we've been away for only a few hours and we're already learning things about each other," Ted said, kissing the top of Margaret's head as he walked past her. "I don't think our different unpacking styles is going to be a relationship deal-breaker."

"I hope not. I won't expect you to unpack everywhere we go, but you're going to have to give me time to do so."

"I can do that. And for now, I'm happy to unpack anyway."

The pair spent some time emptying their suitcases into the wardrobe and the large chest of drawers on one of the side walls. When they were finished, they sat down together on the comfortable couch and stared out the window at York Minster.

"I don't know why I'm so tired," Margaret said. "I didn't do anything today except sit around waiting to get places."

"Traveling is weirdly exhausting, even when it goes well."

"But all of York is out there, waiting to be explored."

"And we're meeting my friend in half an hour at the pub around the corner."

Margaret laughed. "Now that you've said that, I'm starving. Lunch was a long time ago."

"Let's get ready to go, then. I know James is looking forward to meeting you."

"I'm looking forward to meeting him, too."

Ted grinned at her. "Did I mention that he has a cold case he wants to discuss with us?"

ALSO BY DIANA XARISSA

The Isle of Man Ghostly Cozy Mysteries

Arrivals and Arrests
Boats and Bad Guys
Cars and Cold Cases
Dogs and Danger
Encounters and Enemies
Friends and Frauds
Guests and Guilt
Hop-tu-Naa and Homicide
Invitations and Investigations
Joy and Jealousy
Kittens and Killers
Letters and Lawsuits
Marsupials and Murder
Neighbors and Nightmares
Orchestras and Obsessions
Proposals and Poison
Questions and Quarrels
Roses and Revenge
Secrets and Suspects
Theaters and Threats
Umbrellas and Undertakers
Visitors and Victims
Weddings and Witnesses
Xylophones and X-Rays
Yachts and Yelps

Zephyrs and Zombies

The Margaret and Mona Ghostly Cozies

Murder at Atkins Farm
Murder at Barker Stadium
Murder at Collins Airfield
Murder at Dreeym Gorrym Point
Murder at Edgewater Lane

The Isle of Man Cozy Mysteries

Aunt Bessie Assumes
Aunt Bessie Believes
Aunt Bessie Considers
Aunt Bessie Decides
Aunt Bessie Enjoys
Aunt Bessie Finds
Aunt Bessie Goes
Aunt Bessie's Holiday
Aunt Bessie Invites
Aunt Bessie Joins
Aunt Bessie Knows
Aunt Bessie Likes
Aunt Bessie Meets
Aunt Bessie Needs
Aunt Bessie Observes
Aunt Bessie Provides
Aunt Bessie Questions
Aunt Bessie Remembers
Aunt Bessie Solves
Aunt Bessie Tries

Aunt Bessie Understands
Aunt Bessie Volunteers
Aunt Bessie Wonders
Aunt Bessie's X-Ray
Aunt Bessie Yearns
Aunt Bessie Zeroes In

The Aunt Bessie Cold Case Mysteries

The Adams File
The Bernhard File
The Carter File
The Durand File
The Evans File
The Flowers File
The Goodman File
The Howard File
The Irving File
The Jordan File
The Keller File
The Lawrence File
The Moss File
The Newton File
The Olson File
The Phelps File

The Markham Sisters Cozy Mystery Novellas

The Appleton Case
The Bennett Case
The Chalmers Case
The Donaldson Case

The Ellsworth Case
The Fenton Case
The Green Case
The Hampton Case
The Irwin Case
The Jackson Case
The Kingston Case
The Lawley Case
The Moody Case
The Norman Case
The Osborne Case
The Patrone Case
The Quinton Case
The Rhodes Case
The Somerset Case
The Tanner Case
The Underwood Case
The Vernon Case
The Walters Case
The Xanders Case
The Young Case
The Zachery Case

The Janet Markham Bennett Cozy Thrillers

The Armstrong Assignment
The Blake Assignment
The Carlson Assignment
The Doyle Assignment
The Everest Assignment
The Farnsley Assignment

The George Assignment
The Hamilton Assignment
The Ingram Assignment
The Jacobs Assignment
The Knox Assignment
The Lock Assignment
The Miles Assignment
The Nichols Assignment
The Owens Assignment

The Sunset Lodge Mysteries

The Body in the Annex
The Body in the Boathouse
The Body in the Cottage
The Body in the Dunk Tank
The Body in the Elevator
The Body in the Fountain
The Body in the Greenhouse
The Body in the Hallway
The Body in the Igloo

The Lady Elizabeth Cozies in Space

Alibis in Alpha Sector
Bodies in Beta Sector
Corpses in Chaos Sector
Danger in Delta Sector
Enemies in Energy Sector
Fires in Flux Sector

The Midlife Crisis Mysteries

Anxious in Nevada

Bewildered in Florida

Confused in Pennsylvania

Dazed in Colorado

Exhausted in Ohio

Frustrated in Massachusetts

The Isle of Man Romances

Island Escape

Island Inheritance

Island Heritage

Island Christmas

The Later in Life Love Stories

Second Chances

Second Act

Second Thoughts

Second Degree

Second Best

Second Nature

Second Place

Second Dance

BOOKPLATES ARE NOW AVAILABLE

Would you like a signed bookplate for this book?

I now have bookplates (stickers) that I can personalize, sign, and send to you. It's the next best thing to getting a signed copy!

Send an email to diana@dianaxarissa.com with your mailing address (I promise not to use it for anything else, ever) and how you'd like your bookplate personalized and I'll sign one and send it to you.

There is no charge for a bookplate, but there is a limit of one per person.

ABOUT THE AUTHOR

Diana has been self-publishing since 2013, and she feels surprised and delighted to have found readers who enjoy the stories and characters that she imagines. Always an avid reader, she still loves nothing more than getting lost in fictional worlds, her own or others!

After being raised in Erie, Pennsylvania, and studying history at Allegheny College in Meadville, Pennsylvania, Diana pursued a career in college administration. She was living and working in Washington, DC, when she met her future husband, an Englishman who was visiting the city.

Following her marriage, Diana moved to Derbyshire. A short while later, she and her husband relocated to the Isle of Man. After ten years on the island, during which Diana earned a Master's degree in the island's history, they made the decision to relocate again, this time to the US.

Now living near Buffalo, New York, Diana and her husband live with their daughter, a student at the University at Buffalo. Their son is now living and working just outside of Boston, Massachusetts, giving Diana an excuse to travel now and again.

Diana also writes mystery/thrillers set in the not-too-distant future as Diana X. Dunn and Young Adult fiction as D.X. Dunn.

She is always happy to hear from readers. You can write to her at:

Diana Xarissa Dunn
PO Box 72
Clarence, NY 14031.

Find Diana at: DianaXarissa.com
E-mail: Diana@dianaxarissa.com

Printed in Great Britain
by Amazon